Shameful

Innocence

By
Theresa Chevalier

Eloquent Books
New York, New York

Eloquent Books
An imprint of AEG Publishing Group
845 Third Avenue, 6th Floor – 6016
New York, NY 10022
www.eloquentbooks.com

ISBN: 978-1-60860-061-8   1-60860-061-11

Printed in the United States of America

Book Design: D. Johnson, Dedicated Business Solutions, Inc.

Book Dedicated To:

At 66 'Shameful Innocence' is the first novel my father, Werner, has ever read! Also at 66, my mother, Liese, could not sleep at night, after putting the novel down, because she was so concerned for the well being of the characters. They were so real to her! Both of them can't wait to pass on copies to relatives and friends. Receiving such enthrallment and support from my parents is a reward beyond any I would have expected!

Love You Mom & Dad!

Testimonials:

'Shameful Innocence' is a riveting historical drama! The characters are exceptionally captivating bringing to life the very real events in history. Through your work I've gained insight and compassion for what the Russian Mennonites had to endure during World War I. Congrats on a Fabulous Book! Bob Burnham . . . Author of the #1 Amazon Best Seller '101 Reasons Why You Must Write A Book'

"I just finished your manuscript and loved it! I found the characters very interesting and truly enjoyed learning about the Mennonite slice of history you showed. For me, the most compelling element of the story was the *hunger* . . . *y*ou captured the characters' experiences with starvation and hardship with candour and integrity. I came away from Shameful Innocence with a renewed sense of gratitude for the life I have." Maryanne Pope . . . Author of 'A Widow's Awakening' and Chair of The John Petropolous Memorial Fund

. . . a story that gently draws the reader into a world of extraordinary circumstances. Theresa Chevalier beautifully captures the simplicity of her characters' lifestyle while skillfully bringing about profound changes of heart, affected by an endearing heroine that is engaging right up to a truly satisfying ending.

Wendy Simpson—a front-page writer for 'The Abbotsford Neighbourhood Bugel' and author of 'The FM Phenomena Series® for the Fibromyalgia Well Spring Foundation

Chapter

1

The beating of her heart was almost unbearable with the anticipation of what she knew she was about to do. Sarah felt her face burning at the thoughts that were in her mind. But she couldn't stop. The pull was too great.

As she pushed the barbed wires of the fence apart with one hand, she used her other arm to gather her long skirt so she could lift her leg up and over the pokey wire without tearing her clothing. She safely got her first leg through but as she lifted and pulled the next leg she felt the sharp scrape of the barb against the inner part of her other leg. She stifled the moan of pain that was about to escape her lips, quickly looked around to see if anyone was watching her and kept going. She had to hurry to the fruit trees before she was seen by anyone.

As she entered the orchard the sweet smell of apples seemed to just pull her to the center of the field. She closed her eyes and inhaled the delicious aroma, slowing down for only a few seconds, wishing she could capture the fragrance and keep it with her. Past the apple trees she now had to watch the ground for plums that had fallen off the tree too early. Being careful not to squish or slip on one she wove her way towards the walnut trees.

At the edge of the walnut grove she slowed down. She wanted her breathing to be at a normal, controlled pace.

Getting close to the edge of the grove she could see where the rounded mounds of hay almost touched the walnut trees. This was their secret cove. This was where they had first looked into each other's eyes and had both, with a jolt of surprise, realized that the burning inside was shared.

Then she saw Nikolai. The sunlight that streamed through the branches of the tree touched his face and he seemed to glow. He looked so perfect. She came to a complete stop and caught her breath. She felt immobilized.

Sarah remembered every detail of the day he had arrived on their farm with his family. The weather had just started to warm a bit. Spring was approaching after a long hard winter. Much hired help would be needed to run the big farm efficiently. Men, women, and children would work together to care for the cattle, sheep, horses, hayfields, and orchards.

He was sitting at the back of the wagon with his feet hanging over the edge. His big brimmed black hat was tilted forward but as the wagon passed her he pushed it up and their eyes met.

She quickly lowered her eyes and turned her body slightly away as any proper young lady would. Having anything to do with young men at her age was simply not appropriate. As a child, she remembered playing with young boys on the grounds around her house, but Sarah was definitely no longer a child.

Her mother had very sternly made that clear to her three years previously when she had first noticed the warm trickle between her legs. With shock Sarah had received the information that she would now have to deal with this problem every month. In time she had accepted this new ritual of her body and now was at times even proud to be so grown up.

But as she turned her body away from the young man on the wagon she suddenly felt this little stir inside of herself. This feeling totally confused and flustered her.

As days passed on the farm she found herself hungering for information about him. She learned that his name was Nikolai and that his family had a few years previous worked on another farm close to the Caucasus Mountains.

Apparently the lure of mountain's great beauty and the fact that their farm was close to the Caspian Sea had brought them back to the village of Terekeransiedlung. The family was of Russian decent and very hard-working.

Sarah's family was one of the later settlers who had migrated from Germany to Russia. Her father and mother had left their homeland of Germany shortly after their marriage. Her father, Henry, and her mother, Margaret, wanted to follow the religious teachings of the Mennonites. They wanted to have the freedom of practicing the principles of the New Testament in the Bible. Discord between their respective families on these beliefs was something that the young couple had not wanted to deal with.

Together they had decided to join the thousands of Germans' trek to Russia to start a new life. The Russian government had promised them all complete freedom to practice their faith in return for working the barren land. Her father, Henry, was hardworking and idealistic. These characteristics had given him the drive that was needed to work the land into the thriving farm that it was today.

Sarah was the third youngest of eight children. By the time she was old enough to help out the farm was well established. Her chores had always kept her close to the area of the house. She had to help out with the washing of the laundry. Every day she collected all the soiled clothes from her family's bedrooms and brought them to the outdoor wash basins. As she got older she had to help with taking the clean linen off the clothes lines, folding, and putting everything back in the storage cupboards.

Sarah's spirit was adventurous and this work was really not where her heart was at. Complaining was not something that one did without regret. She easily recalled the fear that she'd felt when her father had taken her into his room after occasions of disobedience. Her father's belt always hung over his bedroom door as a reminder to the children that instant obedience was expected.

Even so, while doing her routine chores she would daydream of the adventures that the young men had while out in the hills shepherding the sheep. She would much rather have been working with the animals or even in the orchards. At high noon all the workers on the farm were given several hours to return to their modest cabins for their mid day meals and rest. Chores were done from the early daylight hours till sundown so this rest was much needed to make it through the day.

Children, during this time, were allowed freedom to play away from the living quarters.

Sarah took complete advantage of this time to investigate their entire farm. She would wander through the barns and out to the hayfields. At times she'd spend the entire time playing games amongst the fruit trees. As she got older she became more daring and would venture further and further.

Since the day she had first noticed Nikolai the quest of her afternoons had changed. Every day she would wander around the farm hoping to see him again. Sometimes she would find him still hard at work tending to one of the animals.

Knowing their farm so well she could usually find somewhere to hide and watch him at the same time. Just watching him go through the motions of brushing a horse or carrying water into the barns thrilled her.

The tasks were so simple, so routine, yet watching him go through the motions was something she just didn't tire of.

Sarah kept all of these feelings to herself. She shared a room with her sisters Annie and Frieda, but she didn't dare talk to either of them. Annie was four years older than Sarah and had a character much like their father. She wanted to do everything proper and right. There had been discussions about her marrying a man from a neighboring town. Annie wanted to please her parents in all that she did so she would never question a choice that they made for her. She would not understand all the emotions and turmoil that churned inside of Sarah. Her other sister Frieda was only eleven years old. Although more carefree in nature than Annie, still too young to understand what Sarah was going through.

Sarah's brother, Jakob, had always been closest to her. Being only a year older than her they had grown up almost as twins. Jakob had always been a rough and tumble type of boy and this had suited Sarah just fine. They had climbed many trees together, explored the wildlife that lived at the bank of the lake that was on their property. They'd talked for hours about going on an expedition to the Caucasas Mountains when they grew up. But, he too, had changed as he'd gotten older and at times they almost felt awkward around each other.

When Sarah was nine she spent some time going to school in the village of Terekeransiedlung. There she had made some girlfriends but keeping up friendships was difficult when all the farms were so wide spread. Of the Russian families who had come to work for them during the harvest time, only one of them had a daughter with whom she had shared a common bond. Sarah and Mishka had shared everything.

Often they had been put to work on the same chores. Time had gone by quickly when they worked together. After spending two seasons on the Doerksen farm Mishka's family had decided to move on.

Sarah had been heart-broken. She knew that when these Russian families moved on they often never returned. Life had seemed very lonely since that time. Being thirteen and losing the person with whom she had shared so many secrets and so much fun with had left her feeling very empty and at times resentful. Since then she spent most of her time living inside herself.

So now, at sixteen, she lived in her own world. She hid her feelings and her thoughts from her family. She especially wanted to keep thoughts about a Russian boy to herself. Permission to court someone Russian would never be granted. His family did not share the same religious beliefs as hers. Their God was not her God.

Any relationship between her and Nikolai would be strictly forbidden. If her father had any idea about how she felt he would have asked the family to leave immediately. Sarah was sure of this. So she became very secretive on her afternoon excursions.

*****

Nikolai Chekov's life, up until now, had been a constant struggle just to exist. His family worked hard for their daily meals and they ate just so that they would have the strength to keep working hard. No other way was known to them.

For hundreds of years his Slavic ancestors had worked Russian soil for their existence. They had planted rye, wheat, and barley, hunted in the forests, and fished in the lakes and rivers. They traded these goods with other Slavs. This was in the early 900's.

Then the Vikings started coming from the north and Nomads from the south and battles had begun. Individual principalities gradually formed into a large state and many fighting men joined militaries to fight off these invaders.

Tribal nobility, elders, military leaders, and fighting men now took by force whatever they wanted from the peasants. Princes soon seized the common lands. They gave the peasants small plots to maintain their families. For years they had lived as slaves to these boyars (feudal lords). Nikolai's family now had the freedom to work for who they chose but life had been hard for as long as he could remember. Always packing up and moving to the next farm or city looking for work. He was only seventeen but he felt so tired at times. It was as though generations of hard physical labor was weighing down upon his shoulders.

Nikolai's father, Anton, was tired too and angry with the kind of life that almost every Russian had to endure.

Nikolai remembered the trip to St. Petersburg in 1905. His father had received news that workers were going to meet at the Winter Palace. There the workers would present a petition to the government outlining the people's needs. Thousands of people gathered for this demonstration. Anton had seemed elated to be surrounded by people who desired change as much as he did. Nikolai was seven at the time and he could still remember the fear of seeing so many people. It was a very cold winter day in January but the great throng of people had made it feel very warm to Nikolai. So warm that he could almost not breathe.

Everyone had on thick winter coats and hats and to Nikolai they all looked the same. He had been very afraid that he would lose his parents so he had gripped tightly to his mother's coat.

Then they heard the noise.

It had sounded as though something very loud was crashing almost a pounding noise. They heard a ripple of screams of terror starting at the place where the workers were closest to the Winter Palace and spreading to the back of the crowd where his family stood. Then he heard his father shouting to his family.

"They're shooting at us! The soldiers are shooting! Run!" and with that Anton had grabbed the two youngest children in his arms and started trying to get away.

Nikolai looked at his father's face at that instant and saw something there that he had never seen before. Fear and absolute anger mixed with disbelief.

Nikolai thought, "Why is our army shooting at us?"

But there was no more time for reasonable thought. His mother was pulling at him and he had to walk. He was being pushed at from all directions.

People were falling down in front of them, beside them, all around. Everywhere the snow was red. There were cries of pain and everyone's breathing seemed panicked. His lungs burned from inhaling the freezing air so quickly. His face felt as though it was burning too. "But why?" Then he'd realized that he was crying and the tears were freezing on his cheeks. But there was no time for this now. He must keep going.

Stumbling over people, jumping over their arms, legs. Occasionally stepping on them and having to catch himself from falling. He mustn't fall. Not here. Not in all the blood.

"Aahh!"

Nikolai saw his father falling forward, releasing the two younger children from his arms.

"Nikolai! Take their hands and keep going. I'm alright. I'm coming."

The look on his father's face said that there was no room for questioning. So he took their hands and kept finding a way forward. He could hear his mother helping his father up and crying. But he didn't look back.

They made it to an entrance way of a nearby building. Nikolai pulled the children against the brick wall with him. People were still passing them on the street. He didn't know where to go from here so they huddled together and watched the mass of people cram their way through the street to find safety.

"Mamma! Mamma!" he heard the children shouting and saw them pointing. They were trying to pull away from Nikolai to rush out to meet their mother but he wouldn't let them go. No, they had to wait here in safety for his parents.

As the crowds cleared Nikolai could see that his father, Anton, had his left arm around his mother for support. He was hopping on his right leg and dragging the left one. His face looked almost as white as the snow had been. Completely drained of color!

The sound of gun-fire seemed to have stopped. Now there was the sound of people mournfully crying, calling for help, reaching for help.

Anton motioned for his children to join them and slowly they made their way to the small room which they had rented for their stay in St.Petersburg.

When they got there they watched their mother tend to their father's leg. Everyone seemed to be crying but their father. He still had a look of *anger* and determination on his face. The wound was to the fleshy part of his left lower leg. Although a large area of the skin was missing it didn't appear to be too deep. His mother sterilized it with herbs that they had brought with them and bandaged up the leg.

No one spoke much the rest of that day. The disbelief, shock, and outrage at what had just happened seemed to have numbed all of them.

Two days later his father left to make arrangements for them to leave St. Petersburg. They would go back to the country and work on farms. There was great indignation among the Russian people about what their own soldiers had done to them. And all because they had lost a war to Japan the previous year. The soldiers were angry and out of control.

Revolts had already started in Moscow and Anton wanted his family away from all the horror. He still wanted freedom for the Russian people but not in this way.

Anton had heard that the German settlers treated their workers fairly so that had been his goal. To travel to the European side of Russia and work on the farms there. As the years passed by his zeal to change the way of life for his people slowly ebbed away. He would focus on keeping his wife and children fed and finding shelter for the harsh winters.

Nikolai, too, had accepted this way of life. At times he dreamed of going into the cities and learning a trade but the terror of what had happened at the Winter Palace was still somewhere deep inside of him, keeping him here with his family.

*****

Now it was spring of 1915 and his family was rolling onto the Doerksen farm. Preparing for another summer of arduous work. Everything would be as it had been for years. Different people but the same routine

That's when he had lifted his brimmed black hat to take a look at the farm where he would probably be spending the next few years. As he lifted his head his eyes caught Sarah's.

He felt a strange quiver of feeling rising from within his belly. He felt a sensational stimulation of his whole being. She was so beautiful. Her ebony hair shone brilliantly, like bodies of water struck by moonlight at midnight, and her eyes sparkled like the sea. A few curls had escaped her tight braids during her day's activities adding to the innocent softness of her beauty. Even though her dress was made in such a way as to conceal her from head to toe it could not hide her voluptuous figure. The apron that was tied around her waist only magnified how perfectly formed she really was. The way she held her shoulders back made it easy to see that she was confident and strong. But when her eyes locked on his, he felt her mischievous free spirit. He felt completely captivated by her presence. Then she turned away from him and he felt like jumping off that wagon and running after her. But of course he couldn't. He didn't even know her.

As the days went by and his family settled onto the farm he was continuously aware of her. Nikolai's chores kept him away from the main house so he didn't often see her but she was constantly on his mind. He felt so energized by these new feelings that the work seemed very easy.

Then one day as he was tending to one of the horses in the barn he noticed some movement by the wall of tackle. He stopped what he was doing and looked over but couldn't see anything. As he started to brush the horse he thought he heard something again. This time he didn't stop to look. He just went around the horse so that he could brush the horse and keep his eyes focused on the direction of the tackle wall.

He noticed what looked like a piece of rope through one of the cracks in the wood but he knew instantly that it was one of Sarah's braids. "Sarah," even just thinking her name sent shivers through-out his body.

What should he do? If he went over to talk to her she'd probably run away. If he called out to her he'd probably embarrass her. So he decided just to continue doing what he was doing. "Is she actually watching me?" he thought. "Does she feel what I feel? Do women have the same feelings as men?" As he was working and thinking all of this he could feel the color changing in his face. Now he was embarrassed. "Maybe she'll just think I'm hot from working hard."

When he was finished his chores he left the barn pretending he hadn't noticed anything unusual.

As the days passed he kept hoping that she would be near where he was working. Watching him. Just knowing that she might be, exhilarated him.

Then one afternoon he'd decided to take a rest out by the hayfield under the large walnut tree at the outer edge of the grove. He was tired and preoccupied with thoughts of the afternoon chores as he walked towards the hayfield.

Sarah too was preoccupied. Her mother had just given her a lecture. She wasn't keeping up with her chores and if she didn't start working a little harder she wouldn't be able to have her afternoons free. She'd held her tongue as her mother spoke to her. Promising to do better but angry the whole time. She didn't want to be stuck doing housework.

She wanted to work out in the fields. So as soon as her mother had let her go she had headed for the orchard. Being amongst the trees usually calmed her down.

With these thoughts in mind they had walked into each other. Sarah caught her breath.

"I'm so sorry Sarah. I didn't mean to startle you. I hope you're not hurt," said Nikolai.

"I'm alright. I'm just surprised to see anyone out here," said Sarah.

"I just came to have a rest. I hope that's all right?" asked Nikolai.

"Yes, of course. It's very relaxing under these trees," said Sarah. "Well I'd better leave you alone so you can rest."

"Actually would you like to sit with me by the hay near the shade? We could talk for a while."

Sarah felt very nervous but excited at the same time. She was actually talking to Nikolai and her words seemed to make sense.

She wanted nothing more than to spend the entire day right here with Nikolai. She should probably go but something inside of her was so drawn to him she could only say, "Yes."

"So, have you lived here on this farm your whole life?" asked Nikolai.

"Yes, I was born here, but my parents came from Germany," answered Sarah. "How about you? Where is your family from?" she asked.

"All over Russia," he answered. He spent the rest of that afternoon telling her all about his travels. Somehow it seemed much more interesting telling her than he had felt at the time.

Sarah was attentive to his every word. He totally appealed to her adventurous spirit.

She spoke, too, of her dreams of hiking to the Caucasas Mountains and of how she wished she could work with the animals and on the fields rather than by the house. Conversation between them just flowed.

"Could I meet you here again tomorrow?" asked Nikolai.

"I would like that very much," Sarah answered.

Chapter
2

Sarah and Nikolai now both worked very hard to complete all of their chores. Somehow the tasks assigned to each of them no longer felt so menial. They both put energy into their work that hadn't been there before.

Their parents were very pleased, of course, to see such an improvement in Sarah and Nikolai's work habits. Neither the Doerksen's nor the Chekov's realized that what was driving their children to work more efficiently was actually passion for each other.

Their relationship progressed quickly. They both became proficient at sneaking around the farm to this meeting place by the walnut tree. It was now Monday and they hadn't seen each other since the previous Saturday. On Sundays Sarah had to go to church with her family to Terekeransiedlung. It was a sacred day for her family and no work was done by any of them. After church the family usually invited another family over for a special Sunday supper. Sarah had to spend the time visiting with the children that came over.

But now was Monday. She could see Nikolai again. On Saturday Nikolai had asked her if he could hold her hand. His touch had felt so intimate, gentle and strong at the same time. Today he just took her hand in his as they talked. It felt so natural. Instinctively they moved their bodies closer together.

Nikolai felt quite confident that her feelings for him were just as deep as his feelings for her. So he asked her what he had wanted to ask her since the first time he'd seen her, after lifting that big brimmed hat to reveal the most stunning girl he'd ever seen, "Sarah, could I kiss you?"

She turned to look at him and he could see in her eyes the burning desire reflected that he felt within himself. Sarah didn't answer. She moved her head towards him and willingly surrendered her lips to his. As they kissed the world around them seemed to disappear. All of their inhibitions were gone. Sarah reached her arms up and around his shoulders, pulling him as close to her as she could. She did not want to let him go. Not ever.

They heard some noise coming from the barns and reluctantly pulled apart, breaking the whirlwind that their kiss had started.

Nikolai said, "We'd better go and join the others before they realize we're here together."

Sarah nodded. She could hardly speak. She felt somehow dizzy from the strong emotions that were coursing through her.

"Tomorrow my sweet Sarah. My heart remains with you," whispered Nikolai.

Sarah had regained her voice and said, "And mine with you Nikolai."

They stood up and dusted the hay off of each other so that there would be no tell tale signs of where they had been. Each took a different path back to the living quarters of the farm.

Annie was already removing the clean linen from the wash line when Sarah returned.

"Where were you?" asked Annie. "I sent Frieda out to find you."

Without giving Sarah a chance to answer Annie said in a condescending tone, "Probably with those dirty lambs again."

Not wanting to give Annie a chance to discover where she had really been Sarah said, "And what if I was. The lambs are a lot better to talk to than you are." With that she turned with an armful of laundry and headed for the house. She could hear Annie in the background making a clicking sound with her tongue against the roof of her mouth. Obviously completely disgusted with Sarah.

Sarah could not understand how they could possibly be sisters. They're personalities were so unlike each other.

Sarah would never measure up to Annie's ideals and Annie would never take the time to comprehend Sarah's spirit.

But, that didn't matter now. She had Nikolai. And he understood her and she understood him. He thought that it was wonderful that she enjoyed working out on the farm. They'd even talked about what it would be like if the two of them could start their own farm. They would hire peasants to take care of household chores and she and Nikolai would work outside together. "Side by side," that's what he had said.

That evening when Sarah went to bed she couldn't sleep. All she could think about was that wonderful kiss. She was so tired, her body ached, but her mind would not let her rest. The night was so hot. Finally she decided to get up and go outside. She knew her father would be very angry if he found out she'd gone outside in the middle of the night so she walked as quietly as she could. Holding her breath she opened the door, hoping it wouldn't make any sounds. At last she was out in the cool night air. About twenty feet in front of their house was a tree with a swing attached to one of its thick branches. Sarah decided to go and sit there for a while.

As she was lightly swaying back and forth she looked up into the sky. The sky looked very dark but the moon was full and bright. As she lowered her eyes her gaze drifted towards the direction of Nikolai's living quarters. Was he also thinking of her? Perhaps dreaming of her. She smiled.

What was that? She thought she had seen someone moving at the side of his house but they had disappeared into the shadow. Could that be Nikolai? She stopped moving on the swing and waited to see if there was any more movement.

Then he came out of the shadows and turned completely towards her. It was Nikolai! Sarah was under the shadow of the tree so he couldn't see her. But she knew that he knew that she was there. She could sense it. She got off the swing and quickly ran towards him. When they were both in the shadow of the house he took her hand and motioned with his other hand for her to be quiet by putting his finger to his lips. They looked back towards her house to see if anyone had seen her making her way towards the peasant's living quarters. Everything was quiet.

They stayed close to the buildings and he led her towards the barns. Once inside they looked around to see where they could be together in private. There was a loft above the horse pens and they took some of the riding blankets and made their way up.

As they spread the blankets out Nikolai said, "I couldn't sleep. I was thinking about you. I just want to kiss you again and again."

Sarah was on her knees and went towards him. He was still standing and she took both of his hands in hers and pulled him down onto his knees. She let go of his hands and reached to touch his face. Building within her was a surprisingly new feeling of aggression, confidence.

"Nikolai," she said with a throaty sound in her voice, "let me kiss you."

And gently, ever so gently she kissed his lips. She moved her mouth to his cheeks and then she kissed his eyes.

Nikolai could wait no longer. He put his arms around her and rolled her down onto the blankets. His kisses now became fervent. Sarah responded with equal passion. Her hands freely explored his back. His shirt had become loose and she put her hands inside. His skin was smooth and muscular. Touching him made her feel so aroused. She arched her body towards his. She felt his hardness against her most sensitive area. For an instant she drew her body back in surprise!

But Nikolai reached for her buttocks and pulled her back against his hardness. He rubbed and pushed against her and she knew that she did not want him to stop. His hands reached for her nightdress and slowly lifted it. He pulled himself away only long enough to take the nightdress off of her. Sarah felt wonderful. There was no shame between them. She let herself go completely. Giving way to all the sensations that his hands and mouth were arousing in her.

Their bodies touched and melded, moving in one rhythm. Time neither sped up or slowed down. They were caught in this moment.

And then there was pain. She caught her breath. A slight stinging feeling within her as he entered her. But as Nikolai, slowly and gently, kept moving on top of her she could feel the pleasure and desire deep within her return and she moved her hips to meet his. She felt so free and so complete and with that she moaned, "Ooh Nikolai!" and her body became spasmodic with such pleasure that she thought she would burst.

Nikolai's pleasure was so incited by her moans that he too burst deep within her! They lay in each other's arms completely satisfied. Still connected. Neither wanted to move.

After some time Sarah whispered, "I wish we could stay here forever."

"Maybe we can," said Nikolai, "I want to marry you Sarah."

"Oh Nikolai, I don't think my father would ever allow us to get married," sighed Sarah. "Your family worships Gods, like Perun, the god of thunder, and Veles, the god of cattle. And you wear these beautiful shirts with all this intricate embroidery on the collar and cuffs to protect you against evil spirits. But we are taught that your superstitions are evil. I will probably go to hell just for loving you."

"Sarah, you are much too precious. No God would ever send you to hell."

"Well my God would. Sometimes I just don't understand. We are taught that he loves us and cares for all of us. But we as people still seem to segregate ourselves from other cultures. As if you, just because you are a Russian, are not good enough for us. We are told to share the message of salvation and yet at the same time we are not to get involved with you," said Sarah.

Nikolai responded, "Perhaps if I accepted your God and practices along with mine your family could accept me."

"I wish that it could be like that, but it's just not that simple," said Sarah as she turned to stroke his hair.

"We'd better go back to bed before we're caught. Soon it will be light out," said Nikolai. "Maybe tomorrow we can talk about this some more and figure out how we can be together."

Quickly they put their clothes back on. They returned the blankets to the railings on which they'd hung and slunk their way back to the living quarters. Everything was still quiet and Sarah stealthily made her way back to her room. As she lay in her bed she could still feel the warmth and weight of Nikolai on her. She felt very happy and at peace. She slept soundly.

"Sarah! Wake up," said Annie impatiently. "Come on. It's morning."

"In a minute," moaned Sarah as she rolled over.

"Mother will not be pleased. You're supposed to help prepare breakfast today," said Annie with an unkind edge to her voice.

"Please tell mother that I don't feel well," said Sarah pleadingly.

"Alright, I'll go," said Annie.

Before Annie was even out the door Sarah had fallen back to sleep. Her body was so tired from the night's excursion and ached in places she had not ached before.

"Where's your sister?" asked Margaret their mother.

"She says she's not feeling well," answered Annie.

"Very well. We'll let her sleep. I'll check on her later," said Margaret.

A few hours later Margaret went to check on Sarah. Sarah was still sound asleep and her cheeks appeared to be flushed so Margaret let her be and went to take care of her household. With eight children to look after and all the farm help to keep in order she did not have any time to waste.

Lunch time came and went and Sarah was still sound asleep. Everyone was tired by this time and they decided to leave her be until after the afternoon rest time.

*****

Aggressively Nikolai was woken up by his father. "Come son. We have a busy day today. We need your help with the hay."

"Alright," groaned Nikolai as he rolled out of bed. He knew that he was paying for the night before but anything was worth the time he had spent with Sarah. Just thinking about her stimulated his senses. He couldn't wait to see her that afternoon. He wouldn't think about the future. The thought of a life without her was just too painful. He would focus on today and the pleasure they would share.

Time seemed to go by very slowly as they worked with the hay. There were no clouds in the sky and by mid morning the men were already wiping the sweat from their fore heads. The sun shone forcefully upon them. Not having slept much the night before made the work especially difficult for Nikolai. At times he felt as though he would collapse from exhaustion but he forced himself to keep going. "Just a little bit longer and I'll be able to see Sarah," he mumbled to himself through gritted teeth as he helped to heave a bale of hay onto the wagon.

Finally, meal time arrived. Nikolai took extra care in washing up after all the hard work. He wanted to feel fresh when he saw Sarah. He hurried through his meal and made an excuse to go to the barns. Once there he went inside only to hurry through to the other side so he could escape through one of the side windows so that no one would see him head towards the orchards.

When he got there Sarah had not yet arrived. Nikolai decided to sit under the walnut tree against the tree trunk. After the hot morning sun he craved the coolness of the canopy of shade formed by the massive tree. He wanted to relax but he somehow felt a bit nervous. After what had happened between them last night he wasn't sure how Sarah would react today. Would she still be as open as she had been up until now or would she be embarrassed?

Right now it almost seemed as though everything that had happened between them had been a dream. But he knew that it wasn't. There was no way that he could ever have imagined the amount of sensations and extreme passion that had coursed through his body only a few hours ago. No one had ever told him that there was this type of pleasure to be shared with a woman. He had always believed that the reason people got married was simply to avoid loneliness and have children.

"Do my parents share this type of love?" he asked himself. The answer came to him quickly. Of course they did. He could now remember times when his parents had looked at each other in funny ways that he as a child and even up until now had not understood. Sometimes after those looks they'd asked him to watch the younger children while they went for long walks. He now recalled how carefree they'd seemed when they had returned from "their walks."

Nikolai felt both amazed and yet a little taken back by this realization. He definitely did not want to think about his parents doing what he and Sarah had done last night.

"She's taking awfully long to get here," he said to himself. His body was starting to fell stiff and he knew that he'd been sitting there in the same position for a long time. He got up and walked out from under the covering of the tree looking in all directions for Sarah. "She should have been here by now."

Nikolai started to worry. A knot was forming within his stomach. Hopefully she wasn't sick. What if she's angry at me? Things between them had happened so quickly. Their bodies had reacted with such fervent need that neither of them had taken any time to think about what they were doing. Maybe she now regretted giving so much of herself to him so quickly. But she must know how much he loved her. He felt as though their very souls were united.

His time was up. He had to go back to the field to work. Anguish. There was no other word to describe how he felt. As he worked he was sluggish yet tense. This was not where he wanted to be right now. All he wanted was to go and find out what had happened to Sarah.

Later, what had seemed like eternity in time, as he dipped his rye bread into the thick soup he could almost not eat because of his worry. Usually, by the time they ate their evening meal he was ravenous with hunger. He could not wait to fill his stomach with dark colored, soft yet spongy rye bread that his mother baked. But not tonight. Nikolai could hardly swallow. He listened closely as his mother and younger sister talked about their day, hoping to glean whatever information he could about Sarah.

Sarah was not mentioned and he dared not ask for fear of raising his family's suspicions.

*****

Sarah awoke with a startle. What time was it? Everything looked so bright and the air felt so warm. It couldn't possibly be morning. But her sister Annie lay in the bed next to her sound asleep. "Why is everyone still in bed?" she thought. Then she realized that it must be afternoon rest time.

She decided to stay in bed till everyone else got up to continue their chores. Her body now felt completely rested but she was relishing this bit of time to stretch and be lazy. It wasn't something that was ever allowed but Sarah felt quite complacent about being able to do so now.

"Mmm Nikolai," she murmured to herself. "Ah Nikolai! I was supposed to meet him in the orchards! He must be waiting and waiting," she thought to herself. But it was too late to go now. She was sure of that. Soon everyone would be going back to work and they would be caught. No, she would try to catch his eye in the evening and let him know that everything was alright.

"Girls! It's time to get up and get back to work!" her mother called as she knocked on their door.

Sarah quickly got out of bed and changed out of her night dress into her clothes for the day. In doing so she noticed a bit of a red stain on the back of her night dress. She thought that she must be getting her period so she tucked extra rags into her underwear for protection.

When she walked into the kitchen her mother, Margaret, was busy preparing food for the evening meal. "So you're finally awake," stated Margaret.

"Yes, I'm feeling much better now," said Sarah. "I'm going to go outside and take the washing off the clothes line."

"Alright, as long as you don't have a fever. You did seem quite warm this morning." said Margaret.

"Well, whatever it was it must have passed," said Sarah as she turned away from her mother. She could feel herself blushing. She knew that if her mother saw her face turning red she would know that Sarah was not being totally honest with her so Sarah quickly left the kitchen.

Once outside she looked all around hoping to spot Nikolai. But very few of the men were on the yard. She would just have to wait till the evening.

Later that day when she went into the outhouse she checked her rags but they were still clean. "That's odd," she thought to herself. Usually when her time in the month started her flow would quickly increase and then about three days later it would end just as abruptly. This was something quite strange to her. She wondered if she'd hurt herself down there last night.

Just thinking about last night produced a kind of throbbing feeling 'down there' but it definitely did not hurt. She wasn't even sure what she needed but she knew that just thinking about last night made her wish like crazy that she could be alone with Nikolai right now.

Well, as usual, there was no one that she dared ask about any of these things. She would just have to wait to see what would happen to her body next. If she wasn't in pain than everything must be alright she concluded and decided to go about her day and not worry about the bit of blood.

Long after dinner, after all the dishes had been taken care of, Sarah was free to spend the evening out on the porch or the area in front of their house. She decided to go back on the swing she'd sat on last night under the moon and keep an eye out for Nikolai.

He was the third person to step through their cabin door and instantly she caught his eye. She kept swinging lightly as she looked at him. Nikolai gave her a questioning look? Sarah knew that he was asking her, "Where were you? Is everything alright?"

Sarah slowly nodded her head forward, up and down, and smiled at him meaning yes, everything is fine. Sarah then turned her body towards the direction of the orchard and nodded again hoping that Nikolai would understand that she would meet him there tomorrow.

He smiled back in her direction. He had understood.

That evening they both slept peacefully. Knowing that tomorrow they would once again be able to see each other.

Sarah awoke feeling absolutely wonderful. So alive. So energetic. She even hummed to herself as she worked on some of the flower beds near the house. Life was wonderful. She felt as though she was a whole new person. Alive for the first time. Really alive. She wanted to jump, shout, be silly. "I'm in love," Sarah thought to herself. She was surprised by the thought. While at school she had overheard the older girls talking about being in love but none of their conversation had made much sense to her.

But it certainly made sense now. She loved Nikolai and she was in love with him.

That afternoon when they met under the walnut tree it seemed as though their passion for each other had doubled.

Nikolai held his hand out to Sarah. She reached for his hand and went straight into his arms. Tightly they held on to each other before either of them spoke.

Nikolai loosened his hold on her just enough so that he could look into her eyes as he asked, "What happened to you yesterday? I was so worried. I thought that perhaps I'd hurt you."

"Oh no," said Sarah, "Absolutely nothing we did hurt me. Actually I probably had one of the best sleeps I've ever had. I just couldn't wake up and I guess my mother thought that I was coming down with something so she let me sleep."

"Well you look absolutely radiant. I'm glad you were able to get some extra rest," said Nikolai with great care in his voice.

"If I look radiant it's because I'm here with you," said Sarah. "I feel completely rejuvenated today. Like a whole new person." With that she reached for his face and traced his features ever so tenderly. She couldn't wait to kiss him and reached for the back of his head and pulled his head forward to meet her lips.

Nikolai did not resist. With the sparkle of her blue eyes speaking only of the desire deep within her he was completely entranced by her.

Surrounded by mounds of golden hay and completely sheltered by the enormous branches of the walnut tree they felt no need to hide.

Nikolai gently pushed Sarah away from him as he started to undo the buttons on the front of her dress. He wanted to see her. As he pushed the dress off of her shoulders down to her waist Sarah looked straight into his eyes before he looked at her breasts. Slowly he traced his hand along her neck and down the middle of her chest and out towards her breast.

He moaned as his hands touched her soft, velvety breasts. They were luscious and full. Perfect in his eyes. He felt himself growing with desire as he touched her.

Sarah felt wild with desire as he touched and tasted the sweetness of her skin. Being outside with the risk of exposure seemed to just enhance the fury of passion that was within her. She couldn't control herself any longer. She literally charged at Nikolai and together they fell onto the blanket which Nikolai had the forethought to bring.

Having no idea what would bring each of them pleasure or not they explored each other's bodies completely. They felt completely uninhibited. No shame.

When neither of them could stand anymore of this perusal Nikolai claimed her completely. They moved against each other until their bodies convulsed with pleasure.

Only then did they come to their senses and realize that they were both lying outside, naked, in the middle of the day. Quickly they put their clothes on and sat down on the blanket.

"Sarah, you are absolutely amazing," said Nikolai in astonishment. "I never want to lose you. We have to figure out a way to stay together. Does your father ever mention me?"

"He said once that you were a hard working boy and that he thought your family seemed like decent and honest people." answered Sarah.

"Well that's a good start," said Nikolai in a hopeful manner. "Perhaps in a year's time when he has gotten to know us better he would consider me as a prospect for a son-in-law. I know that our family doesn't have much to offer you in the way of wealth Sarah but I would always work to my utmost to take care of you."

"My father is just so strict. I can't ever see him bending," sighed Sarah. "I'm just not sure how I can talk to him to get him used to the idea."

"Would they consider allowing me to come to your church with them on Sundays?" asked Nikolai.

"If they felt that you were truly interested they might," answered Sarah with a hint of excitement in her voice.

"Years ago we had an older peasant who came with us on Sundays. His wife died while they worked here and he was so depressed afterwards that my father convinced him to come along with us. He promised the old man that he would find hope and comfort there."

"And did he?" asked Nikolai. "Find hope and comfort?"

"Well," said Sarah, "I was still quite young at the time but I know that he did seem much happier after some time had passed. Then he decided to move on. I think he had some children in another town and they didn't even know yet that their mother had passed on. He felt that he was now ready to tell them. When my father said good-bye to him he even embraced him and told him that he had a home with our family any time he wanted. Even that young I remember being very surprised at seeing my father show such affection. Especially to someone Russian."

"Then there is some hope," said Nikolai confidently. "I will tell my family this evening that I am interested in learning about your religion and then as soon as there is an opportune time I will ask your father for permission."

"Won't your family be very angry with you?" asked Sarah.

"Oh they will be angry," nodded Nikolai. "My mother will probably cry and say that she just can't understand why I would want to abandon our culture and everything that we hold dear to us. But I will have to stand firm. I'm seventeen and it is time I made some of my own choices."

"You could lose your family over this Nikolai," said Sarah as she looked directly into his eyes.

"It is a risk that I am willing to take," he answered assuredly. "I will do whatever I need to so that I can marry you."

Sarah could hardly believe that this man would give up his whole world just to spend the rest of his life with her. She was deeply moved by his conviction and dedication. "Then you will need to be very persuasive and we must never let it show that we care for each other."

With this plan in mind they went back to the living quarters each using a different route.

That evening Nikolai approached his parents about his desire to learn more about the religion that the Doerksen family practiced. His parents were absolutely baffled by his announcement. Where had this come from? Where in the world had he come by such an idea? He had not shown any former interest in these German people's religion. Were their own Gods not sufficient for him?

Nikolai stood firm and did not back down from the argument. He was determined to do this and nothing would come in his way. Not once did his parents suspect that love was driving their son. Nikolai knew that his parents would also not welcome a union between Sarah and him so he never mentioned the beautiful daughter of the Doerksen's.

The next evening Sarah listened very carefully as she heard her parents speaking in the next room. She very slowly and carefully pretended to be dusting the shelves outside of their bedroom.

"The strangest thing happened today," said Henry in a perplexed tone of voice.

"Oh really, and what was that?" asked her mother, Margaret.

"You know that Chekov boy, Nikolai," continued Henry, "Well he came to me when I was alone in the barn and asked if he could start coming along to church with us on Sundays."

"Well, that is definitely a strange thing, but perhaps also a good thing," responded Margaret. "Maybe he will accept the Lord as his personal savior the way that old man Leo did."

"It's just that the request came out of nowhere. I just wonder what brought all of this on. Something just didn't seem quite right," said Henry suspiciously. "And the other thing is the government. We Mennonites were told not to approach any of the Russian people with our beliefs."

"What should we do though when the Russian people come to us? It cannot be right to withhold from them the gift of salvation. And the boy was probably just nervous talking to you. You are his boss, after all, and it's probably been his father who's done most of the handlings with you up until now."

"You're probably right. I asked if his family knew of his wishes. He said that he had told them last night. Apparently they are quite upset but he feels that he is old enough to make this decision on his own." said Henry.

"Have you spoken to his father yet?" asked Margaret.

"No not yet," answered Henry, "I told the boy that I would give it some thought and that I would let him know by the end of the week. I guess I'll speak to his father tomorrow."

Sarah could hear them heading for the bedroom door so she quickly slipped into the kitchen pretending indifference when her mother walked in. She felt quite pleased with the whole outcome.

Nikolai had told her that afternoon about the discussion he had with his parents. They had not threatened to disown him and that had seemed like a very good thing in their favor. Now if only the conversation between her father and Anton went well their plans in spending the rest of their life together would be underway. She felt excitement growing within her.

Chapter
3

As the summer progressed everything seemed to be working in their favor. Nikolai joined Sarah's family at church on Sundays and showed great interest in all the sermons. Her father Henry even seemed to respect Nikolai for his strength in resolution to get to know about their faith.

As yet no one had noticed anything unusual happening between Nikolai and Sarah. In church they kept completely apart, not even looking at one another.

Now summer had just slipped into fall and their love and passion for each other had grown with each passing day just as the fruit on the trees, lush and ripe.

Even though they had fulfilled each other's passions and desires for months now, Sarah still had to catch her breath when she saw Nikolai standing in the stream of sunlight. He was tall and ruggedly handsome. His body was still lean because of his youth but his muscles were well formed showing the athletic build that was yet to be his as a man.

This is why she blushed as she snuck across their farm to meet Nikolai. Her hunger for him was something she could not hide. The scrape of the barb wire on her inner leg was long forgotten!

Nikolai could see the depth of love that Sarah was feeling at that moment. She was overwhelmed and could not move. He went to her and took her hands in his never letting his eyes leave hers. This is where their souls connected. In the depths of their eyes. Sarah was so overpowered with emotion that tears started rolling down her cheeks.

Nikolai pulled her close and stroked her tears, "I know Sarah. I love you so much too. It's almost too much to bear and yet it's so wonderful."

Sarah just nodded. Her throat felt closed with the joy of love in her chest for Nikolai.

Nikolai took one of his arms from around her and reached into his pocket. He brought out a handful of the same plums Sarah had been trying not to slip on this afternoon, as she went to see him. "I brought you a gift. I thought that maybe we could save these plum stones to start our own orchard some day. Just as reminder of today."

Sarah smiled and nodded. "I'll treasure them until that day." And then she started laughing.

"What's so funny?" asked Nikolai.

"Oh, I was just imagining Annie's face if she found these plum stones tucked in a handkerchief under my pillow. She would think that I had gone totally mad," laughed Sarah.

Nikolai laughed too. He had seen Annie with her serious countenance performing her chores, going to church. She was like a sheet of ice on the Russian rivers. Moving along but never changing because of the frigidness.

They sat down on the blanket and ate their plums. Enjoying the crispness of the fall air and the scents of ripened fruit they leisurely made love embracing all of nature in this most natural of acts.

*****

Annie was feeling extremely annoyed! Where was that sister of hers? Always off on some adventure on the land and at this age. "At sixteen Sarah ought to be acting like a lady not like a tomboy," she muttered to herself. It was completely irritating to constantly have to wait for Sarah so they could begin their chores. Sarah, in her opinion, was totally irresponsible.

Well, she wasn't going to wait for her this time. She would go out and find Sarah herself. Then she would let her know what's what. Annie couldn't wait to get married. Then Sarah would see what it was like to have responsibility. Sarah would have to deal with their younger sister, Frieda.

Annie headed towards the barns to begin her search. Sarah was probably in there with the smelly animals. She really couldn't see what Sarah found so fascinating about spending time with these creatures or their dirty environment. When she saw no trace of Sarah in the barns she decided to head towards the orchard. No doubt Sarah was probably up in one of those trees just like when she was a kid.

Well, she would have her down in a hurry. This time she would not cover for Sarah. She would tell father and he would deal with her severely. An ugly smirk crept across her face. No, she would not mind at all, watching Sarah squirm.

The silence in the orchard felt almost as if it was crawling over Annie. She shuddered involuntarily. She had better find Sarah soon. She was not at all pleased to be wasting her time out here.

As she approached the walnut grove she heard some strange noises coming from the far end. She couldn't quite place the sounds. Almost like moaning, but not quite like the moaning that accompanies someone in pain. As she neared the origin of the sounds she heard a lower sounding groan and realized that there must be two people there. What was going on? She quickened her pace and clenched her fists. She would certainly get to the bottom of this.

Annie stepped between the mounds of hay and abruptly came to a complete stop. For a second her mind did not comprehend what she was viewing. Then her vision cleared and she realized that she was staring at two naked people completely entangled. The image was too appalling to her and she swung her hand to her mouth and let out a sharp scream.

Nikolai and Sarah were so engrossed in each other that they had not heard Annie approaching. When they heard the scream they both sucked in their breath in fear and turned their bodies to see where the scream had come from.

All three of them seemed to be in a state of shock before they realized who they were staring at.

"Sarah!" shrieked Annie, "Oh my dear God! It's you!"

As soon as Nikolai and Sarah recovered from the shock they instinctively withdrew from one another and reached for their clothes.

"I have to get father," said Annie in a panicking voice, "I have to get father."

"No, Annie, wait!" pleaded Sarah as she started to dress herself. But it was already too late. Annie had already turned away from them and started running towards the house. "What are we going to do Nikolai? My father will beat you and to me he'll . . ." she swallowed hard because she could not say what would happen to her. "Maybe we should run?!"

Nikolai took a firm hold of Sarah's shoulder. "Sarah, we can't run. They would catch up to us very quickly. We don't have enough of a head start. And even if we could get away and they didn't find us death would be certain for us. Russia has been at war with Germany and the surrounding countries for almost a year now. Life in the rest of our country is not as good as here. Your people, the Mennonites, were promised by our government that they would never have to participate in fighting, and so the life on this farm has not been affected."

Sarah started crying now, "What can we do?"

"Whatever happens, Sarah, remember how much I love you. I will always fight to be with you, "said Nikolai in a firm tone. "What we have to do is go and face our families. I will tell your father that I want to marry you."

"He will never agree," cried Sarah. "Especially now!"

Nikolai took her hand and guided her through the orchards back to the house.

*****

Annie stumbled over some fallen branches as she raced towards the house. What she had just seen was absolutely despicable to her. How could her sister behave so wantonly? Surely her parents would now see how evil and uncontrolled Sarah was. This was something that even she herself would never have imagined that Sarah would do.

As she neared the house she could see her father just stepping out of the house. "Father, Father!" she called out.

Henry looked towards his daughter and could see instantly that something terrible must have happened. Annie was a mess. Her hair was disheveled and her clothes looked dirty. Annie was always prim and proper. An obedient child. He quickened his pace towards her, "What's happened Annie? What is wrong?" He asked as he guided her towards the house.

"It's Sarah," replied Annie.

"Is she hurt? Does she need help?" Henry quickly cut into Annie's reply.

"No father," sniffed Annie. Then she blurted out "I caught her with that boy Nikolai! They were naked father. Completely naked! It was evil and disgusting and they were making noises like animals."

"Stop!" yelled Henry. His mind was whirling and he could feel a slow heat churning inside his body. At the same time he realized that they were still outside and that the other farm helpers had noticed the commotion and were listening to Annie.

Across the yard he could see Nikolai's mother turn white and drop the bucket of water that she had been carrying. She turned and ran to find her husband Anton.

Henry wanted to go and kill the boy. All this time Nikolai had acted as though he wanted to become a Christian and instead he was taking advantage of his daughter Sarah. Just as he was about to head towards the orchards Nikolai and Sarah came walking towards them hand in hand.

That did it. Seeing the two of them connected in such an intimate way sent the rage within Henry to an uncontrollable point. He clenched his hands into fists and took big steps towards them, yelling, "Take your hands off of each other, you shameful children! You are evil, Nikolai, and I'm going to kill you!" With that he swung his fist with full force into Nikolai's face. Before Nikolai could even regain his balance Henry was at him with his other fist till he had Nikolai on the ground.

He didn't even notice that the helpers had all gathered around and were watching this. Everyone was in shock. These Mennonites were peace loving people, never raising their hands to anyone. They taught that you should turn and give your other cheek when someone was striking out against you.

Now that Henry had Nikolai on the ground he put his hands around his throat and started squeezing. Nikolai didn't have a chance at fighting Henry off. After years of hard labor on the farm Henry was strong and muscular. Henry's mind was in such rage that he saw only white and knew that he would not stop squeezing until the squirming body beneath him stopped moving.

Sarah was crying and screaming, "Stop father, stop! You're going to kill him. I love him. We want to get married." All the while she was trying to pull him off of Nikolai. Sarah's brothers who'd been out in the barns when the commotion began now arrived next to her. Not knowing why their father was doing what he was doing they now helped Sarah pry him off of Nikolai. Whatever had happened they could not allow their father to kill someone.

Herbert, her oldest brother, now held her father back and was talking to him softly, "Not like this father. Let's go into the house and discuss the problem and then deal with it."

Henry took a deep breath and tried to calm himself. He was shaking. His mind and body were having a difficult time letting go of his need for blood. It took him a few minutes before the white cleared from his vision and he regained a sense of reason.

Sarah was crouched by Nikolai trying to get some response from him, shaking him. Finally he sucked in a quick breath and seemed to regain consciousness. Blood covered his face and he felt very weak.

"Take your sister inside and lock her in her room," ordered Henry to Ernst, Sarah's other brother.

"No!" wailed Sarah, as her brother grabbed her arm and forced her to her feet. "I won't leave him. I love him!"

"You fool," said Ernst as he pushed her towards the house.

Anton, Nikolai's father, pushed his way through the workers that were gathered around his son. He saw Sarah crying and being pushed towards her house. When he saw his son, he stepped quickly towards him and dropped on his knees. "Nikolai!" he exclaimed. Nikolai lay almost motionless. His eyes had a strange glazed look to them and parts of his throat were starting to show the blue bruising imprints of Henry's hands. "What has happened here?" he demandingly questioned of the crowd. As he looked around himself he noticed his boss, Henry Doerksen, dusting loose dirt off of his clothes.

Henry looked at Anton very coldly and answered, "Your son has taken certain liberties with my daughter. You may move him into your living quarters. I will think about this situation for one hour and then I want you to meet me in our kitchen to discuss what is to be done. The rest of you go back to your duties." With that Henry turned and walked into the house.

The mood of the workers was now very sullen. They quietly dispersed and went back to their respective jobs. The rest of the day everyone just spoke in hushed tones. Nothing like this had ever occurred where any of them had worked before. It was truly shameful what Nikolai and Sarah had been up to.

Anton was in shock as he and his wife helped Nikolai into their living quarters. He couldn't believe what Henry had accused his son of. Nikolai had never even mentioned Sarah to them. Winter was coming and what would become of his family now. They had it so good here. They were treated so fairly here. Always enough food for everyone and never ever treated like slaves. They were given time to rest and most importantly they had been treated as equals.

As yet his family had been spared the reality of the war going on around them. Life had been peaceful here. Would they have to leave? Surely they would be drafted by the Russian government.

Nikolai's eyes became focused and suddenly he remembered what had happened. He bolted upright in his bed and called out, "Sarah!"

Anger swelled inside of Anton. "So it's true! You have been involved with Sarah!" accused Anton. "Do you have any idea of the situation you have put our family in? If you weren't already so beaten up I'd like to beat you myself!" he shouted.

Nikolai's mother was crying and came to his defense, "Stop it Anton! There has been enough violence this day. Please let Nikolai speak and tell us what has happened," she pleaded.

"I love her father. I want to marry her," said Nikolai with determination.

"And this is how you planned to go about that? By taking advantage of her innocence and then thinking that you could persuade her father to let her marry you," he shook his head in disbelief.

Nikolai hung his head in shame. His thoughts went back to the image that Annie must have seen when she had come upon them. Was that image now in everyone's mind? Suddenly he felt very embarrassed. What only a little while ago had felt so wonderful and natural between Sarah and him now looked ugly and shameful through the eyes of others. How could he have been so shamefully innocent to think that they could just go on meeting day after day and never getting caught?

He raised his eyes to meet his fathers. "I will go and ask for her family's forgiveness and offer to do whatever they require to make this right."

His son was still so naive to think that he could make this right. Anton softened to Nikolai, "Oh Nikolai, I wish that it were so simple. Mr. Doerksen wants me to come and speak to him about the situation in a bit. I want you to stay right here while I'm talking to him and then we'll see what to do next."

*****

Ernst pushed Sarah onto her bed and quickly turned to close and bolt the door behind him. Sarah pushed herself back off of the bed and rushed to the door trying to force it open. When nothing worked she pounded her fists against it and yelled, "Let me out! I need to see Nikolai!" over and over. When her voice grew hoarse and she finally realized that she would draw no response from her family she put her back against the door and slumped down onto the floor. She felt exhausted. Completely drained, as though she'd been torn apart and everything was falling out of her.

Sarah heard her mother wailing through the walls. She realized that Annie must have told her what she had seen. Her mother sounded as though she were in great agony. How could it be so bad what she had done? She loved Nikolai. What was so wrong in that? She was so shamefully innocent that she did not see the consequences of her behavior in respect to the rest of the family.

Other than her mother's sobbing the house felt deathly quiet. No one wanted to upset their father any further.

By the time Anton arrived to discuss the situation Henry had composed himself and felt ready to deal with him. Henry still couldn't understand how his daughter could have allowed herself to be in such a shameful situation. With all of the workers having witnessed the spectacle they had all made of themselves word was sure to move quickly to their Mennonite neighbors.

He would have to stand before them and beg their forgiveness. He would have to think about that later. Anton was standing in front of him.

Anton held his hat nervously in both of his hands in front of himself, scrunching the brim with his fingers. He bowed his head in profound shame as he said, "Mr. Doerksen, I'm so sorry about what my son has done to your daughter. I . . . I," he stammered, "I know we can't restore the innocence that our children had before this, but we will do whatever you like to make this right." Anton took a deep breath and went on, "I know that inter-marriage is discouraged, but Nikolai would like to marry . . ."

"Stop it! Stop right there! Your son will never be a welcomed part of this family! Sarah, as far as I am concerned is ruined. No decent and upright man will ever want to marry her and I will certainly not allow her to marry a Russian. Normally in this type of situation there would have been a beating required but I feel that I have already overstepped my bounds so all that I require of your family is that you leave. I want you to go far from this region so we will never have to see you again," he paused.

"Yes sir, of course," Anton obliged. His head still bowed.

Henry continued," You may take the rest of the day to pack your belongings. I will provide you with one horse and one of the smaller wagons. You may take enough food supplies to last you for several days. I want you far from Terekeransiedlung before you need to stop for anything. Sarah will remain locked in her room until you are gone. You must leave first thing tomorrow morning."

Anton felt so grateful. "Oh, thank-you so much Mr. Doerksen. You are doing far more for us than you need to after all that has happened. I will get started right away," and he turned to leave.

"One more thing," motioned Henry with his pointing finger, "Tell that son of yours to stay in your cabin until you're ready to leave tomorrow. I don't ever want to see his face again," he finished threateningly.

Anton nodded as he hurried out of there.

His wife waited at the open door as Anton stepped inside their modest home. She closed it quickly behind him and motioned for Anton to sit on the wooden chair by the bed. They waited for him to speak.

"Nikolai, before I say anything I want you to restrain yourself. I don't want any outbursts from you or any confrontation. Do you understand?"

Nikolai nodded, but his eyes had a wild look in them, as though he would burst out of their home at any second to get to Sarah.

"Do you understand?!" Anton repeated very firmly.

Nikolai took a deep breath and let his body relax as he answered, "Yes father. I will control myself."

"All right. Mr. Doerksen wants us to leave his farm and never ever to return. He especially requested that he never see your face again Nikolai and that you stay inside until we are ready to go tomorrow."

Nikolai's face contorted as he wailed, "No! No! That can't be. Please father, didn't you tell him that I wanted to marry Sarah?"

Anton answered, "Of course I did, but he did not want to hear a word about that. He said that there was no way that she would ever be allowed to marry a Russian, especially now. Now you can't do anything more foolish Nikolai. We must all suffer now because of what you have done but Mr. Doerksen is being very generous. He is giving us a wagon and a horse and some food supplies. I don't want you to do anything to ruin our family's chance of survival. Do you understand?"

Nikolai just nodded. The pain inside of him was too great to even speak. He didn't even realize it but tears were streaming down his face as he grasped the full meaning at what his father had just told him. He would never see Sarah again. How could he even think of living without her? Maybe they should have tried to run away together. At least, had they not survived, they would have been together.

His mother had her arms wrapped tightly around him, "Shh Nikolai," she whispered in his ear soothingly. "It will be alright. Things will make sense in time." She pulled him onto the bed and they sat there together. She, cradling him as she had done in infancy and him mourning the loss of one that meant more to him than anything else in the entire world.

Sarah was left alone in her room that entire night. Long after dark her youngest sister Frieda brought her some supper and the chamber-pot. Ernst their older brother held the door open for Frieda and guarded it so that Sarah would not be able to leave. They'd been instructed not to speak to Sarah so none of her questions were answered.

Sarah could see that Frieda was very distressed by this whole situation so she thanked her kindly for bringing the food. She didn't want to worry Frieda.

Although she should have been hungry after all the events she just couldn't eat. What was happening to Nikolai? How could she make her family understand if they wouldn't even talk to her?

Annie and Frieda must have slept somewhere else that night because they never came to bed. Sarah tried to sleep but she just couldn't stop thinking about all that had happened. Close to morning she fell into a restless sleep, plagued by dreams that made no sense at all.

Earlier than usual she heard noises outside. She could hear people talking and what sounded like the clip-clop of a horse pulling a tired wagon. She strained to hear what was going on but everything was too hushed. Her own house was still completely quiet. No one had yet gotten up or started any of the usual chores. What was going on? She just couldn't make any sense of it.

Then she heard what sounded like the people climbing on and the wagon leaving their property. Just as the sounds of the wagon and horse were fading away she distinctly heard shouting, "I love you Sarah! I love you!"

"Nikolai! Nikolai!" she screamed as she realized what was happening. How could they leave? Her father, he must have sent them away. "Let me out! Let me go with them! Please father, please!" She felt like a caged animal. She banged her fists against the door and the walls and shouted.

Through all of this she was completely ignored. No one stirred. Of course they could all hear her but they dared not talk to her. After several more hours had passed her family got up for the day.

This time Annie was sent in to fetch and empty her chamber-pot and bring her some breakfast. Annie kept her head high and her eyes averted from Sarah. She felt absolutely no compassion for what Sarah was going through. Such immoral behavior deserved no acknowledgement just severe punishment. As far as she was concerned, Sarah, with all her free spiritedness could remain here till she completely succumbed to their rules of society.

Sarah sat on the chair in their room watching Annie with complete defiance. She would not let Annie see the defeat that she felt. As soon as the door was once again locked behind Annie, she crumpled. She dragged herself back onto her bed and let the pain that was within her soak her bedding. She felt completely broken. She felt so weak and helpless and empty.

Nikolai was gone. What did it matter now if she was locked in her room? She could stay here forever. What purpose was there in life without him? Life would never be the same for her again. She felt as though her spark had been extinguished.

For two days the family left her alone in her room. Henry wanted to make sure that Nikolai would be far gone before his daughter was released. He didn't want to take any chance of her trying to go after him.

On the third day Annie came in and informed Sarah that she was to get herself cleaned up and go speak to their father.

Sarah decided she might as well obey. Maybe she could still persuade him to change his mind, although she felt quite hopeless. From lack of sleep, food, and fresh air she felt very weak. It took all of her strength to wash down her body and change her clothes.

When she came into the kitchen, father was already sitting at the head of the table. He motioned for Sarah to sit at the other end. For the first time Sarah felt a quiver of fear deep within her. He looked so reserved and indifferent to her. She could not feel even an ounce of love or warmth coming from him.

"Sarah, from now on you will sit at that end of the table. I cannot stand to have you any closer. You have caused our family great shame. " Henry spoke matter of factly.

"Father I," Sarah interjected.

"Quiet! I don't want to hear anything you have to say. We have tried to raise you to be an upright young woman and you have gone and done something so sinful. There must be something very evil inside of you," he continued.

Sarah just bowed her head and nodded quietly. She could feel hot tears forming inside of her just waiting to be spilled.

"You will have to come up to the front of the church with me and beg their forgiveness. By now I'm sure the whole community will know what has gone on here. You will be shunned by everyone for your entire life Sarah. No man will ever want to marry you now and I will also never allow it." He emphasized the word never. "Never!" making it sound like eternity. "Had I had any knowledge at all that you liked this boy I would have sent him away the same way that I sent Mishka's family away!"

Sarah found her voice and spoke with astonishment, "You sent Mishka away? Father, how could you? We were such good friends! We were closer than sisters." Sarah was completely stupefied by this revelation. She started thinking back to that time when Mishka's family had decided to move. She now recalled that it really hadn't made much sense. They had made a good life for themselves on the Doerksen farm. They'd gotten along well with everyone. "Father, why?" she repeated with resentment and bitterness in her throat.

"Because you were becoming too involved with them. I did not want you to start to accept their life-style as your own. We worship a living God Sarah, not statues and icons. God has given us specific instructions on how to live a pure and clean life. I had hoped that by now you would have understood that but obviously there is no respect in you for God Almighty," he answered in dismay.

The bitterness stirred the fire back to life within Sarah. She no longer felt fear but great anger at her father. "If God made all of us, Father, than why is it so wrong for one culture to marry with another? Should we not all be equal in his eyes? Or is it just your eyes, Father? Do you see us as better than them? Just because we were privileged enough to be given this land and can have control over all the peasants."

How dare she speak to him like that?! How could she be so different in her way of thinking? Well, he would put an end to this nonsense right now. "Sarah, I will not have you speaking to me that way. For now you will remain within our house. All your chores will be inside only. There will be no more wanderings around the land by you."

For Sarah this was the same as a prison sentence and Henry knew it. For her life was outdoors, not behind the confines of a building.

Henry stood up to leave, "Go and see you mother. She will tell you the chores that you are now to be responsible for. "

Life for Sarah, as she had known it to be, was over. Any respect that she had had for her Father was gone. He obviously had no love for her. If he had he would not have sent away people that had meant so much to her. She didn't care that she would never be allowed to marry. For her there would never be anyone other than Nikolai.

Chapter
4

Gone was the crispness of September air, replaced by a sharp chill. Winter seemed to be coming early and the cold environment matched the cold heart within Sarah. Life was dull and hopeless. She spent every day scrubbing and cleaning up after her family. Annie, of course, had never looked happier. She seemed on occasion to even go out of her way to leave extra mess for Sarah.

Sarah did not complain. She knew that her life would not change and there seemed to be no point in making anymore waves.

No one would listen to her anyway. No one even spoke to her except with orders.

Going in front of the people of their congregation had been completely humiliating. Having to beg their forgiveness, when in her heart, she knew that could she go back she would probably repeat everything in the same way, had been very difficult. But in order that her family would still be able to face their community, she had tried to give it an honest effort.

On Sundays she still went to church with her family, but now she always sat at the back, with her head held down. The other young people with whom she had often spent time with during social gatherings had been forbidden to associate with her by their families. Sarah could see that people often stared at her and whispered things about her. She was almost feared. As if some of her wickedness would rub off on them.

She was completely isolated. Only her brother Jakob and Frieda had managed to find some time when they were alone to talk to her and give her some encouragement. Jakob had confided that he too at times wrestled with feelings of desire for girls but after seeing what that would lead to would wait until he was allowed to marry. He assured her that he still loved her but that he wouldn't be making too much effort to talk to her for fear of repercussions to himself. Maybe when they were older life would change and things would seem more normal again. Sarah had just nodded in agreement. She did not want him to get into any trouble because of her.

Frieda had given her a big hug and told Sarah that she missed playing outside with her. She didn't understand why father didn't want her talking to Sarah. Was Sarah really that bad? Sarah just told her that she should listen to father and that in her heart she would always be there for Frieda. Everything was very complicated right now but when Frieda was a grown woman she would explain it all to her. Frieda had been happy with this and gone back out to play.

Days passed by, one fading into the other. Life for Sarah was monotonous. Sunshine had left her continence. Every day she felt so tired. All she really wanted to do was stay in bed and sleep. Of course she wasn't able to. Instead she had to force her weary body to respond to everything that was required of her.

Today would be no different from other days. But as Sarah pulled herself out of bed she felt a very queasy feeling in her stomach. She had to swallow to keep herself from heaving. She managed to get herself dressed and went into the kitchen to help with preparations for the morning meal.

While stirring the eggs the nausea returned. She felt her cheeks flushing and as the smells from the kitchen assailed her she started to heave.

"Sarah, what's wrong?" asked her mother in surprise. "You look horrible. Come, let's get you to the outhouse, before you get sick in here."

Sarah just nodded in consent. She was trying to hold her breath so the she wouldn't have to smell all the aromas that seemed to be bothering her so much.

Outside she started to feel a bit better. The cold air was clean and sharp and odorless. Soon her heaving subsided and she was able to catch her breath. Since she hadn't yet eaten anything nothing came up.

Her mother had stayed with her the entire time. "Are you feeling better now?"

"Yes mother. It was all the smells in the kitchen. For some reason the thought of going back in there just makes me feel very ill."

Margaret leaned herself against the outside wall of the outhouse. She clasped her hands to her face as she said, "Oh, my dear God! Not this yet too."

"Mother, what is it? What are you talking about?"

"Sarah, I think you are pregnant. What are we going to do? As if it wasn't shameful enough what you have already put us through. Now we will also have to deal with an illegitimate child." Margaret sank to the ground, leaning against the outhouse, and cried out of pity for herself and the rest of her family.

Sarah was stupefied. How could she be pregnant? Didn't women have to be married first? She had always thought that people just got married and somehow a woman's body would know that it was time to be with child. "Mother, I don't understand. I'm not even married. How can I be pregnant?"

Margaret removed her hands from her face and with shock stared at her daughter. Just then she realized her own mistake in all of this. She had never told Sarah about the intimate act required between a man and a woman to produce a child. For that matter she had never explained this to any of her children. One just didn't speak of these matters. It was assumed that once married a couple would figure this all out. Had Sarah known that her wanton activity could lead to having children, perhaps she would have refrained.

Margaret seemed to be in a daze so Sarah repeated herself, "Mother, why do you think that I am pregnant?"

Margaret pulled herself together and looked into her daughter's eyes as she spoke, "Sarah, what you did with Nikolai, is what made you pregnant. When a man and a woman come together in that way, that is how babies are made."

Sarah felt herself blushing as memories of passionate afternoons flashed in her mind.

Margaret saw the shame and for the first time felt some compassion for her daughter. "Sarah, I know now that you had no idea what you were doing or what it would all lead to. For now let's just keep this between us. I need to think about what I will say to your father. You can stay in bed today and I'll get Frieda to bring you some tea and dried buns. Come now, it's too cold to stay out here to talk." Margaret put her arm around Sarah and ushered her back to the house.

Once inside Sarah did as she'd been told. She lay in her bed thinking about what her mother had said. Was she really carrying Nikolai's child within her? The thought was both frightening and exciting. Her mind whirled with all that this realization could mean. She would have a part of Nikolai with her for always. How wonderful. She felt her spirit start to lift and some of the joy return. There would be someone for her to love and to love her back. She would not be alone forever. She fantasized about what it would be like to hold a small baby and cuddle her child in her arms.

With these thoughts in mind she drifted into a peaceful sleep. She gave way to the weariness that had overtaken her body and allowed herself to rest.

*****

Sarah awoke to the sound of her parents arguing in their bedroom down the hall. She could not make out what was being said but knew instantly that her mother was telling her father about the child. Panic and fear welled up inside of her. What would her father do now?

The thought of punishment sickened her and she felt the nausea assail her once more. How could a baby make a person feel so awful?

She decided she'd better put on something warm and run out to the outhouse again. Perhaps if she could actually vomit she'd feel better.

Outside the sky was quickly darkening and Sarah realized that she had slept most of the day. She quickly made her way to the outhouse but before she had reached it she started retching and her body forced her to expel all that was within her stomach. When the heaving finally stopped she searched for a small branch to cover up the vomit with dirt and leaves. Although her throat felt quite raw and she had a most horrible sour taste in her mouth she did feel better.

Sarah took a minute longer just to breath in the fresh clean air and then decided that she had better go back into the house to face whatever fate her father had decided for her.

Margaret was just coming into the kitchen as Sarah came in through the outside door. "There you are. Sarah, your father will now speak to you. You can go and see him in our bedroom."

"Yes, mother," she replied obediently. Sarah knocked on his door.

"Who is it?" asked Henry.

"Sarah, father."

"Come in," he replied.

Sarah walked in and closed the door behind her.

"You can sit down over there," he told her pointing to the chair in the corner. She did as she was told and folded her hands in her lap and waited for him to speak. "Your mother tells me that she suspects that you are with child. We are, of course, very unhappy about this. Since there is nothing that we can do about this problem we will just have to accept it and deal with it. Sarah, life will now get even more difficult for you and us. This child will be a constant reminder to us and everyone in the community about your wanton behavior."

He took a deep breath. He did not want to admit that this was one consequence that he had not even thought of when he sent Nikolai away. He had been so angry the thought that there may have been the chance of pregnancy had never even occurred to him or his wife.

"I want you to know that just because you are pregnant you will not be pampered. Everything that was required of you before will still be required of you now."

"Yes, father," answered Sarah. A part of her was so happy that she didn't care if she had to continue working hard. "I will do my best."

"Good. Morning sickness is a normal part of pregnancy and you will have to work through it. I will not assert any other punishment on you because I feel that you will suffer a lifetime of humiliation through your child. It will be a very painful lesson."

Henry slumped down onto the bed. Some of the fight within him had deflated. It was as close to compassion as he would get. "You may go now. And Sarah close the door behind you. I need to be alone to pray." After she'd closed the door he poured his heart out to the Lord. He begged for forgiveness for his daughter and for himself. He asked for understanding as to where he had gone wrong. Nothing had ever felt so painful to him before. And yet the love that he should have felt for his daughter still did not come. His own inability to forgive constricted the warmth of love that God could give him.

Chapter
5

Sarah stopped icing the cookies for a minute and watched all the commotion going on all around her. The house was filled with people doing last minute preparations for Annie's wedding. Some of their neighbors had come over to help and for the first time in months it seemed that the house was filled with warmth. Everyone was excited to have something festive to break up the monotony of the long, cold winter. Of course, as a Russian farmer it was tradition to have weddings in the winter. Spring, summer, and fall were just too busy a time with planting and harvesting.

Sarah's belly was just starting to protrude a little and a few of the women had given her disdainful looks. Sarah had lowered her eyes and blushed, not only from shame but also from anger. They just thought that they were so much better than she. But were any of them without sin? She thought not.

Not once did any of them even bother to ask how she was feeling or what she was going through. But she wouldn't dwell on this. She had to think about the child that she would have and the life that she would give it.

As she stood watching people hurrying about she felt a strange flutter in her lower belly. It took her by surprise and she caught her breath making a bit of a sound. Her mother who had come up behind her noticed Sarah's quick intake of breath and the reaction of placing both hand on her belly.

Margaret knew instantly what her daughter was experiencing. She placed her hand on Sarah's lower back and whispered quietly in her ear, "That was your baby kicking you."

Sarah looked with surprise and wonder at her mother. Her mother put her index finger to her mouth signaling Sarah not to say anything but at the same time gave her a knowing smile. Feeling your child move inside of you for the first time was just such joy and such a miracle. The child inside of Sarah was pure and innocent and just as precious as all other children. She did not condone her daughter's behavior but she, for one, would not shun this child.

Feeling the love that radiated from her mother a single tear slid down Sarah's cheek. It seemed that for the first time in her life she shared something with her mother and it felt so good that it hurt. Knowing that Sarah needed a bit of time alone to regain her composure Margaret said, "Why don't you go and get changed for your sister's wedding while I finish up here?"

"Thank-you Mama," was all she managed to say before she left the kitchen. Everyone was so busy, fixing hair, hemming dresses, preparing decorations, that they hadn't even noticed the emotions that had transpired between Sarah and her mother.

Sarah was thankful to get a few moments to herself before having to face the stares of all the people she was sure to get when she arrived at the church. She washed her face in the small water basin in her room. It was ice-cold but it felt good on her eyes. She was crying again but this time for joy. Knowing that her mother would be there to share with her what she was going through was such an unexpected gift, it left her deeply moved.

*****

Sarah sat on the hard church pew with her hands folded in her lap and her eyes looking towards the floor. She'd looked over at Annie standing in front of minister with her husband to be. Annie still looked so serious and morose. Shouldn't she be happier? She had seemed nervous throughout this past week. Sarah wondered if her sister would ever allow herself to feel any joy.

She couldn't help but think of Nikolai at this time. If only it could have been the two of them up there right now. She certainly would not have been able to contain the joy that she would have felt. What was he doing now? What was he feeling? Did he miss her as much as she missed him? She hoped and prayed that he had not joined as a soldier in the war that was going on.

A tear slid down her cheek as the familiar ache closed in on her chest. She could still picture him perfectly in her mind. He was tall, and although quite slim you could see the physical strength that he possessed. His fair colored hair seemed to shine when the sunlight hit it. Without warning she felt the familiar yearning to touch him and be touched by him.

She blushed at the thought and quickly tried to re-focus her attention on the ceremony. At least the people in the church would have no idea what she'd been thinking or feeling. Everyone now just assumed that she was consumed by guilt over all of her actions.

Sarah looked at Annie and wondered at how strange it must feel to marry and give yourself to someone you hardly knew. Even if she wasn't in the situation she was now in she would never have agreed to this type of marriage. She was thankful that she had known true love. To Annie the act of consummation would probably always be a chore and just breed more bitterness. Sarah felt sad for her sister.

The couple walked down the aisle to the front door of the church to form a receiving line. Sarah's family followed them out. Not too much time was spent. It was bitterly cold and everyone wanted to hurry to get back to the Doerksen farm for refreshments.

Back at the house Sarah tried to stay out of everyone's way. No one spoke to her or even acknowledged her presence. She felt as though she may just as well have been one of the farm animals. Even they were treated better. She swallowed the lump that was in her throat. She had to be strong. This was certainly only the beginning. She would probably have to face this for the rest of her life.

*****

February had arrived. The Russian peasants on the Doerksen farm had celebrated Candlemas Day as usual. Everyone had tried to enjoy the fact that the days would now become longer and soon the heavy cold of winter gone once more. But underneath the festivities there was a tension in the air. The war was taking its toll on Russia.

They knew that they had it well here on the Doerksen farm. Things were not so well though for their fellow countrymen. Everything was being taken from them to feed the soldiers at the battle front. Peasants were hungry and unhappy. They had heard that the railroads were being used to ship military supplies to the soldiers. This meant that food and fuel was not being supplied to the cities.

The peasant families were worried about their young sons. Young men were being drafted and sent to the front lines. Not having been properly trained as soldiers this certainly meant death for them. So they did what was required of them on the farm but the tension and worry was easily felt.

Henry Doerksen was not worried though. He knew that the Russian people who worked for him were completely loyal. The workers on the farm had told him that since he had always treated them so well that they would stick by his family with whatever was to come.

Henry was worried about his son Herbert. Herbert was spending more time in Terekeransiedlung and trying to gather all the information he could about the war. Up until now the Doerksen's had not been affected by what was going on around them but Herbert thought that it was just a matter of time.

Mennonite people did not fight and part of the agreement of working the land in Russia was that they would not be called upon to work as soldiers. Herbert felt very edgy about everything that was going on and wanted to be involved. He announced to his father that he would be joining other young Mennonite men in helping the injured Russian soldiers. He loved the land in which they lived and wanted to do what he could to protect it.

Herbert was a grown man now and Henry knew that he had to let him go. He knew that his son would be helping others and this gave him some comfort. To actually get involved in the fighting would be a sin and totally against their beliefs.

Although Russia was at war with Germany, the German Mennonites in this region were totally dedicated to Russia. They now had entire families here and a whole new way of life. They prospered.

Sarah had no doubts as to where her heart lay. She was devoted to a young Russian man, carrying his child, and she would help his people any way she could. She fantasized about her brother meeting Nikolai, telling him about the child, and that he would come back for her.

It seemed that her father had softened to her and perhaps now he would be ready to allow her to marry Nikolai.

She no longer felt sick now and actually felt quite strong. She could work in the kitchen without being offended by any of the food odors.

Without Annie and Herbert it almost felt as though her family was becoming a tighter unit. Her parents missed them deeply but at the same time it almost seemed as though they realized even more how precious their children were to them.

Sarah once again spent more time with her younger sister Frieda, who was very happy to be allowed the freedom to talk to Sarah whenever she wished. Perhaps it was because it was still winter and everyone stayed indoors more they could monitor their children better. Whatever the reason was, Sarah was thankful. She desperately needed the companionship.

Her sister Frieda had been informed as to why Sarah's body was changing and had accepted all the facts nonchalantly contrary to what the parents had always thought. They had felt that if children knew about personal acts between a man and a woman they would become preoccupied with the idea. Not so with Frieda. She had processed the information and moved on to other daily activities. Being the youngest she had not had much to do with babies but she looked forward to the arrival of Sarah's.

Chapter
6

The sun felt soothing and warm on Sarah's arms as she reached up to pin the wet clothes onto the clothesline. The clean smell of the freshly washed laundry mixed with the warm sun was a pleasurable experience for Sarah. It just felt so good to be outside again. They were nearing the end of June and Sarah had once again been allowed to deal with outdoor chores. Her belly was so prominent now that she figured her parents must have thought that there was no way she would make any trouble.

The child within her moved continuously now, sometimes kicking so hard that it felt quite uncomfortable against her other organs. Sarah didn't mind though. "Soon I will see you my little one," she spoke softly to her belly as she touched it lovingly.

Being outside on a day such as this she thought of Nikolai. It had been almost a year ago that she had seen him for the first time on just such a day. At times she could almost not remember what he looked like, but she could remember exactly how he smelled and how she had felt being near him. Her heart always softened at these memories. She would never forget him but now at least she felt as though she could still go on with life.

Life on the farm seemed much quieter now. Many of their young workers had been drafted and there would be no influx of new workers. The pace of life seemed to have been slowed down considerably. Russian men were dying and the Russian people were starting to feel great discontent with their government. So far they had not yet heard from her brother Herbert who was voluntarily helping the injured soldiers on the frontline.

When her father went into town and had to deal with Russians he was not treated well. He felt completely Russian at heart, but he was not trusted now. The Russians felt that since he was originally German that he was now probably a spy and that all these Mennonites were their enemies.

The peasants who had spent years working for the Doerksen's remained loyal and held firm in their promise to protect and serve the Doerksen family in all that lay ahead.

Sarah finished with the laundry and went inside for a drink. Sitting in the kitchen with a glass of water she felt completely out of breath. The baby was so big now it seemed that her lungs could never quite fill with as much air as was needed to complete even minor tasks.

She was almost done for the day. Tomorrow was Sunday so she still had to do some house cleaning and food preparation. Her family would be going to church and wanting to do as little as possible in the way of chores. For her that meant a day of rest. The last few Sundays she had stayed home from church. People just looked at her with disdain and seemed to feel that it was disrespectful that she was even there. The tiny village of Terekeransiedlung had never yet faced such a situation and was completely abhorred with Sarah.

Evening arrived and Sarah was completely exhausted. She felt weariness right to her bones and was quite grateful when she could go to bed.

*****

Sarah awoke to a warm wash of sunlight on her face. Lazily she opened her eyes and turned towards the window to gaze outside. It was a beautiful day and at that moment she felt quite at peace and content. The house seemed unusually quiet so she got up to see what was going on.

It seemed that everyone had already left for church and let her sleep in. In a house where there was always so much activity it felt very strange to be there all by herself, surrounded in stillness. Even outside everything seemed eerily quiet.

Sarah decided that after she ate she would go out for a walk through the orchards.

She had not been allowed to go here since last fall and even now was a bit afraid about the consequences should her father arrive home before she returned. But she felt so invigorated from the extra sleep that the pull of the beautiful trees and the memories of what had once been was too great. Without even realizing how she had gotten there she was standing on the same spot where she and Nikolai had made love for the last time.

Crying like she hadn't cried in a long time she allowed all of her emotions to reach the surface. Sarah said good-bye. She now felt that she would most likely never see him again and the pain was once again unbearable.

She sank to the ground on her knees feeling spent once more. As she tried to pull herself together and contain her emotions she felt a sharp pain shoot over her belly and into her lower back. She sucked in her breath and grunted at the surprise of the pain. After a few seconds the pain ended and she could breathe again. She stood up and decided that she had better get back to the house. Too much time had passed and her family would probably be back soon.

After walking for just a few minutes she was engulfed in another intense burst of pain. She had to hold onto a tree just to keep on her feet. "Oh, Lord, what is happening now?" she spoke to herself.

As she continued on her way back to the house so did the pains, lasting what felt like an eternity, then giving minutes of respite in between. By the time she reached the edge of the orchard and could see her home she was completely covered in sweat.

Elizaveta, one of the older peasant women on the farm, noticed Sarah clinging to a tree and knew instantly that Sarah was in labor. She rushed over to help Sarah to the house. Sarah clung to the old woman, grateful to have someone with her. Elizaveta kept touching her belly and speaking rapidly in Russian to Sarah trying to tell her that her baby was coming. With all the gesturing Sarah finally understood what was happening and although relieved also quite frightened.

Elizaveta helped bring her into her house and into her room. There she had Sarah lay down on her side and stroked her shoulder trying to convey to Sarah that all would be alright now. She left to get some water and a wash cloth and proceeded to wash Sarah's forehead and arms.

When the pains stopped, Sarah tried to relax and think about something else. Surely this wouldn't last for very long. She had to stay strong and focused until the baby came.

After what seemed like hours of time to Sarah she heard her family outside and she relaxed a little, feeling reassured that everything would be alright now.

Elizaveta left her immediately to tell her mother that Sarah was in labor. Margaret came rushing in to check on Sarah. As she stepped into the room she could see that Sarah was in the middle of a contraction. Having experienced this many times herself she went over and took her hand not saying anything. Talking during a contraction just broke one's concentration and seemed to make the pain even worse. When this contraction was over she said, "We sent your brother Jakob to get the midwife from town. She will stay here until your baby arrives.

Everything will be all right."

"Is it supposed to hurt so much, mother?" Sarah asked.

"Yes, but while it's hurting just try to relax so your body can open the way for the baby," Margaret answered. There still seemed to be a good amount of time to rest in between contractions so Margaret guessed that there would probably still be a fair amount of time to pass before the child would be born.

By the time Jakob returned with Lieschen, the midwife, it was already starting to get dark out. The contractions still seemed to be at the same interval and it seemed that it would be a long night.

Lieschen had helped deliver many of the Mennonite women's children, but never to anyone who was not married. Coming over she had felt a bit uncomfortable but had decided that should she not go and things did not go well than she would not be looked upon in a favorable fashion. Besides, with the war going on, and the shortage of supplies she could use whatever the Doerksen's gave her in exchange for her work.

When she walked into the bedroom and saw this young woman in so much pain, she felt her own heart soften, and felt guilt over not having wanted to help.

"Hello Sarah. I'm Lieschen and I'm going to help you bring this child into the world."

Sarah just nodded.

Lieschen started to pull the blanket down as she said, " I'm going to have to remove your underclothes to check how far along you are."

Sarah looked to her mother for affirmation who nodded at her and said, "It's all right Sarah, this is the only way we will know when you're ready to start pushing." As she spoke she went over to close the bedroom door.

Sarah felt very vulnerable and ashamed as Lieschen lifted her dress to her chest and exposed her entire naked belly and proceeded to touch and prod her. Her mother had come back to hold her hand but had turned her face and body away from her as not to cause her any further embarrassment.

"Sarah, I must now put my hand inside of you to see how far you've opened," Lieschen said.

"Do you have to do that?" Sarah asked. No one had ever touched her there other than Nikolai and this felt much stranger.

"Yes, I do. I know it's not very comfortable but if you try to relax it'll be much easier, " Lieschen answered.

Lieschen moved her fingers over Sarah's vaginal area for a second and found the opening. Gently she inserted her fingers and reached until she found the area where the baby's head was pushing down. Just as she was trying to decide how far the cervix had opened Sarah started moaning. Another contraction was coming. Lieschen stopped moving her fingers and just held her hand in place until the pain had stopped.

She knew from her own personal births that this kind of probing during a contraction just seemed to intensify the pain. When the contraction was over Lieschen continued feeling the cervix. The opening at this point was only at two fingers width. This young woman has a long night ahead of her she thought. She gently removed her hand and went to wash up before she came back to cover Sarah.

"Sarah, I know that the pain you've had so far has already been quite intense and for what seems like a long time, but your body still has a lot of work to do. Your mother and I will take turns staying with you during the night. If you feel that you can sleep a bit, that's alright," said Lieschen.

Sarah nodded as another contraction came on.

"Margaret, could you prepare a bed for me? I'll stay with Sarah for now," said Lieschen.

"Certainly," said Margaret, " but I would like to take the first shift with Sarah. I don't think that I could sleep right now anyway."

"I understand," said Lieschen. Sarah being Margaret's first child to have a baby was probably quite nerve racking for the new grandmother to be. Margaret would know all too well the many things that could go wrong. The child could be turned in such a position that being born might not even be possible, or the cord could be around the child's neck, suffocating it before it ever even took its first breath.

Lieschen had already been at several such births where too many things had gone wrong and there was nothing that could be done. It was absolutely horrible to watch the hours of torture before either the child or both the child and mother could survive no more.

Fortunately she had been privileged enough to be at many wonderful and miraculous births before ever having to witness such horror. Had her first experience as a midwife been so sad and traumatic, Lieschen had often wondered if she would be doing this now.

"Spend your quiet times in prayer," Lieschen said to Margaret before she left the room to lie down.

Sometime during the middle of the night Sarah's pains subsided. Margaret being quite weary by now had Sarah turn over onto her side and told her to try to sleep for a bit. Margaret lay down beside her, gently placing her arm over the part of Sarah's belly that was now directly under her breasts, so not to put any extra pressure on Sarah's body. This was the closest physically that Margaret had been to Sarah since Sarah was a child. It felt very soothing and comforting.

As she felt Sarah's breathing slow down and relax she thought of how much fun they had all had watching Sarah as a young child. Sarah had always come up with things to say and do that were just not like her other children. They had to watch her very carefully so she wouldn't hurt herself on her little adventures.

Climbing fences when she wasn't supposed to, playing amongst the horses or the cattle, where she could easily have been trampled, wandering too far on their property, and the list could go on. Margaret smiled as she remembered these things. Slowly she too relaxed and dozed off.

A few hours later, as the sun came up, Sarah woke up feeling great pressure on her bladder. She had to get to the outhouse. As she gently started to get off the bed her mother woke up. "Where are you going?" asked Margaret.

"I need to go to the outhouse," said Sarah.

"You'd better stay inside and use the chamber pot," said Margaret. "I'll help you keep your balance."

"Alright," said Sarah. She felt quite embarrassed to do this in front of her mother but at this time the need was too great to give embarrassment much thought. She stood up and walked away from the chamber pot back towards her bed. Just before she was about to sit down she heard something like a slap. It felt as though she'd been kicked in her lower back. A second later, what felt like warm water, came gushing down her legs.

Margaret too had heard the sound. "What was that?"

"I don't know but I'm all wet," said Sarah as she stood completely still and looked down at the puddle on the floor.

"Your water broke," Margaret told her. "I'll get something to dry you off."

Seconds later Margaret came back in the room and saw Sarah on her knees on the floor, right in the puddle of amniotic fluid, hanging on tightly to the edge of the bed, holding her breath.

"Breath," Margaret commanded her.

"I can't," said Sarah through clenched teeth. "It hurts to much!"

"Slowly," said Margaret in a gentler voice as she stroked her head. "It's almost over."

Finally the contraction ended. Margaret cleaned Sarah and put a fresh night dress on her. Just as she had her settled back in bed the next contraction hit. This one seemed even more intense and lasted even longer. Margaret had told her to try to relax as much as possible, breathing in as normal a manner as she could so that she wouldn't become all tingly and pass out. Sarah focused only on this during the pains. How much more would she have to endure? "Is it time yet, Mother?"

"I will go and wake up Lieschen," answered Margaret. Lieschen was surprised to see daylight when Margaret woke her.

"You didn't get me all night," said Lieschen, slightly annoyed, realizing that Margaret would now be very tired.

Margaret sensed why Lieschen was a bit annoyed with her and answered, "Sarah's contractions stopped during the night and we both slept for a while. She woke up at sunrise needing to relieve herself. Right after her water broke and her contractions started right away. She's in much more pain now in her back as well as across her whole stomach. She's begging to know if it's time yet."

"Alright," said Lieschen, a bit calmer now. "I'll quickly go to the outhouse, then boil some water so I can properly clean my hands."

By the time Lieschen joined Sarah and Margaret in the bedroom other members of the household started to wake up.

Frieda knocked on the door and asked, "Has Sarah had her baby yet?"

Margaret opened the door slightly and said, "Not yet Frieda, but we think that it will be very soon now. I will come and get you when it's here. You run along now and start your chores. You can help your brother Peter in the barn today if you like."

Frieda's eyes lit up. "All right," she answered and ran off.

Margaret knew that Frieda also enjoyed tending to the animals much more than performing the household chores. This way Frieda wouldn't have to worry about the painful sounds coming from the bedroom.

Lieschen was just finishing examining Sarah when Margaret closed the door and came back into the room. "Sarah, you will surely be holding your baby in your arms by supper time today. The baby's head is pushing down nicely and you're about half way opened."

"Only half way?" Sarah thought to herself. The pain with every contraction was excruciating and she already felt that she could barely go on. "It hurts so much in my lower back," she stated to Lieschen as another contraction subsided. "Can I try sitting up?"

"Of course," answered Lieschen. "Margaret, could you get some extra pillows? We'll place them behind her back to prop her up in bed. And then you should go and have something to eat. It could be a long day and I don't want you to feel weak."

"Thank-you," said Margaret. It had already been many hours since she'd eaten and she felt quite hungry.

After they'd made Sarah more comfortable, Margaret went to have some breakfast. "And take your time too," offered Lieschen as Margaret left the room.

Henry was still sitting at the kitchen table when Margaret entered. He had an anxious look on his face. Margaret sensed that he was concerned about Sarah. As their eyes met Margaret answered him before he even needed to say anything. "Sarah is doing alright. Everything so far is progressing normally."

"Good," said Henry. "It just feels as though she's been in labor for a long time already. I thought that maybe I should stay close to the house today in case anything was needed."

His concern was quite touching for a man who conducted most of his days in a very formal and what could appear to be a cold manner. Margaret gently touched his arm and said, "I love you Henry." Although he was not a man accustomed to public affection, Margaret knew the passion within him. And she truly loved and respected this man.

Henry stayed with her while she ate her breakfast. Sitting still for too long was just not a part of his nature though, so as soon as she was done, he left to work around the yard. Margaret took some time to clean in the kitchen, then went back to be with Sarah.

Hours passed, but the progress was slow. The day had grown quite warm and with all the exertion of her body, Sarah felt very hot and sweaty.

Margaret and Lieschen took turns staying with her, wiping her down with a cool wet cloth.

It was almost time for dinner when Sarah felt great internal pressure on her vaginal area. "Something's pushing on me!" she exclaimed.

"Don't add to the pushing!" ordered Lieschen as she quickly went to check the cervix one more time. "All right Sarah. It's time to really focus and work hard. With the next contraction I want you to push as hard as you can. Try to push in the same spot as you feel the pressure right now."

Sarah just nodded because another contraction was already starting. She closed her eyes and started pushing. She didn't feel as though anything differently was happening. When it was over she asked if they could sit her up again. During the day she'd changed position many times. Right now she was laying on her right side. They hadn't even gotten her properly propped up yet when the next contraction came. Margaret and Lieschen were each on one side of her helping her to hold her body in a sitting position.

When this contraction ended they finished arranging the pillows around her and Lieschen placed extra towels under her buttocks. Margaret let her squeeze her hands as the contractions came and Lieschen massaged the vaginal opening to help it stretch. The massage actually helped to numb the pain a bit as the contractions hit. Lieschen knew that with a first baby it was sometimes quite difficult for the mother to figure out which muscles to use for pushing. Even though she could now see the top of the baby's head things could still take quite some time.

During the short periods of rest between the contractions they could hear the workers and family come in from the fields. Dinner time came and went but still no baby. Sarah had not managed to move the head downward even a slightest bit. Lieschen now felt that something had to be done to help move things along. Sarah was starting to get quite tired and weak. Lieschen could feel her losing hope. She did not want Sarah to give up.

She told Margaret to get one of their woman workers to come in to help. Margaret asked Henry to summon Elizaveta. Elizaveta, being one of the older women, would have much experience with childbirth, therefore probably the most helpful.

Lieschen took a large sheet, folded it fan style, and placed it across the upper portion of Sarah's belly. She knew that this would not be a very pleasant experience for Sarah but she needed help.

"Alright ladies," said Lieschen, "As soon as the next contraction comes and Sarah starts pushing, I want the two of you to help pull down with the sheet. When she stops pushing, tightly hold the sheet in place, so that the baby can't move back." While speaking she was also showing them what she meant so that Elizaveta would understand.

Elizaveta nodded her head. She seemed to know exactly what Lieschen wanted her to do.

As the contraction came, Sarah pushed as hard as she could internally, while the ladies pushed externally with the sheet. Being at this point in pregnancy her entire stomach area was very sensitive to touch. Sarah braced herself at the uncomfortable feeling of all the pressure. As the contraction ended she could definitely feel that the baby's head had moved a bit further. And when she relaxed the pressure of the sheet kept the baby in place.

"Sarah, you need to work very hard with the next one! Give it all your strength!" Lieschen ordered.

Together they all pushed as hard as they could. Sarah screamed as the baby's head finally entered the birth canal. "Ahhh!" It felt as though her vaginal area was on fire. As though a burning log had been placed inside of her. She couldn't move away from the feeling though. The ladies were tightly holding the baby in place.

"One more good push, Sarah," said Lieschen in a very firm voice, "And the baby will be here."

The next contraction was unbearable. From deep within herself, Sarah grasped all the strength she could find, and pushed again. Lieschen used her hands to work her way past the baby's head to help with the shoulders. With a gush of amniotic fluid following the baby seemed to pop out.

With confident expertise Lieschen used her free hand to catch the head and shoulders.

"You have a baby boy, Sarah!" she said with elation.

Sarah took a deep breath as she leaned back and looked at the baby Lieschen was bundling. She was so amazed at this small child who'd come from her body that she didn't even notice that her body was still having contractions to expel the afterbirth. She watched Lieschen clean the inside of the baby's mouth. Then she held her son upside down and gave him a little pat on his bum. He immediately gasped for air and started crying. Then she laid him back on the bed, cut the umbilical cord, and tied it off. Lieschen tightly wrapped a narrow band around the entire belly and back of the baby to keep the belly button area from popping open.

Margaret too, seemed to be in shock. This had been quite the experience. She had never witnessed anyone else have a child.

When Lieschen was finished preparing the baby she said to Margaret, "Why don't you sit down in the chair for a bit. You can hold your grandson, while I clean Sarah."

Margaret numbly nodded and did as she was told. It had been many years now since she had held such a little one. The boy was still crying and as she tried to calm him down she felt the reality of it all. She was now a grandmother. She had a grandson. Although just a newborn he felt very solid. Holding him felt so good.

Margaret walked over to Sarah with the baby. "Look at your son Sarah. He's beautiful."

Lieschen finished with Sarah. Sarah was lying down on her side. Margaret placed the baby in Sarah's arms. He felt so warm. So good. His face was a bit red, but he looked truly beautiful. She could hardly believe that she was holding a baby in her arms. Her own baby. "I will name him Nicholas."

"That is a good name," said Margaret. "A nice and strong sounding name for a boy his size." It was the German version of Nikolai. Her husband, Henry, might object to the constant reminder of Nikolai, but Sarah at least had the right to name her child as she pleased.

Sarah smiled at her mother in thankful appreciation.

"Now I think that boy of yours is hungry. He hasn't stopped crying." said Margaret. Margaret helped Sarah to adjust her nightdress so that her right breast was completely exposed. While Nicholas once again opened his mouth wide to wail she quickly pushed his head towards Sarah's breast, landing his mouth right onto the nipple. He seemed kind of surprised. He wasn't sure what he was supposed to do.

As he clamped his jaw closed a drop of the sweet liquid which precedes breast milk dropped onto his tongue. He quite enjoyed this taste. It didn't take him too long to figure out to clamp and release with his jaw, while sucking and swallowing at the same time.

Sarah marveled at how natural this felt. Although he sucked so hard that it hurt, she also felt very comfortable doing this for her child. She already felt so connected to him.

"Since he's quiet I'll go out and tell the family," said Margaret. "Lieschen, I'll get one of the boys to take you home on the wagon. I'm sure that your family is missing you by now."

"Thank-you. If Sarah has any problems or if something doesn't seem quite right with the baby, don't hesitate to get me."

The three women left the room. Sarah bent her head forwards so that her cheek could feel the top of her baby's head. It felt so soft and tender. She'd been told not to nurse too long on one side so she carefully rolled Nicholas over her belly as she also rolled to her other side. She was definitely still very tender and sore in her vaginal area. As she used her legs to turn herself she noticed that they too felt very weak, almost rubbery. Nicholas didn't like the fact that he'd been removed from the breast and once again started fussing. This gave Sarah the perfect opportunity to push his head against her other breast. As he closed his mouth he latched on again. Content.

Henry and the five children currently still at home were all anxiously sitting around the kitchen table. They'd all heard the baby crying. It had almost felt as if they'd all been holding their breath until that moment. Finally they could breathe a bit easier.

Margaret smiled at her family as she and Lieschen walked into the kitchen. She knew that they were all awaiting to hear about the baby so she wasted no time in telling them, "Sarah, has a beautiful and healthy baby boy!"

"Can we go see him?" asked Frieda excitedly.

All eyes turned towards Margaret's, asking the same thing.

"Yes. As soon as Sarah's done nursing. That boy came into this world screaming for food," answered Margaret.

"Just like the rest of us Doerksens," announced Ernst patting his stomach, "Always hungry."

This broke the tension in the room as everyone laughed and started chatting.

"Well Ernst," said Margaret, "Then why don't you and Frieda prepare a snack for everyone while I go check on Sarah."

One by one the family took turns visiting with Sarah and the baby.

When Nicholas looked directly at his grandfather Henry, he could not resist picking up this innocent baby. Even Henry's heart seemed to have been softened by the arrival of this child.

Sarah smiled at her father. She was thankful that he would not scorn her child.

"I'm very glad that both you and Nicholas are alright," said Henry.

"Thank-you father," said Sarah with emotion in her voice. Sarah now knew that her family would stand by her and support her.

Chapter
7

Before they could see them, they could hear them. Soldiers marching home from the front lines. Large number of soldiers, at times a greater number than battalion strength, came streaming home from the front fully armed, with machine guns, and horses.

They poured into villages demanding and taking food, fodder, clothing or whatever they wanted.

Sarah quickly grabbed her toddler, who'd been playing under the huge tree in their front yard, and hurried into the house.

So much had happened in the world around them in the past year.

The current czar of Russia had been accused of crippling the war efforts because he had removed many capable officials from high government offices and replaced them with weak, unpopular men.

Early in March of 1917, the people revolted. In St. Petersburg, riots and strikes over shortages of bread and coal grew more violent. Troops were called in to halt the uprising, but they joined it instead. So did the aristocrats, who had turned against the czar. On March 15, 1917, Nicholas II, who had lost all political support, was forced to abdicate.

Sarah's brother Herbert had also come home from helping as a Red Cross worker. He had seen firsthand what was going on in the cities country around them. He was desperately warning the Mennonite people of what he believed was coming their way.

Everywhere, that Herbert had been, there were speeches, demonstrations, slogans without end, music and jubilation. Many of the demonstrators seemed to have no real idea what they were marching or yelling for. But the one clear idea that Herbert realized everyone understood was that the Czar had abdicated and now there was freedom. People were weary of the war. They wished an end to it and that peace would now come.

Kerensky was now the head of the provisional government. He'd had or so it seemed, obtained control of the situation throughout the country. The new government also did not fully grasp how desperately tired the broad masses were of the war and how deeply they hoped for peace and fundamental transformation of the Russian political and economic system. Kerensky rushed from city to city, front to front to encourage everyone to "fight to a victorious end of the war." But his efforts were in vain. Soldiers, by the thousands, were deserting the front.

During this time, a small group of revolutionaries called the Bolsheviks, started to form. Their leader, Vladamir Lenin, convinced the Bolsheviks that they should try to seize power. The Bolsheviks were telling the masses at home and the soldiers at the front to support them, for they alone would be able to give them "peace, bread, and land."

Just yesterday one of Herbert's friends who'd also worked at the Red Cross stopped by their farm on his way home. He told them that the revolutionary Red Guard workers, soldiers, and sailors had stormed the Winter Palace in St. Petersburg and arrested the members of the Provincial Government. The Bolsheviks were now in control.

*****

Within minutes of Sarah entering the house the soldiers marched onto their property. Sarah quickly found Frieda and told her to take Nicholas into their room to play. Henry had already talked to the soldiers and told Margaret to start preparing food. Sarah busied herself peeling potatoes. Henry and Herbert went out to kill some chickens for the soup.

"We will not have enough food to last us the winter if this keeps on," whispered Margaret to Sarah as she prepared the other vegetables for the soup.

Soldiers were already entering their home and making themselves comfortable. It was near the end of the day and everyone was tired.

Sarah watched through the kitchen window while she worked. Their property was overflowing with soldiers. Many were heading towards their barn and the peasants quarters. The smell of these men was indescribable. It was obvious that they had not bathed in days. The soldiers seemed oblivious to their condition. All they wanted right now was rest and food.

Sarah heard Nicholas giggling and turned around to see a soldier lifting him into the air making silly noises. The joy on the soldier's face was clearly evident. Sarah smiled. These men had not seen their families in a long time. They also did not know that Sarah was an unwed mother and that Nicholas was an illegitimate child. Nicholas was not being shunned.

Nicholas was now one and a half years old. For them this time had been quite good. Although they'd had to give quite a bit of their harvest to the government for the continuous war they'd still had plenty of food for themselves. Her family could not resist the bubbling nature and charm of little Nicholas. Sarah had on many occasions noticed that even her father couldn't help but smile at Nicholas' antics.

For Sarah, Nicholas had brought immeasurable joy. She'd loved every moment that she'd gone to her room to lie down to nurse him. His warm little body would snuggle in so close to her and often with his free little hand he would reach up to touch her hair. Usually he wouldn't let go. He'd fall asleep like that. When he was sound asleep she would gently pry his fingers loose so that she could leave the room to work on chores.

Frieda was still enough of a child to thoroughly enjoy playing little games of peek-a-boo or holding on to his hands trying to teach him how to walk. This past June just before his first birthday he'd figured that part of life out. Now of course they were chasing him everywhere they went.

Looking at Nicholas she was still often reminded of Nikolai. He definitely looked like his father and when he made certain expressions they were a complete replica of Nikolai. Her heart still yearned for Nikolai but her outlook on the world had once more softened. She felt hopeful for the future and wanted more than anything to give her son a wonderful life. She loved showing Nicholas new things. His excitement of seeing the animals or finding a pretty flower was contagious. She could see the world anew through his eyes.

Seeing Nicholas accepted by this soldier brought Sarah great pleasure. Although her own family and the farm workers treated him well this was not so when they went into town.

When they were in shops or at church the other mothers would not let their children play with him. Nicholas would be so happy to see another little face and then the mother would whisk her child away. Nicholas would get a confused look on his innocent little face and sometimes he'd start to cry. Sarah always quickly tried to mollify him by distracting him with something else that he might find exciting.

It was truly an awful feeling. It hurt her deeply that her son had to deal with this. She didn't know how to change this or if such a thing was even possible. These people were so set in their ways and beliefs. So she avoided as many trips into town as she could. On the farm they were happy. They were safe.

*****

Henry came into the kitchen with the slaughtered chickens. He told her brothers Ernst and Jakob to go into their cellar to get some bags of stored apples. They were to start handing them out to the soldiers resting in the barn and in the house. Hopefully this would show good will and keep them happy for a few hours until the supper was cooked.

Sarah could not recall ever seeing her father help in the kitchen but decided that it was best to keep quiet and not say anything. This was obviously a serious situation and there seemed to be urgency in preparing this meal.

Nicholas started fussing. He was also getting hungry. It was much past their own family's meal time but they would all have to wait.

When the soldier who'd been playing with Nicholas received his apple he cut off a slice, peeled it and gave it to Nicholas. Nicholas did not hesitate to take this generous offering. Quiet once more Sarah was able to relax and continue on with her work.

*****

Several hours later the soup was ready. Henry had placed a table out on the porch to place the pot of soup on. Sarah and her mother stood outside and ladled out portions to the soldiers as they came by with their bowls. Somehow everyone was fed.

Finally they had everything cleaned up and were able to sit down in their kitchen for their own meal. There was only one bowl of soup left so they all took turns dipping their bread.

"Tonight we will all sleep in Sarah's room," Henry announced. "The soldiers are already sleeping in all the other rooms." He said this with a look in his eyes that said no one was to protest.

*****

Morning came too soon. Sarah's shoulder bones and hip bones ached from sleeping on the hard floor. She'd given her bed to her mother hoping that Margaret would have a good sleep.

Outside they could hear the soldiers bustling around and making preparations to leave.

While having their own dinner last night they'd boiled eggs to give to the soldiers this morning. This time her father and two of her brothers stood at the entrance of their property to hand these out to the soldiers as they filed by.

A few hours later Henry and the boys came back into the house. He was very upset.

"They took our best horses with them and our hay wagon fully loaded with fodder. How are we supposed to do our planting and harvesting this coming year?" he said more to himself than anyone else.

Their family had been quite sheltered from the effects of the war until now. Herbert, though, had by this time witnessed much tragedy and put their loss in perspective. "Father, these men have been fighting for years. They've gone days without food. They've seen many of their comrades die. We all survived. If taking some of our supplies will help them rebuild their lives, then let them. Next year we will just work twice as hard and we'll be fine."

Henry looked at his son with admiration. Herbert had become a strong man with a good heart. "You are right, Herbert," said Henry. "God will continue to take care of us."

Everyone relaxed and sat down to enjoy their breakfast. Just as they were finishing there was a knock on the front door. Henry stood up to see who it was.

Abe Toews, one of the overseers who lived right in town, walked in all flushed and breathless. "We believe that a group of bandits is heading our way. Two nights ago they were in Stawropol, a few towns over, and completely destroyed it. They took everything they could get their hands on. When people tried to stop them they were shot down!"

"Dear God! That's brutal! What is everyone planning to do to protect themselves?" asked Henry.

"Well, some of the people are already packing up what they can and are planning to move to the town in the other direction and just wait until the bandits are through," answered Abe. "Others believe that if they don't resist and just let the bandits take what they want, they will be fine."

Sarah, feeling anger arise in her, because of this injustice, asked, "Who are these bandits?"

"They are groups of peasants who believe the Bolshevik slogan "Plunder the Plunders" and now want to take what they feel is owed to them," answered Abe.

"And we are the plunderers?" asked Sarah.

"Yes, because years ago the Czarist government gave our people so much land to farm. The peasants believe that it should belong to them. The Bolshevik government believes that everything is now owned by them and encouraging the peasants to take back what is theirs and to live wherever they want." answered Abe. "I'd better go now. I have two more farms to warn before I go home to pack up my own family."

"Hopefully we'll see you in a few days," said Henry as he said good-bye to Abe.

This would be a difficult decision to make. Should they stay on the farm or pack what they can and hope to be safer somewhere else. And what if the bandits didn't even come in this direction.

"What would you like us to do father?" asked Herbert.

"I'm just not sure, "answered Henry, "but I think that to start with we should have a meeting with all of our workers and explain to them what is going on. So if you boys can get everyone to meet in the barn in ten minutes maybe we can come up with some ideas."

When her father and brothers had left for the barn Sarah turned to her mother. "Are you all right mother?" she asked, "You look very tired, almost ill."

"I think I'm afraid Sarah. We are sitting here in our warm house and everything is calm and peaceful, but I think that our world will be turned upside down," Margaret stated. "I'm just not sure if I'm ready for something like that."

"Mother, I will be strong for both of us. You've worked so hard and for so long taking care of all of us, and always still finding ways to show us love." Sarah had a young son to take care of and protect and she would work to her last breath to make sure that her family was safe.

"Mother, why don't you lay down for a while? Frieda and I will bake some buns and prepare lunch so that we can be ready for whatever father decides."

At lunch Henry told them that the peasants on their farm completely supported the Doerksen family. They felt that they had always been treated very well and richly taken care of. There was a small bridge at the entrance of their property and some of the peasants were going to hide in the bushes and try to take the bandits by surprise. Hopefully scare them away. If the bandits did get through then the Doerksen's were to hide in the cellar.

The boys spent the afternoon making the cellar comfortable. They brought in straw for cushioning and covered it with blankets so that they would all be comfortable for the night. Some of the peasants had suggested burying tools and necessary farm equipment in the orchard for safe keeping.

When night came their property seemed deathly quiet. Sarah's brothers would take turns staying up during the night to listen for any commotion. After all the preparations they'd made for this inevitable event, sleeping was very difficult. The danger just felt so real.

Nicholas could not fall asleep either. Sarah had a difficult time keeping him still beside her. When her brother Ernst came down from keeping watch she asked him what time it was. He told her that the sun would soon be coming up. Sarah decided to take Nicholas to their own room for the rest of the night so that everyone could get some sleep. She told her brother Jakob, who'd be keeping watch next to wake her if anything happened.

As soon as they were in their own bed he relaxed and fell asleep beside her. She, too, must have fallen into a deep sleep, because the sun was already high in the sky when Nicholas awoke her with his playing around beside her.

Margaret was in the kitchen preparing lunch when Sarah came in to feed Nicholas and herself. "Is it already lunch time?"

"Yes, the two of you were sleeping so well, we didn't want to wake you. We don't know how many more nights we will have like this so you might as well get as much rest as you can." answered Margaret.

"Where is everyone?" asked Sarah.

"Father sent Ernst into town to see if there is anymore news about the bandits," replied Margaret. "We've also sent Jakob to warn your sister Annie to prepare themselves for trouble. We're not sure if anyone from town was sent to tell them about what's been happening. Herbert seems to think that because Annie and Werner just live in a small cottage with no valuable possessions at this time that they'll be left alone."

Now, in the daylight, everything seemed as though it was normal. Herbert had warned them all though not to let their guard down. He felt that it was just a matter of time before one of these partisan bands made it their way.

When Ernst came back from town he confirmed Herbert's warnings. There was still a group heading towards Terekeransiedlung.

That night Nicholas seemed a little more comfortable in the cellar. Frieda had taken him down there in the daytime to play with him to make it seem like a friendlier place. It felt extremely cold tonight though. To make the house seem deserted they had not lit a fire for warmth. Even with Nicholas snuggled right up against her, Sarah could not generate body heat. Everyone else seemed to be asleep tonight. They'd all been so exhausted from the lack of sleep the previous night.

It was Jakob's turn to keep watch through the kitchen window. He'd put on everything warm that he could find but he was still freezing. There was just enough daylight beginning that he could see the white stream of breath as he exhaled. He felt pity for their workers hiding in the bushes outside. They must be even colder than him.

Before he could see or hear anything he felt it. Just like when the soldiers had marched onto their property, the ground now seemed to rumble. As the bandits came closer he could hear the sound that the wagon wheels made on the earth and the almost even clip clop of the horses working their way towards them. Instantly his stomach knotted up and he instinctively moved his body to the windows edge so that just half of his head was exposed as he watched.

The front line crossed their bridge on horseback. As soon as the bandits had made it this far the yard came to life with their workers jumping out from behind the bushes. They charged at the bandits hollering and using shovels and clubs to scare the horse and beat the bandits.

The bandits, who at this point, had already had much experience attacking small German army detachments, were not fazed in the least. Even their horses seemed controlled during this pitiful endeavor. The men slid off of their horses and manually fought the peasants. The bandits far outnumbered the peasants still working on this farm and easily pushed their way forward.

As soon as Jakob saw the glint of a saber he rushed to the cellar door. He carefully removed the part of the wooden floor that hid the thin rope handle and dropped his body into the cellar. The cellar was only about five feet deep so that when he stood up his head stuck out of the opening. He could easily reach the handle placed on the underside of the cellar door to pull it shut. Before doing so, he remembered to reach around to the front of the door and replace the piece of wood to conceal the rope.

Everyone was sound asleep. Being more used to being below ground and slightly more relaxed because nothing had occurred the previous night his family had been resting well. There was absolutely no light in here and Jakob had to feel his way towards where his father was sleeping.

"Father," Jakob whispered as he gently shook Henry, "wake up. The bandits are here."

It took Henry a few seconds to realize what Jakob was telling him. Then he quickly sat up. "Alright, let's wake everyone up, so that no one is taken by surprise, if the bandits make it into the house."

Sarah, who had not yet fallen into a deep sleep, woke up as soon as she heard her father and Jakob whispering. "I'm already awake, but I will just lie still so that Nicholas stays asleep for as long as possible. I think it will be much quieter then.

Slowly everyone was woken up and sat up on their hay beds. They stayed under their blankets because it was so cold and quietly waited and listened.

Everything was deathly quiet. The cellar seemed to be completely soundproof.

The farm workers had surrendered. The bandits had gathered them all into a group and demanded to know where the owner of this property was. The yard watchman told the bandits that the owner and his family had left and that they did not know where the owner had gone.

Of course the bandits did not believe a word of this and became quite angry. They repeatedly hit the watchman and started pushing around and intimidating the other peasants. The workers all held fast to their resolve and did not give up the location where the Doerksen's were hiding.

Finally the bandits got tired of harassing them and put them all into one of the worker's cabins with several guards surrounding it to make sure that these workers did not cause them any trouble.

One group of the bandits headed toward the Doerksen home and proceeded to attempt to break in. It didn't take too long before they'd broken the wooden window shutters and were inside. Their eyes glowed with delight when they saw that everything in this home was still intact and filled with possessions. They built a fire, lit the lamps and at a comfortable pace, took everything that they wanted. Their own wives would love these dresses and dishes with floral prints. The beds were stripped and any extra blankets were loaded onto the wagons.

At this point the Doerksen's could feel that people were walking around upstairs in their home. Sometimes they could hear a thud, but everything was still very quiet. So they waited. The workers were supposed to come and get them when all the bandits were gone.

The bandits were in no hurry though. Who was there to stop them? No one. The Bolshevik government was encouraging them to take back what they believed to be theirs. This was a comfortable home, they would enjoy it.

After three or four hours of loading the loot the men were tired and decided to relax and enjoy some of their homebrew, samogonka, that they always brought along on these occasions to celebrate. They became loud and boisterous.

Some of their laughter could now be heard through the cellar floor. Nicholas woke up and started crying because everything was still dark. They all took turns whispering to him and trying to make him feel comfortable. Frieda played one of his favorite peek-a-boo games with him while Henry peeled and sliced up an apple in the dark. Apples were one of his favorite treats so he became quiet as soon as he had a little taste.

It was much warmer in the cellar now and they guessed that it must be about noon. They had thought for sure that by now the bandits would have moved on but did not dare to open the cellar door.

*****

Annie woke up at daylight. Werner was still sound asleep beside her. Getting up this early was not necessary during the winter months so she didn't want to wake her sleeping husband.

She felt so restless though. Ever since Jakob had come by to warn them about the approaching bandits she'd been worried about her family.

Their home was a small two room cottage and if she were to leave the warmth of the bed to start building a fire in the other room, surely she would wake Werner. She decided to lay still and try to wait at least another hour.

Finally she allowed herself to leave the bed. She had to do something, to keep busy, to try to still her fears. Of course Werner heard her.

"Annie, what are you doing, up so early?" Werner asked.

"I'm worried about my parents. I think that we should go there and see that everyone is alright," Annie answered.

"Alright, but why don't you come back to bed first for a little while and warm me up, before we leave," Werner seductively suggested.

Annie was still not very comfortable with this part of married life. Werner had proved himself to be a hard working man, like her father, which she completely respected.

He did not treat her harshly or with disrespect, but when he wanted to become amorous with her, she just felt herself stiffen up.

He was always gentle when he touched her, but because of her resistance, she still always felt some pain when he finally entered her. She felt that this was part of her duty as being a wife, but wondered if at some point a man's desire lessened and this would not be required of her. She did wish to have children though and knew that this was necessary in order for her to conceive. They'd been married for two years now and people were starting to ask when they'd be seeing little ones in their arms.

With this thought in mind she headed back towards the bedroom. Maybe she could just think of other things until Werner was satisfied. She tried to put on a little smile, hoping to mask how stiff she already felt inside.

How her sister Sarah could have been such a willing partner towards Nikolai was totally beyond Annie's comprehension.

As she lay there and Werner started to touch her underneath her clothes the picture of Sarah and Nikolai held her captive and she stiffened even more.

Werner felt her becoming more rigid and stopped. He felt hurt and angry. He'd learned to admire this woman. She was very dedicated to him, took excellent care of their home, and was outwardly quite attractive. He could not understand why after all of this time she could still be so cold towards him.

Trying to control the hurtful rejection in his voice he asked, "Annie, what just happened? You seem terrified or something."

"I..,I'm sorry," she stammered. "I just started thinking of my family again," Annie lied.

Werner could see that this answer was only a half truth but decided not to push her any further.

As he pulled her dress back down to cover her up he said, "All right, why don't we just get ready to go there then. I'll hitch the horse to the wagon and you prepare us a good breakfast to tide us over until we get there. "

Annie just nodded in agreement. She felt even worse now than if they had made love. She could tell that he was deeply hurt, but had no idea what to say or how to rectify her problem. Usually, when it was over, Werner would gently hold her in his arms, and stroke her head. She did really enjoy this part and always felt a nice warmth inside when he did this. She was able to relax.

Now there was only coldness between them.

Werner dressed quickly and headed outside. As soon as he left Annie started to cry. She cried so deeply and sorrowfully and could not stop. She could not remember the last time she had cried over anything. It felt as if something inside her was breaking.

When Werner came back inside he was shocked to see Annie bent over the stove cooking their eggs and sobbing like a child. She was always so in control of herself, with very little emotions of any kind ever showing.

Werner immediately walked over to her. He gently removed her hands from the handle of the frying pan and fork and moved them off the heat. Then he held her in his arms as she continued to cry.

"It's alright Annie, "he said to her softly, "We'll work through this."

"How?" she cried. "I don't know what's wrong with me. I love you but it just doesn't feel right to show my love in that way."

"Maybe we could talk to someone, like a doctor, or a pastor, or maybe even just your mother," Werner suggested.

"I'd be so embarrassed to talk to anyone about this," Annie stated.

"I know," Werner answered. "For now why don't we just relax and not worry about it. Maybe we can think about it for a while and other solutions will come our way."

Werner led her over to their small table and helped her to sit down.

"Now, let me feed my wonderful wife, so that we can leave and check up on her family." Werner said in as light spirited a tone as he could. Husbands never brought the food to the table but sometimes exceptions had to be made. Maybe this was the beginning of his wife opening up and showing some feelings. He would do anything to see genuine happiness on this woman's face.

When they went outside to leave a light snow had started to fall. Werner went to the shed to get some extra blankets to keep them warm along the way. It would be at least three hours before they arrived at the Doerksen farm.

The tension between them had been broken and conversation between them was light and easy.

After about an hour Annie even put her arm around Werner's waist and rested her body against his while they travelled on the wagon.

As they crossed the small bridge onto the Doerksen property they noticed that the place was unusually quiet. It felt almost deserted. The two inches of snow that had fallen during the morning hours nicely hid all the activity that had torn up the soil during the dawn hours.

The few bandits who had still had their wits about them before going to sleep had made the peasant workers move their loaded wagons into the barn and under the fruit trees to protect their new belongings from the coming snow. So now all the pillaging that had taken place there was hidden from view.

"This feels very strange," noted Werner. "Do you think that your father decided to flee after all?"

"I don't think so," answered Annie. "Let's go inside and see if they're all there."

Werner quickly tied the horse to the porch railing and went over to help Annie down.

Werner knocked on the front door before opening it to let Annie step inside.

One of the bandits who was sleeping near the door woke up from the knock and quickly stood up to stand behind it just as Annie and Werner stepped inside.

"Mother, Father!" Annie called as she walked in. Just as Werner's body was past the door the bandit quickly pushed it shut with the back of his body and held his pistol aimed at the couple.

Annie screamed from the sudden noise and Werner instantly turned back towards the door to find himself face to face with the pistol.

Having been outside in the bright snow light their eyes did not instantly see all the men sleeping in the room. Some of the men started moaning and rolling over to see what all the commotion was.

Annie and Werner simultaneously felt the danger that they were both in. They realized that they were surrounded and escape seemed impossible.

"Well, well, what have we here?" asked the bandit pointing the pistol at them. "Look at this boys. A pretty plaything for us to enjoy before breakfast." He said this while stroking his erection. Even in her heavy mantel and with a hood covering her head he could see that underneath all this that Annie was quite lovely.

Annie's eyes widened and she instinctively took a step back in horror only to feel the arms of a very strong man reaching around from behind her and pinning her to him. "Werner!!" she said in a loud panicky voice.

Werner out of a strong desire to protect his wife charged for the lewd man at the door but didn't even get to touch him as someone sleeping near his feet reached out and pulled them out from under him. He landed flat on the floor with a thud. The heavy clothes he had on cushioned the fall. The man at the door laughed. Playtime was about to begin.

Before Werner could even move four men had surrounded him and pinned him down. "That's a pretty nice coat you have there, Werner, "sneered the bandit at the door. "Men why don't you take that coat off of Werner and let me try it on. He won't be needing it after today."

Werner struggled to keep his possession but it was no use. With more of the bandits waking up and seeing that they would have an opportunity to humiliate these Mennonites his struggles were futile. The bandits were on him like piranhas ripping all the clothes from his body. A wild look entered their eyes as their excitement increased. They pulled him to his feet and shoved him to the center of the room.

The man at the door put his pistol away and put up his fists. "All right tough guy, let's see what you got," he taunted. The shame and embarrassment of being naked only lasted a second. As soon as this man taunted him anger and adrenaline kicked in and he moved forward to punch this evil man. The man at the door blocked the punch and kneed Werner right on his exposed groin. The pain was so intense that he doubled over, his hands instantly reaching to protect himself. As he bent down the man grabbed his shoulders and kneed him once more on the face.

Werner went flying backward and landed on his back. The bandits laughed. Werner was a hard working farm man who had never had to physically fight anyone. He had never even heard of this type of fighting.

Annie who'd been holding her breath during all this started crying. Werner's face was covered in blood. "Stop, please stop!"she begged. "You can have everything we have. Just let us go, please!"

"Oh, don't worry, pretty lady, "someone answered, "We will most definitely take everything that you have and then some."

Werner rolled onto his stomach and tried to stand up. As soon as he was on his feet someone else took a swing at him.

This time he managed to stay on his feet and punched back. Being unencumbered by clothes he was able to move quite quickly now and dodge some of the blows coming his way, even getting some hits in himself. As soon as this man was tired he stepped out of the way and another placed himself before Werner to take his turn.

After facing about three opponents Werner, too, became quite winded. He started slowing down. He was not going to win this.

The next man hit Werner in the side of his neck. Werner crumpled to the floor unconscious. Annie's eyes opened in horror and she lurched forward to go to him but the man holding on to her would not release her.

"Well men, I think that was just the beginning of our fun. Two of you drag him to the main bedroom and tie him onto the chair in there. When he comes to he can watch and see how real men take care of their woman," sneered the bandit who had surprised them when first entering.

The lust in their eyes was frightening.

Werner was carelessly dragged to Annie's parent's bedroom. They placed him on the chair. His hands were tied behind his back and then secured to the chair. Several ropes were used to secure his shoulders and upper body to the chair so that he could not wiggle around. Next they tied each foot to one of the feet of the chair to prevent him from standing up when he came to.

Annie was pulled into the room behind Werner and tossed on the bed.

When she tried to get up the man who had pushed her onto the bed straddled her hips and held her hands down. "Please, don't do this," she begged.

"Shish," he said as he put his pointing finger to his mouth. "Now, if you don't cause us any trouble, this will be much better for you," he said as he pointed to the man standing beside them. The man beside them took out a very sharp and deadly knife and pretended to slit his own throat as he pointed to her husband sitting on the chair.

Annie got the message and nodded. Her fear was so great now that her voice felt trapped deep within her.

The room was filled with bandits. All eyeing her excitedly, smiling, and giving their approval to the man sitting on her to get started. Slowly he unbuttoned her coat.

Annie tried to hold it shut but two men from the other end of the bed instantly kneeled down and grabbed her arms and held them behind her. With the coat still on her but now wide open the man on her gently but firmly touched and stroked her rib cage almost touching her breasts but not quite. You could feel the excitement growing in the room.

Annie felt herself tense up. This was happening to her and she could not make it stop.

After what seemed like minutes he reached up further and cupped her breasts. Squeezing gently at first, then harder, and finally pinching her nipples. Annie screamed from the pain!

He moved off of her and sat her up. Three of them worked to take the coat off of her, one of them claiming the coat as a prize to his girlfriend. While they had her in a sitting up position they undid her dress from the back.

Then she was pushed back down on the bed so that all eyes could watch as her body was exposed.

Annie struggled to stop them but every time she moved there were more hands on her to hold her in place. Her dress was pulled down from her shoulders and removed to her waist. The bandits made grunting sounds as soon as her breasts were exposed. The same man was straddling her once more and now touching her bare skin in the same way he had previously with her clothes still on.

"Annie!" Werner screamed from the corner of the room. He had just become conscious and was now witnessing this man straddling his wife and touching her half naked body. "Get off of her you filthy dog!" he shouted.

With that the man standing beside him slapped him in the face and spat on him. "You are the filthy dogs, now shut up!" He tore off a piece of the bedding, shoved it in Werner's mouth, then tied another strip around his head to keep it in place. "Now you won't be able to spoil our fun."

Annie turned her head in the direction of her husband and looked him in the eyes for the last time. There was worry, despair, and frustration in his eyes for not being able to protect her. She felt so ashamed she turned her head in the other direction.

The man on her now slid off of her landing his knees on the bedroom floor. From here he had the man standing beside her untie one of her shoes while he untied the other and took it off.

From his position on the floor he easily pulled her dress and underclothes off. Her legs were held apart by a man on each side of her.

The man who'd been putting on this show with her now stood up and removed his own pants and footwear. Once done he came back to kneel between her spread legs.

Annie squeezed her legs together as hard as she could to keep him away but it was no use. He would have his way with her. He started touching her breasts again but now running his hands all the way down her belly to her pubic bone. Annie cringed. After about a minute of this he let his hands fondle her entire pubic area and trying to insert his fingers into her vagina.

Annie once again tried to hold her vaginal muscles tightly together to keep his probing fingers out of her but he just pushed harder.

"Ah, she's a good and tight one men. You will all really enjoy her," he said.

By this time all the men were urging him to get on with it and to mount her already. Many of them were stroking their own erections, hardly able to wait for their turn.

"All right, all right," he answered. "Alright bitch, now you will feel what it's like to be with real men." He positioned himself above her and used his hand to guide his penis into her. When she tightened up he just pushed harder causing her pain on her delicate tissue. Because he was not the one holding her in place entering her was quite easy. She really couldn't struggle enough to get away from him.

"You can all let go of her now!" he almost shouted. "I want to feel this bitch move underneath me."

As soon as they let go Annie started struggling to free herself. She used her arms to push at him, and tried to use her hips and legs to turn herself free. She even tried to claw at his face, but he held himself so tightly against her, that she could not budge him. All of her movement did the work for him, causing just the right friction to bring him to orgasm. He let out a moan as he collapsed on top of her.

"Thanks bitch, that's one of the better ones I've had in a while."

Annie started crying. She felt just horrible. So ugly. She was so tired. As soon as this man rolled off of her the one who'd been standing beside them took his place. Through her tears she did not instantly see what they were doing and before she even had a chance to move she felt him inside of her.

The sperm from the previous man had lubricated her and insertion was now easy.

She felt herself become hopeless. Her strength was gone. She did not fight him at all. He was already so excited from watching his comrade that it did not take him long at all to reach his ecstasy.

Werner bound and gagged could not watch anymore. He could feel Annie slipping away as new men took their turn on her. His stomach was retching but with the cloth in his mouth he gagged and choked on his vomit. Tears were rolling down his face. He was so angry. He wanted to kill everyone in the room.

Annie was gone. She turned inward, tuning out everything that was going on around her. She was awake but no longer conscious of what was happening to her or of the pain her body was in.

When they turned her over onto her stomach and positioned her on her knees so that they could now penetrate her anally she was no longer aware of what was happening to her.

She did let out a reflexive scream at the pain of this intrusion but this was her outward physical body only. Her spirit, her center, her rationality, was gone.

When everyone who wanted a turn with her was finished they turned her back onto her back and just left her there on the bed. They could see that there was no longer a need to restrain her. She just lay there like a rag doll.

Even though they realized that she would not be aware of what they would do to her husband they still wanted her to witness this one last shame.

The man who had originally held them hostage at the door now approached Werner.

Werner was looking at Annie, tears streaming down his face. Just that morning he had finally gotten closer to her.

Something hard inside of her had broken, allowing them each a glimpse of hope that their future as a couple would now be filled with more warmth. The hope was now gone. Forever. Annie would never have a chance to flower. She would be buried deep within herself. He now mourned the loss of her in the same way as had she been dead.

With these thoughts he felt the sharp pain of the saber as it was plunged into his belly and through his back to the point where the metal hit the wooden chair. He sucked in his breath and looked up in shock at the man who had just done this to him.

The bandit looked back into Werner's eyes with total hatred. As he held Werner's stare he began to pull the saber back out, using both arms to push downwards on it with full force. As he cut through more of Werner's insides and flesh, Werner screamed. The sound came out all gargled because he was still gagged.

For the bandit the fun was now over. He was disgusted with Werner. Once again he held the handle of the saber in both hands and swung it at Werner's neck. In mere seconds the head was off and falling to the ground.

"All right men, this party's over. Let's finish packing and move on," he said.

*****

Several hours later the peasants who still worked on the Doerksen farm were released and told to enjoy all that had been left behind on the farm. It now all belonged to them. Except for the initial injuries while battling to save the farm, no more harm had been done to them.

They decided to wait for at least an hour before telling the Doerksen's that it was safe to come out. They wanted to make sure that the bandits were well underway. By the time they made their way to the house it was almost evening. Everything was dark inside and lifeless. They lit some of the oil lamps and went to open the hidden cellar door.

In the cellar all had been quiet for so long. The Doerksen's had no idea of what time of day it was. When the door opened from above they all held their breath in anticipation. Would this be the bandits or their worker's letting them out.

They were relieved to see the friendly familiar faces.

One by one they made their way out of the cellar. It felt so good to be able to stand up straight and stretch their bodies. The cellar was only about five feet deep and only little Nicholas had been able to enjoy a fully upright position. Everyone seemed to talk at once. The mood was almost festive. Their plan to keep the Doerksen family safe had worked.

"So, what does it look like outside?" asked Henry above the hubbub.

Everyone quieted down as Leo, the current head worker answered, "Well, from what we can tell, the news is not good. The barns look empty. The tools which were hidden were not found, so we still have them. They've left us a few of the older horses and a bit of cattle, but all the rest is gone."

Henry looked quite devastated by this answer. They had all worked so hard and for so long to acquire all that they had. He could not even begin to fathom what would make these bandits want to just help themselves to what others had worked for. Henry slumped down onto a chair.

Herbert walked over behind his father and placed both his hands on Henry's shoulders to comfort him. While he spoke he gently massaged his father's neck, "Father, I know that it must feel to you as though you must now start again from the beginning, but it will be alright. All of your sons are now grown men and we will do the work. We're all well and alive. Maybe this way when other groups come by they won't bother us, because there is nothing left for them to take."

The children all nodded in agreement to this. It seemed like a reasonable assumption.

"Let's clean up some of this mess and make a light meal before we head off to bed," announced Margaret. She knew that as long as her Mennonite husband was kept busy he would have a renewed hope and purpose. His thoughts would become clearer. "Sarah, you and your sister Frieda can start cleaning here in the kitchen. Elizaveta and I will tidy the bedrooms. "Henry, you and the boys build the fires and see if there is anything that needs to be taken care of outside. It feels as though it will be a very cold night tonight."

Henry nodded to his wife. She certainly knew him well. Some fresh air and a bit of a wander around outside would definitely clear his head and brighten his spirits.

Just as he started to rise out of his chair they heard a blood curdling scream come from Elizaveta. Elizaveta had already left the kitchen with a lamp and headed toward the owners bedroom. They heard the lamp hit the wooden floor and the glass break at the same time as the thump of the old woman fall to the floor.

Sarah reached down to pick up Nicholas before she followed the rest of her family to the bedroom. The scream had frightened him and he started crying.

Margaret instinctively grabbed Frieda as she rushed by her to see what was the matter. She looked at Frieda and said "No, you wait here with me."

Herbert was the first to rush down the hallway and could see Elizaveta's body blocking the doorway. The lamp that he was holding cast the light in just the right direction that he could make out the shape of a body sitting on a chair. It took him a second to realize that the head was missing.

He quickly stepped over Elizaveta and turned around to block the doorway with his own body. Having seen much of the horrors inflicted on the human body by the war he was not in shock and realized that he had better take quick control of the situation.

"What happened in there?" asked Ernst as he tried to see past his brother.

Without answering him Herbert said, "You and Jakob move Elizaveta to the kitchen and tell mother to see if she's all right. Everyone just back up so we can help Elizaveta." As the old woman was moved out of the way Herbert closed the door behind him and also moved into the hallway.

His father looked at him with questioning eyes. "Someone has been murdered in there. Only father and I will go in," he announced.

Herbert wanted to spare his family the ugliness that was sure to face them in that room.

"Father, it does not look good. Please, brace yourself before you go in," said Herbert.

Herbert slowly opened the door and let his father walk past him into the bedroom. Before raising the lamp high enough to see he closed the door behind him. "Oh, my God!" he exclaimed as his eyes saw the figure of a naked woman lying on the bed.

They immediately walked over to her. She lay completely motionless, except for the involuntary shaking of her body. "It's Annie!" moaned Henry. "Oh, my Lord. What has happened here?" In the dull light they could not see the bruises that were starting to form on her body. Henry touched her arm, "Annie, Annie," he softly called. "It's all right. We're here now. What's happened to you?"

"She's cold father and in shock," said Herbert. "We need to cover her up." He could not see anything to cover her with so he put the lamp down and took off his own coat and covered her.

Now he raised the lamp again and walked over to the corner where he could now see that the man tied to the chair was also naked. The smell of the puddle of blood on the floor permeated the room and Herbert started to gag as he got closer. He could see the head laying about a foot away from the chair facing the direction of the wall.

He stepped around the puddle and positioned himself so that he could look at the face of the dead man. "It's Werner!" he said louder than he had intended to. Seeing Annie on the bed he should have suspected that this might be Werner, but the thought had never even occurred to him.

"He must have been trying to protect Annie," said Henry while still holding her hand. She made no gesture of recognition. "Let's wrap the blanket that's underneath Annie around her and carry her to the other bedroom. Then you and Ernst find a sheet or something to wrap Werner in and bring him to the barn. I'll get Jakob to help me build a coffin for him."

They wrapped her up and Herbert carried her with ease to the other bedroom. Henry guarded the door and made everyone wait before explaining what had happened. While still standing in the hallway he said, "I think that Annie was raped by the bandits and that Werner tried to protect her. Annie is still alive but they killed Werner." He paused for a moment to let everyone absorb the information. "They must have come to see if we were all alright and been caught by the bandits. How is Elizaveta?" he asked looking at Margaret.

"She'll be all right. I put her near the stove with a hot cup of tea." Margaret answered.

"Good, then you and Sarah should see to Annie. Ernst, you help your brother clean up our bedroom. Jakob, I will need your help in the barn. Peter and Frieda can finish straightening things out and preparing a bit of food," said Henry.

Sarah went to prepare warm water to bathe Annie with. Annie would probably feel better if she was cleaned. Elizaveta entertained Nicholas while Sarah worked. When she had everything she needed she went to join her Margaret and Annie in the bedroom.

"I think Annie wet herself just now. The blanket near her bottom is all wet and warm. I've looked all over your room for a change of clothing, but I can't find anything. Could you look through the other rooms for something for her to wear?" asked Margaret."I'll start cleaning her."

Sarah looked in the other bedroom but could find no clothing. Everything had been taken. Even their dirty laundry. She went to Elizaveta. "Elizaveta, all of our clothes have been taken. Could you see if any of the workers have anything left that we could put on Annie?"

"Of course," Elizaveta answered. "In the cabin that we were kept in nothing was touched." She hurried out. In no time she was back with a clean dress and underclothes for Annie.

"Thank-you so much," said Sarah. It felt strange to take something from one of their workers. Usually it was her family passing things on and the workers were always most grateful. She could see that Elizaveta was most joyful to be helping them and almost kind of proud. Sarah accepted the clothes most gratefully.

"Elizaveta got us some of their clothes to put on Annie, mother. Everything of ours seems to be gone," said Sarah.

"It is going to be a cold and long winter," said Margaret solemnly. "Annie, must be so sad from seeing her husband murdered. I just can't believe that he's gone."

"Maybe she can tell us what happened once she's dry and warm," said Sarah hopefully.

Several hours later the family finally came together for their evening meal. Coming out of the cellar they had all felt safe and quite clever for outsmarting the bandits. But it had not been so. While they had been tucked away some very horrible things had been going on right above them.

The realization that this was probably just the beginning of the terror that would befall them hit home. No one was very hungry.

Tomorrow they would bury Werner. How many more would have to die before there was once again the peace that they had enjoyed for so many years?

Chapter
8

Sarah looked at her new surroundings. Her entire family now lived in a wooden house that had once been used as a work shed. It was very simple and plain, basically one big open room.

The day after burying Werner her father had decided that it would be safer to move the family into their neighboring village Astrojowka. Most of the inhabitants of this village were of the Lutheran faith and he hoped that they as Mennonites would blend in.

They had packed the most necessary of their belongings that remained and set off with the remaining set of oxen. Their workers who still remained loyal to them would stay on the farm and provide for themselves as best as they could. Henry had made one return trip to the farm to see how much he could still take to sell.

Sarah was still haunted by the things she had seen during their flight. An entire family had been slain by the roadside. This family, too, must have been trying to escape. Even the children had been hacked at till they were dead. The lust for blood in these bandits was immense.

They could not get to Astrojowka quick enough. Hopefully all of this would be over before Nicholas could remember anything. Sarah wanted to keep his world as happy as possible.

Her family had made an effort to celebrate Christmas. Margaret had baked the usual peppermint cookies, they lit candles, and sang Christmas hymns.

During these days of celebration they had heard news of more robberies and homes taken hostage and people beaten and killed. The German evangelical of Astrojowka had prepared a lookout on top of their church steeple. As soon as the watchman thought he saw a group of bandits coming near he was to ring the church bell to warn everyone. At this point everyone was to run into their homes, grab their weapons, and go to their assigned locations surrounding their village. They hoped that they would be able to keep the bandits away from their homes.

The cloak of danger still surrounded them and it had been difficult to make their hearts feel the joy of the Christmas season of previous years.

Her parents had also hoped that Annie would snap out of her comatose state of existence from the smell of the cookies and the warm glow of the candles. But nothing had changed. Annie did not speak or do anything for herself. If food was put in her mouth she would go through the motions of chewing and swallowing, but she never reached for anything herself.

Sarah and Frieda took turns throughout the day to bring Annie to the outhouse. Here Annie would occasionally relieve herself and yet at other times she did her business wherever she was, without any guilt or shame. They had to change her almost as often as her young son Nicholas. Sarah felt so sad for her. Annie had been such a strong and proper type of woman. Whatever those men had done to her must have been beyond Annie's comprehension.

Sarah felt sad that she had never really had the chance to get to know Annie. And now it seemed that would never happen. Perhaps now that she herself was older and different she would have been able to understand Annie more.

Sarah determined that she would do the best that she could to take care of Annie. She also decided that should a similar fate happen to herself during these times of terror that she would not allow her mind to leave. She would do the best to protect herself and at all times remind herself that she must live for Nicholas. God had given her this precious gift and she felt truly honored to have this precious child to raise.

In this simple home they had tried to establish a routine that would make their life seem as normal as possible.

Everyone had found odd jobs to do for their German neighbors to bring in little bits of money to keep their family going. Twice a week Sarah walked to a neighbor a few miles from their home to help with the washing. This was not always a pleasant task with the cold winter days but she too had to do her part to help support the family. Her mother, Margaret, stayed home and took care of Nicholas and their own family's needs.

A feeling of unsettlement seemed to be over the whole land. People were definitely not breathing easily. Every time she left the home Sarah felt tense and apprehensive. There wasn't a day that went by now without someone warning her to be careful and on the lookout for danger.

Leaving Nicholas during these times was especially difficult for her. She wanted to be there to comfort him should anything befall her family.

So much had changed in the last few years. She could hardly believe it. And now they were packing to flee once more. News had reached them that a few weeks ago the central Colony, Nikolaijewka, had been overtaken by an uncountable number of bandits. It had been a bloody event and many had died.

The bandits were so angry that some of their own men had been injured that they were vengefully motivated to strike again. One after another more of the surrounding villages were attacked. So far Astrojowka had been spared, but their day was surely coming too.

Last night two riders had come into town to warn Jakob Wiebe that a retaliatory army of one thousand men was on the way. By tonight the entire village should be vacated. Mr. Wiebe knew these men personally and the news was taken very seriously.

Their wagon was packed full and ready to move on. Sarah had helped her mother hide money in their clothing by sewing it into the hems and other inconspicuous places. Just before midnight they left their home with their loaded wagon and all they could carry to join the large procession. It was a pitch black night, very eerie, and yet somehow Sarah felt as though the darkness would hide them from the evil.

A few families had chosen to stay behind, not quite believing what would befall them, and not wanting to leave so much of what they had behind. Sarah's family had, through their own hardship, already concluded that none of their possessions were worth the personal torture to be endured by these lust driven bandits.

Talking to others along the way they learned that many had left some of their most essential items at home. Because of the rush in having to pack and panicking in fear they had not been able to think straight. Many realized that they had even left their lanterns still burning on their kitchen table and their front doors wide open.

Their life until now had always been slow and routine. Getting up early to milk the cows, going in to a big breakfast, these daily occurrences had been taken for granted. This is how your father before you had lived his life and this is how your children would continue into the future. Everything that they had worked for was now left behind.

There was no time to look back.

Their thoughts could no longer be on what was left behind but rather on what was in store for them in the future. They were all in a life and death situation now.

Sarah wondered if they would make it alive to the next town. Would they feel any safer when they got there? They could even be robbed by bandits along the way? It was in the middle of the night and she was tired. Her brothers helped her with carrying Nicholas. She had to stop thinking like this and just concentrate on the task of moving forward.

She decided to use her thoughts for prayer instead. She prayed for the strength to continue and asked God for protection. In time she did feel some of her anxiety leaving.

Before Nicholas she had always felt completely immortal. Daring to do just about anything without fear. She'd been head strong and courageous. Now she felt that she had to watch her life choices carefully. She could not put herself in a situation that would take her from her precious son. She knew that her family would take care of Nicholas the best they could should anything happen to her, but it was just not the same.

A child needs his parents. And she still believed that she would get the chance to raise him differently than she had been raised. She wanted him to have more freedoms. Freedom to be himself without condemnation. Freedom to look at others as equal. Freedom to love whomever he chose.

Sarah resolved to stay focused and strong. She would not waiver in her goal to take her son to safety. She wanted him to have the chance to enjoy life in peace. Just as her earlier years had been. Carefree and adventurous.

Occasionally the train of fleeing people slowed down to give others from outside their village a chance to hook onto their train.

By the middle of the night travelling became even more difficult because of the rain. The train was stopped so that a few wagons could be cleared to make room for the old, the sick, and the children. Everyone else had to continue walking.

Sarah's mother, Margaret, was given one of these spots and she took Nicholas on her lap till they reached Kasi-Jurt.

By dinner the next day they arrived in Kasi-Jurt. Here they were welcomed with open arms. Once they'd been cleaned up a bit and had been fed they were given the best rooms to rest in.

Even though Nicholas had slept a lot on the way as soon as Sarah lay down with him he was asleep. She, too, could not remember ever being this exhausted. They did not know how long they would have this luxury of lying in a bed so Sarah savored every moment. Having her son close to her was so peaceful she just allowed herself to have a wonderful sleep.

When Sarah woke up in the morning the rain had stopped and Sarah was thankful that they would enjoy another day. Her thankfulness soon took on an even deeper level as news reached them as to the fate of the town that they had just left behind.

The bandits had arrived in Nikolaijewka heavily armed. They had big intentions of teaching these German people a lesson in revenge for fighting back during their previous raid and injuring some of their men.

The bandits had broken windows and entered the homes. When they realized that the homes were empty and that the entire town was deserted they were furious.

The bandits had managed to find the few residents which had stayed behind and took all of their fury out on them. Their bodies were stripped and everything was taken from them, shoes, clothing, and money. The residents were beaten and humiliated.

A young servant girl had been kidnapped and dragged along to use later for their own pleasures. Margaret cried and cried because she knew that the same thing that had been done to her precious Annie would now be happening to this young girl. How could people possibly become so barbarian? Even in the animal world this type of torture never occurred. Males would fight for their right to be with the female, but this seemed like an honorable system.

People became monsters. She could understand the peasants desire to fight for a better life. A fight for their own land. Like the war that they had just survived. Men had gone to fight other men with honor. Where possible women and children were left alone.

At what point did these people get to a place where only torture and wickedness would satisfy them? And once started on this path could satisfaction even be reached? She prayed that her people would always remember their humanity, no matter what situation they were in. She prayed that she would be able to still show kindness if she were to come face to face with these bandits.

The entire entourage spent ten days in Kasi-Jurt. During this time they rested and built up their strength to continue their journey for safety. Some of the people traded items that would not be of great necessity to them, like clocks, with more necessary items such as lanterns, blankets, and cooking supplies.

Their progress to Kasafjurt was steady and without incident. Because of the extra days that they had spent in Kasafjurt they had been able to prepare and organize better for the travelling. This made moving along much easier.

On March 3, 1918, Lenin had lost the Ukraine to Germany. These German troops had now moved into the homes of the families in Kasafjurt.

As the train of people reached the outskirts of Kasafjurt they were met by one hundred of these German soldiers. The town had been warned that hundreds of refugee wagons were underway to seek help from them.

They had requested that the soldiers find out exactly what these refugees wanted. The soldiers were to prevent these refugees from putting their town into a chaotic state.

Had these Kasafjurt townspeople realized that harboring these soldiers would only worsen their own plight in the future with the bandits, they would perhaps have been kinder. They were optimistic that the German's and Austrians would bring them machinery and many goods. They also believed that these German soldiers would not be defeated by the Bolsheviks.

Before long though they would also come to realize that instead of bringing them anything these German and Austrian troops would take grains and all kinds of food stuffs from them and ship it back to their respective countries. Making these Mennonites even poorer than they had been during the war.

The troops also perpetrated many deeds for which the Mennonites would later pay a great price when the Bolshevik government came into full power. The German troops arbitrarily arrested real and alleged enemies, such as terrorists and brigands, while in the Ukraine. If after debate they thought that these enemies were guilty they would summarily execute them.

These acts later engendered the Bolsheviks against the German Mennonites which still remained on Russian soil. The Bolsheviks did not trust the Mennonites as being loyal to their mother country, Russia.

So now the refugees had to present their requests to these soldiers. All they wanted was to take a train to their next destination of Suworowka. They would camp on the outskirts of town until enough boxcars could be secured.

They had expected to leave Kasafjurt within a few days, but securing enough boxcars had been more difficult than expected.

Finally the amount of boxcars required were secured and filled with all of their belongings including cattle and horses. After a week of camping in miserable conditions they were able to roll away on the hard rails toward Suworowka.

In Suworowka they were warmly welcomed and made to feel comfortable. They were totally dependent on the kindness of others for living quarters. An old friend of the family, Mr. Kornelsen, had heard while doing business in Suworowka, that the Doerksen's were one of the refugee families staying here.

Mr. Kornelsen came to visit them and invited them to come and stay with him and his family in Kalentarowka, the next small settlement. His small homestead had as yet been untouched by plunder at the hands of the bandits, German army troops, or the Red or White soldiers.

The Doerksen's had secured for themselves a small haven. Spring was on the way and it felt as though peace might be upon them. Henry and his boys helped with clearing more of the Kornelsen land and started spring planting.

Life was different here but good. Sarah spent much time playing outside with Nicholas and the younger Kornelsen children. Nicholas was now almost two years old. He was a tall, strong, and intelligent young boy. He could come up with the most amazing stories and questions. He never failed to amuse anyone.

Mrs. Kornelsen, who had for many years taught school in the Mennonite colonies, spent three hours each day instructing her older children and Frieda.

Because there were so many capable hands in the home even Margaret was able to take more time to rest.

Everyone was doing well except for Annie. Her mental state had not improved at all. Although she was extremely thin, they had all noticed that her abdomen was steadily increasing in size. Annie was pregnant. This brought on a whole new set of worries and questions. Would Annie have enough natural instinct left to deliver the child? Was this the baby of her husband or one of the bandits? Would Annie have any interest in the child?

Sarah felt especially sad for Annie. She knew how much Annie and Werner had wanted to have a child of their own. Now it seemed that neither of them would have the joy of watching their child grow.

Sarah made sure to take Annie out into the warm sunlight everyday, hoping that somehow the heat would penetrate her frosted over continence, and make her come alive once more.

Spring was here and had brought with it much hope for a new life for all. In the evenings they would all gather around the kitchen stove and talk about their hopes for peace in this country that they loved.

Chapter
9

They were completely taken by surprise. On a warm summer's night just as they were preparing for bed the house was surrounded by a group of bandits.

Terror instantly took a hold on the families. They had discussed what they should do if in this situation and had decided not to retaliate, but to be submissive. From all the things they had heard it seemed that the more people fought and tried to hang on to their possessions the more violent the bandits became with those people.

The Kornelsen and Doerksen family would try to show these bandits utmost respect.

Everyone was ordered outside. They touched hands and looked into each other's eyes to show and acknowledge love as they obeyed the command.

The fear greatly increased when the bandits identified themselves as Makhnovich.

Nestor Makhno had in a short period of time become a notorious gang leader. He had become leader of the broad masses of peasantry and encouraged them to take it upon themselves to vent their unbridled fury and age-old hatreds against each and everyone who had allegedly exploited them in the past.

Makhno also formed an alliance with the Bolsheviks. His men attacked the German army detachments which had been sent out to collect grain and restore estates to the German landowners living in the Ukaraine. The Makhnovich interrupted rail communications, looted these restored estates, and killed landowners and their families.

Sarah had overheard Mr. Kornelsen saying that this rabble mass of men were plundering the already crucified country, raping women, and wreaking a frightful revenge upon all whom it hated or disliked.

The men who would originally capture the towns would first seize everything they could get their hands on and then engage in drunken revelries. As a rule the looting would start in the business section of towns then fan out to the residential areas. The men, women, and children of the towns would be kept busy gathering the loot and filling wagons. This would go on for days.

No one from the Doerksen or Kornelsen family had gone into town in the past week and they all wondered if their whole town had been seized by the Makhnovich. If it was, there had been no warning.

And now this most feared group of bandits surrounded their home.

The men in the family and children were ordered to go to the barn and make themselves comfortable. Margaret, Mrs. Kornelsen, and Sarah were told to stay behind and prepare them food and places to sleep. The men were assured that nothing would happen to their women as long as they did as they were asked.

Sarah was well rested and strong from the peaceful spring that they had enjoyed and gave her father a self confident nod that she was strong and capable of carrying out these requests.

Once everyone was ushered to the barn and the three women were left standing alone with the bandits the bandits started to dismount from their horses.

Because of the darkness of the night it had not been easy to see the condition of the bandits. Now the more capable of the group went over to the weaker ones and started helping them off their horses.

Sarah looked with astonishment as she saw one of the riders just slump forward and start to slide off of his horse.

Without thinking of herself she lunged towards him in time to capture him in her arms to prevent him from hitting the ground.

One of the bandits nearest to her had caught her sudden movement out of the corner of his eye. His first thought was that she intended to inflict harm on one of his fellow gang members. As he rushed towards her to stop her he realized that her arms were extended in a way as to catch something.

He managed to stop himself from hitting her just in time. Sarah gave him a defiant look and said, "Well, don't just stand there. Help me bring him in the house."

The bandit just nodded in shock and helped her lift this sick man and drag him into the house. Sarah told him which way to go to her room and together they placed the sick man on her bed.

Margaret and Mrs. Kornelsen had been told to stop gawking and get to work in the kitchen.

They had as yet not been treated roughly and started to relax a little as they went about familiar work.

Sarah went to get a lantern to get a better look at this sick man. Before she even made it to the lantern she could already feel little things moving on her body. She rubbed her arms and head but could not stop the creepy itching sensation.

When she brought the lantern near the sick man she could see that he was covered with lice and fleas. They were crawling all over his body. On top of his clothes and on all his exposed skin. He was covered in red spots and his body had felt very warm to her when bringing him inside. He kept mumbling as though in some sort of delirium. He also seemed to be having a difficult time breathing.

Sarah knew right away that this man had typhus. Because of all the crowding, uncleanliness, and miserable conditions that these men lived in typhus was an expected symptom. Her brother Herbert had spoken extensively on the subject of trying to stay clean while helping the injured soldiers so as to prevent typhus. She knew that this was a deadly bacteria.

As she looked at the bandit who was still standing in the room with her she noticed that he too was covered with crawling fleas and lice. His eyes told her that he knew what he would be enduring. He'd seen his friends lose their appetite, complain of excruciating headaches, then endure this high fever, skin rash, and go through bouts of delirium.

She had the power in this situation and realized it as she said, "I will take care of your sick men and of you when you get sick, if you tell the rest of your group to keep their distance from my family in the barn. Let my father know that you have typhus and that they are to stay away." It would already be too late to save her mother and Mrs. Kornelsen from exposure. With this large group of men in the house it would already be infested.

The bandit looked at her challenging eyes and remembered the compassion that she had shown his friend earlier. He believed that she would provide the best of care if he agreed to her request. "Alright, you do everything you can for my friend Nikolai and I will try to keep your family safe."

"Nikolai?!" Sarah asked as her confident exposure crumbled. "Nikolai Chekov?" she heard herself softly question as her eyes opened wide with anticipation. This man on the bed was so dirty and covered in red spots that she had not seen anything recognizable about him at all.

"Yes," answered the bandit in astonishment. "Do you know him?"

Sarah looked across the room at the man on the bed and nodded her head as she leaned against the wall for support. She couldn't believe it. This was her love. Nikolai. He was here in her home, in her bed, and seemed so near death.

"Of course," said the bandit. "You must be the beautiful woman Sarah that he has so often spoken of."

Sarah was so deep in her own thoughts that she hardly even heard the bandit speak.

"I am Alexander. I fought beside Nikolai in the war and when we realized that we had not increased our worth any in this society we joined the Makhnovich. Thoughts of finding you and making you his wife helped him through many tough times."

Sarah started focusing and pulling herself together as she listened to what Alexander was saying.

"Nikolai, said that you were not like the rest of the Mennonite people. You do not see yourself as superior.

With the way you just helped him from his horse you just proved that. Out of respect for Nikolai's feelings towards you I will personally make sure that everyone on this homestead is treated decently," said Alexander. "You ask for whatever you think you may need to help us overcome this disease."

"Thank-you," Sarah answered as Alexander left the room. Slowly she walked over to Nikolai and placed the lantern on the small table that was near the bed. She looked at his face and reached out her hand to gently touch him. "Nikolai," she whispered. "Please, come back to me. I have so much that I want to tell you." Tears slowly rolled down her cheeks.

His face had matured. His bone structure was now more prominent.

Although he was now only twenty years old, he looked much older. She could see the experience of all that he had already endured in his lifetime.

Even though Nikolai was unconscious Sarah could still feel their souls connect. A warm wave coursed through her body. "I love you Nikolai and I will do anything I can to help you." Sarah squeezed his hand and got up to get to work.

Sarah wiped the tears from her face and straightened out her clothes to make herself look and feel as confident as possible. She went out of the room to tell her mother that she would be helping the sick and get water. The first thing she would do is clean him up.

Alexander had already told the women in the kitchen that Sarah would be tending to the sick men. He'd also instructed two of his men to help her get whatever she needed. The three of them went to the well to get water and filled the barrel near the house.

When this was done she took a bucketful inside and went back to Nikolai. Sarah asked one of these men to help her undress Nikolai. He didn't seem too pleased with the task but helped her anyway.

The bandit then took Nikolai's clothes outside to be cleaned the next day.

Nikolai did not appear to be a weak man but he was very thin. Sarah used a washcloth and bathed him as well and as carefully as she could.

Occasionally he would moan and shiver. The cool water against his skin gave him the chills.

Sarah covered him with her blanket and checked to see that no one was looking. Then she gave him a soft kiss on his cheek. "I'll come back to see you later," she whispered.

Sarah went throughout the house and did the same thing for all the other men who had been showing the symptoms of typhus from the body louse.

Sarah asked the men who were still capable of caring for themselves to remove as many of their own clothing as they could and to wash themselves. It would probably be too late to prevent them from getting typhus, but maybe by sterilizing everything, they could prevent it from spreading.

Sarah and the other two women worked well into the night feeding everyone and making everyone as comfortable as possible. A bit of room was left against one of the walls in the kitchen and this is where they finally sat down to get some rest for the night.

Mrs. Kornelsen seemed especially tired and soon fell asleep.

Finally a moment to herself and now Sarah couldn't relax. She started thinking about her son Nicholas in the barn without her. My son? Our son.

She hadn't really thought that she would get the chance to see Nikolai again. Early on she had assumed that it would be just Nicholas and herself to face the world. If Nikolai survived would things change for her? Of course he would survive! After all these years they were finally together again. She wanted to spend every minute of his life with him. She wanted to tell him all about Nicholas. Would he be as happy about their son as she was? Just so many thoughts.

And Nicholas. Would he have gone to sleep alright? Would he be worried about her? She had never yet not been there for him for the night. She hoped that Frieda was assuring him that his mother was fine and would be back very soon.

She had been so busy helping the sick men that she'd hardly even thought about Nicholas. She missed him so much right now.

Margaret noticed her daughter moving around uncomfortably. "Is the floor too hard for you too?" Margaret asked.

"Well, it is mother," Sarah answered, "But there is also something else on my mind."

Sarah moved her head very close to her mothers and looked straight into her eyes as she quietly whispered," Nikolai is here, mother."

Margaret quickly gasped in surprise. Sarah put her forefinger to her own mouth motioning her mother to stay quiet.

"Really?" asked Margaret.

"Yes, he's the sick man in my room," answered Sarah. "That's why all the bandits have been so decent to us. I discovered from Alexander that it was Nikolai that I had helped from the horse. Mother, he's been talking about me all these years. Alexander says that thinking of me has kept him going."

"Oh, Sarah," said Margaret. "You still love him, don't you?"

"Yes, just as much as ever mother. I don't want to lose him again," she said with an incredible ache in her chest.

"I'm so sorry that you've had to spend all these years without him," said Margaret as she stroked Sarah's shoulder. She could feel both the love and deep anguish coming from Sarah. She herself had shared so many good years with her husband Henry. How could they have denied their own daughter the same joy? There would always be hardship in life but when sharing it with someone you loved it always seemed bearable.

Lying in Henry's arms at night seemed to make all of their problems diminish. Losing all of their possessions was nothing in comparison to losing the people they loved.

"I don't know how my life may have been different had I been allowed to marry Nikolai, mother," said Sarah, "but I do now want to see if I can make a life with him."

"Sarah, I will do whatever I can to help you," said Margaret, "but for now we had better try to get some sleep. Tomorrow, we will have lots of work to do with trying to sterilize all of those clothes and killing these irritating little creatures."

Morning came much too soon. As Sarah awoke and became orientated to where she was she realized that every part of her ached from sleeping on the hard floor. She rubbed her left hip where she was especially sore. She must have slept the whole night on just that side. Sarah noticed that some of the men were already up and talking so she decided that she'd better wake her mother and Mrs. Kornelsen.

Sarah gently shook the other women and told them it was time to wake up.

She knew that most of these men had by now already committed atrocious acts towards many other German people and she wanted to do whatever she could to keep them happy, hopefully thereby keeping her family safe.

Margaret, being the eldest, of the three women seemed especially stiff and sore. This did not stop her from quickly making herself mobile. She just hoped that they would be able to provide enough food for all of these men during the duration of their stay. Last night they had boiled extra potatoes and this morning all they had to do was fry them up with a bit of salt. She quickly had breakfast underway.

Before doing anything Sarah realized that she needed to make a desperate trip to the outhouse. On the way she noticed that everything outside still seemed quiet and peaceful. The sun was already quite warm and she decided that they had better get to the washing right away so they could hang everything out to dry quickly in the hot afternoon sun.

On the way back from the outhouse she saw her father walking towards her. She didn't know if she could prevent the lice and fleas from finding their way towards him or the rest of the family but told him to keep his distance.

"Sarah, how is everything in the house?" asked Henry.

"Just fine father. We're being treated well and respectfully. We should have some breakfast out to you in a bit," answered Sarah. "Was Nicholas alright without me last night?"

"He was actually quite excited. Frieda told him that they were having a special sleepover with the animals and he liked that."

"So he slept alright?" asked Sarah.

"Just fine," Henry assured Sarah. "He just curled up next to Frieda and they whispered and giggled till he finally got tired."

"None of you are covered in body louse yet?" asked Sarah.

"No. Somehow we managed not to rub close to any of the bandits," answered

Henry.

Henry kind of hung down his head to avoid his daughter's eyes, "I wish that we could do more to help, but they don't trust us men. They feel that you won't physically retaliate."

"Father, I know. It's alright. I'm strong and I've been taught to work hard. Please just keep Nicholas happy and occupied and away from those of us now covered in these infectious lice," said Sarah with confidence and conviction.

"I'm so worried that the three of you in the house will get typhus now too, "said Henry. "I'm not sure that keeping our distance will make any difference and if your mother gets sick, I do not want to leave her side."

Henry rarely spoke this openly about his feelings but Sarah could see in his eyes and hear in his voice the love that he felt for Margaret and how much she meant to him. Sarah understood completely.

Sarah gave her father a look that showed she understood exactly how he felt. "If mother gets sick, I will get you."

Henry was all choked up. "Thank you."

With that Sarah went back to the house. Feeling relieved and knowing that Nicholas was in good hands she went about checking on the sick men.

For some of them the severe headache and muscle pains were just starting, for others their fevers had broken during the night, and now they seemed to be extremely cold. She did what she could for each one to make him more comfortable.

Then she noticed a man lying in a strangely stiff position, his eyes and mouth were wide open. Before walking across some of the other sick bodies on the floor she looked up and caught Alexander's eye.

"What's wrong Sarah?" he asked.

"I think you'd better look at that man in the corner over there," she said as she pointed. Together they both walked in the stiff man's direction.

Alexander already knew that he was dead. They had already lost a few of this group while on the road.

"He's dead," announced Alexander as he took her arm to hold her back. He didn't know why he was trying to protect this woman. While marauding other villages he had taken his pleasure with someone he fancied no matter what their protestations might be. He had felt quite satisfied knowing that they too were finally suffering. But with Sarah, he cared. Was it just out of respect for their mutual friend Nikolai that he felt protective of her? No, he could feel the genuine love from her heart. This woman could change a man.

"We're going to need your men from the barn to dig some graves," said Alexander to Sarah still holding her arm.

"Graves?!" she shrieked as she pulled herself free from him to run to Nikolai. The full realization of how serious their predicament was just hit her. Sarah was in a panic. Not Nikolai, please God, not Nikolai. She almost threw herself on him when she saw that he was still breathing and alive. "Thank-you God, thank-you," she whispered.

Margaret had followed Sarah into the room when she saw the rush that Sarah was in. Margaret put her hands on Sarah's shoulder and just massaged her back for a moment before saying, "Sarah, you had better come and eat something. We have lots of work to do today and you need to stay strong. I, too, will pray for Nikolai. It's all we can do now."

Sarah nodded. She knew her mother was right. She had more than just herself to think about and care for.

That day four out of the thirty bandits that had come to find rest and comfort in their home died.

Clothes had become so scarce during these turbulent years that everything was removed from their bodies before being buried.

The women boiled the clothes and tried to get them on the clothesline to dry before the clothes became infested with more body louse. The task was much greater than Sarah had imagined. She herself wore as little as possible to not give these creatures a safe haven for rapid reproduction.

As more of the bandits died Sarah became truly aware of how dangerous the situation was that they were in. She, too, could become sick. What if her mother got typhus? Would her mother be strong enough to make it through? Spending too much time thinking about the 'ifs' and all the consequences was much to debilitating. She had to continue focusing on the tasks at hand.

Throughout the day Sarah checked on Nikolai. She used a washcloth dipped in cool water to try to bring down his body temperature. Although his condition did not worsen it also did not improve. He still had no idea who was caring for him.

That night when the women lay down to sleep they were so physically drained that it did not matter how hard the floor felt. Any place to lie down and rest was good. Sleeping was not a problem for any of them.

Deep in her sleep Sarah heard her name being called, "Sarah!", "Sarah". At first it sounded as though it came from a far distance. As the sound neared her she awoke. It had sounded so real she sat up to listen. She was sure that someone was calling her. Then she heard his voice.

"Alexander!" Then a silent pause. "Alexander!"

Quickly Sarah got up. Nikolai was awake!

It was wonderful to hear his voice. She could feel content her whole life just listening to his voice.

It was amazing how much pleasure could be derived from just the sound of someone's voice.

As Sarah entered the room she was careful not to disturb any of the other men sleeping in the room. Alexander slept in this room too but his sleep was so deep that he had not yet heard Nikolai.

Sarah approached the bed and whispered, "Nikolai, It's Sarah!" She could not contain the excitement in her voice. She kneeled on the floor and gently took his hand. "I'm so glad you're awake."

Nikolai felt a bit confused. "Sarah?" he asked. "My Sarah?"

"Yes, I'm here," she answered.

Slowly his mind started working. "Am I having a dream?" he asked. Nikolai reached out his hand to touch her face. "You feel so real."

"Nikolai, I am real," Sarah answered. "I've been taking care of you. You've been very sick."

"But, how did you get here? Before I became sick I know that we were a long way from Terekeransiedlung." Nikolai stated.

Before Sarah could respond Nikolai exclaimed "Oh, my God!" His mind had just accepted the reality of this situation and he couldn't believe it. This was too much. "How you got here does not matter. You are really here!" he said as he reached out to touch her face. "I've dreamed of a day like this," he softly said.

"Me too," Sarah whispered. "I have never stopped thinking of you or loving you."

Nikolai pulled her towards him and she let herself fall into his arms. They were both crying. They both felt such sweet joy.

After a few minutes Nikolai started shaking. The next stages of typhus were starting in his body.

"What's the matter?" Sarah asked.

"I feel very cold," Nikolai answered. His body now felt just as cold to the touch as before it had felt hot.

"I will lie down beside you to keep you warm," said Sarah as she started getting on the bed.

"No, you will get sick too," stated Nikolai.

"Nikolai, it's already too late. I've been working with all of the sick men and the louse infested clothing. I may get sick anyway," Sarah answered.

"Sarah, I don't want you to get sick. I couldn't stand it if anything happened to you," Nikolai whispered as he stroked Sarah's hair.

"We've had plenty of food here and I feel very strong. Even if I get sick I believe that I will survive," Sarah said with confidence.

Nikolai relaxed under her arms. Sarah did sound very strong. Suddenly he felt very weak and tired. "I think I need to sleep for a bit. I'm feeling very tired. You must be exhausted too," he whispered with the last bit of strength that he had left.

"Yes, let's sleep," Sarah agreed. Sarah felt as though she was exactly where she was supposed to be. Being near Nikolai she felt completely at peace. This was home, home for her soul. What anyone would think when they awoke in the morning did not matter.

*****

Alexander was the first to wake up. Out of habit he first looked over at his best friend Nikolai to see if he had survived the night. He instantly recognized the shape of the woman lying entwined with Nikolai. A gentle smile touched his lips. They looked so beautiful together. So at peace, locked together.

Alexander quietly left the room. Times like these were precious and few and he would not let anyone disturb Sarah and Nikolai.

In the kitchen Margaret was just starting to wake up. She had such an awful headache and the pain in her muscles was so severe. This had to be from more than just sleeping on the hard floor. She tried to sit up but the task seemed almost impossible. Margaret turned over to talk to Sarah and said her name as she did so, "Sarah?"

"Sarah is in the other room," Alexander answered her."She's sleeping by Nikolai." He said it with such firmness that it was apparent that no questioning was to be done and that the situation was to be left alone.

"Oh," said Margaret with surprise. She wondered if Nikolai was worse or better. Nikolai's time here on earth could be short and she would not deny her daughter what could be his last days. She would not make any excuses either to Mrs. Kornelsen or anyone else.

As Margaret turned to her other side to wake up Mrs. Kornelsen she started coughing. Mrs. Kornelsen heard her and woke up.

"Margaret, do you have a bad headache and does your whole body ache?" asked Alexander.

Margaret just nodded as she continued coughing. Mrs. Kornelsen looked at her with fear in her eyes. Now they were starting to get it too. She quickly got up and stepped back as though some distance could possibly spare her the same fate.

"Margaret, that's how the typhus starts. You can go and lie down where I was sleeping. You will just get worse from here." Alexander stated with more compassion than he was used to giving in the past years.

"Yes, I know," said Margaret. "Thank you for your bed." It took all of her strength to get up off the floor and carefully walk to the bedroom. As she walked into the bedroom the beginning of morning light shone in the window illuminating Nikolai and Sarah on the bed. Margaret stopped for a moment. She , too, noticed the peace that surrounded the couple. She would savour this sight in her mind.

Alexander looked at Mrs. Kornelsen. She was just standing there as if in a daze. Maybe she was just realizing that she, too, might soon be suffering horribly. Realizing that her children could be left without their mother. Alexander could see that this woman did not have the same mental resolve as Sarah did to keep fighting and working for self preservation till the very end.

Mentally, Mrs. Kornelsen was a weak woman. Alexander instantaneously lost respect for her. His own mother had died when he was just a young boy and he had always felt angry with her for not trying harder to stay alive and be there for him.

His mother had been sick for what had seemed a long time and there came a point at which she seemed to just give up. When he would enter her room to see her she would just lay there and blankly stare out the window.

Just waiting to die. She would give him absolutely no response, no twinkle in her eye, no gentle pat on his hand. Nothing. She had made him feel unworthy to live for.

Seeing Mrs. Kornelsen in this mode of self pity made him boil inside. It took everything he had inside not to lash out and physically hurt this woman. They needed her.

"Mrs. Kornelsen," said Alexander. No response. "Mrs. Kornelsen!" he said in a much louder tone.

"What?" Mrs. Kornelsen asked as she kind of shook her head to come back to the present.

"I was speaking to you," Alexander stated.

"Oh, please forgive me," she said submissively, "I didn't hear you. Could you please repeat it?"

"Yes," he answered. "I was just saying that I will help you this morning until Sarah is up and about and maybe we'll have to get that other young girl, Frieda, to help you women now that Mrs. Doerksen is ill."

"Oh no, please!" begged Mrs. Kornelsen. "She's the only female capable of looking after all the children out there. I'll work twice as hard, we'll manage."

"All right," Alexander conceded. At least he'd lit a bit of a fire under her. Some motivation to keep her focused on the tasks at hand rather than the sorrowful future which was a very realistic possibility.

*****

Brilliant sunlight warming Sarah's face stimulated her to wake up. She was reminded of the times she had spent entwined with Nikolai on the hay under the walnut tree. Warmed by the heat of the sun and their passion for each other. Right now she felt just as satiated.

Nikolai must have sensed her thoughts. He turned to face her and the look in his eyes spoke of the same thoughts which were in her heart. "I will take those moments with me to eternity," he spoke to her softly as he took her hand and gently put it to his lips. "God has granted me my last wish."

Worry creased Sarah's brow, "Don't say that Nikolai! We will have much time together now, you're getting better now."

"Shhh, don't worry," Nikolai consoled Sarah. "I will work as hard as I can to become strong and conquer this disease, but I wanted you to know that I kept asking your God, that if he was real and had any power, that he give me just one more precious moment with you. Now you're here, and I just can't believe it. If I were to die today," Nikolai stressed the If word," I would die very happy."

"Well," said Sarah coyly, "I have some news for you that could make you even happier and give you even greater reason to fight hard."

"That isn't possible," declared Nikolai.

"Oh yes it is," Sarah whispered. "You have a beautiful and wonderful son."

Nikolai's mouth opened in astonishment. "We had a baby?!" he whispered in amazement. "I'm a father? Oh, Sarah, I wish I could have been there for you!"

"Thank-you Nikolai," Sarah said with great sincerity. "That means a lot to me. Oh, Nikolai, our son has meant so much to me. He gave me reason to go on after you were gone. When I looked at him and I saw a reflection of you, my joy for life was returned to me. He has brought me much happiness."

"Tell me all about him," said Nikolai as he touched Sarah's hair.

"Well he's two years old now and his name is Nicholas," started Sarah.

"Now there's a good name for a boy," smirked Nikolai.

Sarah smiled back, "Yes, and he looks just like you too. He's very bright and just wants to know about everything around him. He can come up with the most silliest of comments and questions. Everyone has to watch what they say around him."

"And how has your family been towards him?" Nikolai interrupted, wondering if his son would have been treated as a bastard child, especially since he was the son of a Russian. Nikolai's stomach instantly tightened for her response believing that it would most likely be negative. He could feel his anger building, getting ready to be defensive.

Sarah felt the change in his body. He pulled himself stiff and backed away from her slightly. Sarah looked him straight in the eyes and said, "They've been wonderful to Nicholas." Nikolai relaxed. Sarah was telling him the truth. "He captured their hearts right from the start. Even my father couldn't hide the joy that Nicholas' antics brought him."

"The typhus!" Nikolai said in horror. "I've brought typhus to my son!"

"No," reassured Sarah, "Nicholas and the rest of my family and the family who own this house are staying in the barn. We're hoping to protect them."

Once assured Nikolai let his head go back on the pillow and relax. He was once again completely exhausted from even just this bit of exertion of talking.

Sarah could see that he was still very weak. "You just rest now. I will go and cook you some breakfast so that you can gain back your strength."

"I would really like just to see him, "Nikolai said to Sarah before closing his eyes to rest.

"And you will. You will see your son." Sarah said to him as she got out of bed.

Across the room the sun now shone brightly on her mother. Sarah quietly inhaled her breath in astonishment and whispered to herself, "Oh Lord, please, not my mother." Sarah walked over to Margaret and knelt down beside her.

"Mama, it's Sarah." Sarah gently took her mother's hand. "Stay strong mother and fight this. Please!" Sarah urged.

Margaret lightly squeezed her hand in acknowledgement. She had heard her daughter pleading for her to live. Right now her whole body ached so badly and she felt as though she was burning up. She would have to concentrate on just enduring this pain.

"I'll be back in a bit," said Sarah. She remembered that her father had requested to be informed should her mother become ill. As much as she hated the idea of exposing her father to typhus, and taking a chance on losing him, she would honour his wishes.

In the kitchen it seemed that everything was well underway. She was astounded to see Alexander sitting at the table peeling potatoes. Alexander saw the bewildered look in her eyes and ignored it as he said, "You can take over here now. I will go help outside."

"Would you be so kind as to inform my father that mother is ill?" asked Sarah.

"He's already been told," answered Alexander as he rose from the chair to allow Sarah to take over. Now Sarah was thoroughly astounded. First she was allowed to sleep in, then she finds her mother resting in Alexander's bed, rather than just suffering on the hard floor, and now he's already had the foresight and compassion to tell her father about her mother.

"Thank-you," was all that Sarah was able to say without crying. She was deeply touched by Alexander's kindness. After losing so many people that were close to you a lot of people would probably turn bitter and cold. Alexander seemed to be becoming more compassionate. Sarah wondered why. She looked him directly in the eyes to see if she could see an answer there.

What she saw was genuine warmth and caring from a friend. He cared for her!

Comprehension showed in her eyes as she said "Thank-you," again. Henry walked into the kitchen and their exchange was ended.

Without thinking Sarah rushed over to Henry and gave him a hug, "Father!"

Surprised, Henry hugged her back for a long second before gently pushing her back. Theirs was not a family accustomed to physical gestures of affection. Sarah would always be different.

Alexander left the kitchen just after witnessing Henry's uncomfortable realization that his daughter had just hugged him with free abandonment. Alexander smiled to himself as he went outside. That's why he liked her. She was a free spirit. True to herself and not at all worried about what others may think of her.

He could see why his friend Nikolai had never been able to just take his pleasures with any of the women they'd captured. Nikolai's anger with the Mennonites was not that deep. His love for Sarah had kept him humane.

"Father it's so good to see you," said Sarah still holding on to Henry's hand.

"You too, Sarah. I'm so glad that you're still healthy," said Henry. He started to let go of Sarah's hand and turned to find Margaret.

Sarah gripped Henry's hand more tightly. "Wait father. Before you go in there I have to tell you something."

Henry turned back towards Sarah and this time he gently squeezed her hand. "If it's about Nikolai, I already know that he is here. Alexander told me. He said that Nikolai has been very ill and that he respects your relationship with Nikolai and that I am to do the same. I told him that I have a wonderful grandson named Nicholas and that I would treat his father with compassion."

Sarah could no longer contain her tears. They now flowed softly and steadily down her face. Here they were amidst years of war and sadness and yet there were such wonderful things happening. God was gracious.

This time Henry let go of his reserve and hugged Sarah until she let him go and said with much emotion in her voice, "Go and be with mother."

Sarah was completely empowered by love. She was bursting with joy and with energy. The work that she did was a labour of love. It did not feel like work. Everything was pleasure. She arranged through Alexander to let Frieda take Nicholas to play outside within view of Nikolai's window that afternoon.

Together Sarah and Nikolai sat by the window and watched their son play. Nicholas seemed quite content and happy. He was still nice and round and healthy looking. Sarah could see that Frieda had been making sure that the centre of her life was eating well and being protected.

More tears rolled down Sarah's face that afternoon as she shared the joy of having and loving a son with Nikolai. Nikolai, too, was moved to tears. They held hands and wiped the tears from each other's faces, oblivious to the fact that five feet away from them sat her father, watching them share this moment, while also trying to comfort the love of his life. He, too, could now see the depth of love that Sarah and Nikolai shared.

It had been a good day. A wonderful day.

Her brother Ernst had been sent into the town of Suworowka to purchase flour. With this many people to feed supplies were starting to run very short. While there he'd been told that many people in the town were sick with smallpox and that they should stay on their farm until it passed over. Hopefully no one that he had dealt with was contagious.

Lying next to Nikolai, the joy of all that she had right now, allowed her not to worry about the future. This moment in time was perfect. Sarah slept peacefully and soundly.

Over the next two weeks Nikolai gradually improved. Day by day he became stronger. Margaret, too, seemed to be over the worst of the symptoms, but she was still too weak to leave her bed. Henry never left her side and waited on her hand and foot. Miraculously no one else had contracted typhus and it seemed that the bug had been eradicated.

For the bandits that had now survived typhus, life on this small homestead was becoming mundane. Since their health was returning their desire for lust and adventure was also returning. Even Alexander seemed to become restless.

Plans would soon be made for them to move on. Supplies were running very short and the Kornelson's were worried about their own survival through the coming winter. This invasion had been a peaceful one and they were all grateful for that.

Just as things were becoming normal Ernst developed a high fever and was physically completely exhausted. He complained of back pain and muscle ache and seemed to spend that first entire night vomiting.

Since everyone on the farm now intermingled, the bandits whose health had finally returned were terrified of this new sickness. Their bodies were still weak from the typhus but even so they wanted to leave immediately.

It was too late.

Smallpox is a highly contagious disease and it was making itself known in their part of the world.

While packing up their wagons and saddling their horses the men quickly became ill.

Only a handful of the bandits which had survived the typhus did not contract smallpox.

Sarah prayed that Nikolai would be immune but this was not to be. He, also, was back in bed in severe pain. It was truly awful to be once again surrounded by so many sick people. The entire Kornelsen family was sick. Of her own family her beautiful son Nicholas was spared the torture, as was her brother Herbert, Jakob, and Sarah herself.

Two to five days after the onset of the fever and pain, a rash developed on the face, the palms, and the soles of the feet. A week later the rash developed into pus filled pimples.

For almost everyone there these pustule pimples ran together followed by a return of the fever and infection. As the pustules healed they become black and crusted falling off the bodies. The new skin was tender and sensitive.

During the few days where it seemed that everyone was recovering from the first disease, typhus, Sarah had finally felt that is was safe to bring their son, Nicholas, into the house to live with them. Before Nikolai had become ill with smallpox they had a wonderful time uniting as a family.

The evenings were once again starting to become cooler, but on the days where the sun shone Sarah would put a blanket under a tree for Nikolai and he would sit and watch his son play. Nicholas took to his father immediately. He must have sensed the genuine love coming from this man because he did not with hold any of his affections.

If Nikolai asked him to come over to give him a hug he would run as quickly as he could on his stout little legs and lunge into his father's open arms. He would wrap his own little arms as tightly as he could around his father's neck. If he hurt himself while playing he would seek comfort in Nikolai's arms.

At night they slept with Nicholas snuggled between them. Such sweet joy!

Now, not even a few weeks later, Sarah was once again trying to get comfortable on the hard floor. Nicholas was already sound asleep beside her. Although he asked questions about what was going on, "Why can't Father play?", "Why is Uncle Ernst's face turning black?" Sarah's simple answers seemed to satisfy him and he was able to have fairly normal days.

Sarah had a difficult time trying to get to sleep. She had spent hours in the day sweeping up black pieces of skin which had fallen off the sick bodies. The sight and smell of all these sick people and decaying skin just turned her stomach. The sound of pain that they were in when the new raw flesh, now exposed, touched anything was just haunting. As she tried to sleep, these were the images in her mind.

Although she had been blessed with continued health, throughout the days she could just feel the aches and discomfort of all those around her.

Watching her sister Annie go through this was the worst. Annie was still in her other world. Annie did not cry. She did not moan. She did not feel anything that was happening to her. She just lay there as though already dead. Annie would not drink anything or eat.

When Sarah touched Annie's belly for movement of the growing child within she could not detect any. If the child was still alive it was as motionless as its mother. There was absolutely no will for survival in Annie's spirit. Sarah would hold her hand and beg her to come back but it was hopeless. There was no response.

In the last few days Sarah sensed that Annie would not live and instead of asking Annie to fight, she now spent her time with Annie saying good-bye. She talked to her about the better days on their own farm and about the things that had been important to Annie. She told Annie that everything here on earth would be alright. That if she was ready she should go on and join her husband and child. Sarah told Annie that she loved her.

Annie's body had left this world on this day. Her spirit had already gone on ahead many months before. Sarah was filled with mixed emotions. She was mournful of the fact that the family would never have the pleasure of getting to know Annie's child. Nicholas would have had a cousin and playmate. She was sad that Annie had missed out on so much joy and wonder that was in this world, but she was also glad that Annie would now have peace.

Sarah truly believed that Annie was now being comforted in the loving arms of a Heavenly Father and united once more with the spirits of her husband and child. Sarah knew that in order for her own survival she had to stay focused on this wonderful benefit of death.

Sarah's two brothers Herbert and Jakob, who had also remained healthy, had dug a grave for Annie and used whatever wood material they could find to build her a coffin. That afternoon they had buried her and said their goodbyes.

Herbert had taken over as head of the family and read scripture and prayed. Only four of the family had been strong enough to be present for her burial.

Margaret, her mother, was also not doing well. She hadn't even had a chance yet to recover from the typhus when she'd started showing symptoms of smallpox.

Occasionally in a state of delirium Margaret would try to pull the uncomfortable black scabs off her body before it was time for them to fall off, causing bleeding. Henry, even in his own suffering, was still trying to care for his wife. If he heard her moving around and speaking nonsense he would force himself out of his half sleep and try to hold her still and from injuring herself.

Sarah's stomach was in a knot worrying about Nikolai. Where would she find the strength or desire to go on in this world if he did not make it?

As soon as Ernst had gotten sick, Nikolai seemed to sense that this sickness would also have devastating effects upon himself. In the days before he started suffering from the fever he spent all of his energy trying to strengthen and encourage Sarah to live her best life possible even if he was no longer there.

Of course, Sarah had not wanted to hear any of it. She wanted to believe that their happiness and life together would be forever. She wanted to live the best life possible with him in it. Nikolai begged her to think only of their son and to focus on Nicholas to give her reason to live. He assured her that seeing her and knowing about Nicholas was the greatest gift that God could have given him here on earth. If this was his time to leave he was very sad to leave them, but he was also so thankful for all this time they had spent together. He no longer felt any anger or hate, only peace.

Nikolai did not want her to have anger or hate either, and he wanted her to find and always strive for a peaceful existence.

Nikolai was thrilled with the strong spirit of their son and he begged Sarah to continue nurturing him the way that she had until that point. He wanted her to enjoy every precious moment that life had to offer.

Nikolai wanted her to continue loving with all her heart and to always allow herself to share that love.

Although Sarah had not wanted to hear any of this, she had listened. She was not ready to accept the idea that Nikolai would no longer be here for her in the flesh.

So many had died around her in this past month and the world was changing by the minute.

All of this occupied Sarah's thoughts and she could not relax. It was overwhelming.

Sarah looked over at her sleeping child and gently stroked his hair so that she would not wake him. Yes, it was truly a miracle that he had been spared all of this suffering. Sarah took a deep breath and allowed herself to calm her body and mind. Sleep finally came.

Chapter
10

Thinking back on the last three years Sarah did not know how she could have survived without the constant life force of Nicholas by her side. Even with all that had happened he still did not seem to be scarred and maintained a spark. When all had felt hopeless, Nicholas was the centre that gave them hope.

The winter of 1918 had been a devastating blow to the entire family. The ones who were still alive couldn't grasp why they had been spared death and how were they now to cope with losing so many that they had loved so deeply.

Sarah had been with Nikolai when he had exhaled his last breath. Although she had sensed that he was at complete peace it wrenched her apart saying good-bye to him. His death had rendered her immobile. She had clung to him for hours after he died, screaming to be left alone with his body, when her brothers had come to take him outside for burial. Frieda with all her good sense had taken Nicholas away from the house so that he wouldn't be frightened by his mother's grief.

Her father who was still trying to recover from the small pox himself had not said a word. He felt Margaret slowly giving up her fight to stay in this world and was quietly enduring his own sorrow at watching her go.

Although Nikolai had exhaled his last breath, Sarah still sensed his spirit in the room, and this gave her great comfort. Sarah cried, and she prayed, and she talked to him.

When previously she had been forced to let him go, she had not been given the opportunity to whisper last words of everlasting love. Now no one would take this from her. Their souls had been made for each other and she knew that at some point they would connect again.

Even this time with his spirit had been incredible, giving her an inner strength that years before she would not have thought possible. She herself felt that she had left this world to say their good-byes.

Hours later, when every tear had been cried, when she had felt him leave the room to move on, Sarah came back to the present world. Gently she removed herself from his body, and went to find her brothers to help her prepare Nikolai for burial.

Herbert and Jakob were shocked to see Sarah so composed and functioning. They had no idea how she had managed to bring herself from a screaming fanatical state to now being completely task oriented and in control.

They had thought that everything would now be up to the two of them and their sister Frieda. They would have to continue looking after the sick and take care of little Nicholas. They knew how much Sarah had loved Nikolai and they had thought that she would be in a mentally non functioning mode for months maybe years.

Sarah knew that her love had been pure and complete and that their love for each other was still there. Even though physically they would never be together again that did not matter. Their spirits were united.

Several days later Margaret succumbed to the complications of small pox as did Sarah's brothers Ernst and Peter.

Frieda had been absolutely devastated by her mother's death. She had just crumbled. She was a fourteen year old girl that had needed much support and comfort but no one was there to give it to her. Everyone that had survived these horrible illnesses was barely coping with their own grief.

It had been a complete shock when weeks later Frieda had started developing the symptoms of small pox. By the time Sarah and her brothers had realized what was going on with Frieda it was too late. Frieda's illness was too far along to allow her to listen to words of reason to give her the strength to live.

With Nikolai's death Sarah had been able to find some peace, some closure. But with the death of Frieda, Sarah felt great qualms of guilt. Frieda should have been able to live through the sickness. Sarah felt great guilt for not having realized how mentally weak Frieda was. Sarah had been so wrapped up in her own world of devastation and pain that she had not been able to see beyond that to what was happening in Frieda's world.

Herbert and Jakob had lived their entire lives just focusing on all that was going on physically that they seemed to have no idea what to do with all the emotions that were in the air around them. Give them shovels and rakes, axes and bales of hay. With these items they knew what to do. But how to stop the family around them from falling apart? This was beyond them.

It had been a devastating time for the family that remained. Henry, especially, was a completely broken man because of the death of his wife. He no longer had any of the drive for leadership in his family. Henry had become quiet and thoughtful, totally unmotivated to make any decisions for himself. At night they would have to tell him that it was time for bed and he would just give them a kind of quizzical look, nod in understanding, grumble some kind of acknowledgement and go to bed. In the mornings one of them would always go to wake him up.

Herbert, who was the oldest of the siblings, had taken over as head of the family. He never failed to make any decisions without consulting Sarah first. His sister had become an amazingly strong woman and he completely trusted her judgement. Together they had comforted Jakob and Frieda after the deaths of their mother and brothers. Together Herbert and Sarah had assured Jakob that they would all be alright and taken care of.

Shortly after the death of Nikolai, Alexander had taken the rest of the bandits and moved on to unite with the Makhnovich. Watching the heart of this young woman had changed him.

He knew that he could no longer go and take from these Mennonite people as he had before. He could no longer torture and kill those that could possibly have the same heart as Sarah.

Before he left Alexander had thanked Sarah for all that she had done, and for loving his friend Nikolai so much. He had told her of his plans to unite these remaining bandits with the bigger group and then leave the group to make a life on his own. Sarah had told him that she would pray for his safety. Would the Makhnovich let him survive or would they call him a traitor and kill him?

Alexander did not know the answer but he could no longer be a part of destroying complete towns and causing this devastation so he would take his chances.

Alexander had also warned Sarah that without him there already claiming this homestead that her family was also once again in danger. She had taken his warning seriously and together Herbert and Sarah had decided on what to do to keep the family safe.

Mr. Kornelsen with three of his children had survived the smallpox and typhus epidemic. He had offered to let them stay the winter but the food remaining was now very scarce and the Kornelsen's too had suffered enough.

The remainder of 1918 and all of 1919 had been very nomadic years. Packing up and moving from town to town. Many people had died during these years and homes usually had room to spare for the Mennonites travelling about trying to stay alive. They worked whatever odd jobs they could find to keep food on their table and clothes on their backs. Their possessions by the end of 1919 were meagre.

The clothes on their bodies was all that they had left. When those became torn or a button fell off, nothing could be done. There was no thread available to fix anything. Some people had discovered how to use silk worms to create a thread that was just thick enough to fix something.

Sarah had felt herself extremely blessed when people would pull out some little outfit that they had hidden away and give it as a gift to her growing son Nicholas. They were so cut off from any type of normal lifestyle that nothing new was available to them.

By 1920 the Doerksen's had made their way to Molotschna. Molotschna was one of the first Mennonite settlements established in Russia and therefore bigger and safer.

Along the way they had been accosted many times for their remaining possession but physically left alone. Days after leaving a village they would hear how villages were attacked by bandits, homes gone into, entire families slain, then everything burned to the ground. By this point they feared everyone, the White Army, the Red Army, and the bandits. If one group thought for any reason that you were somehow supporting one of the other groups you were considered a traitor, and could be killed on the spot.

Proving your innocence was impossible.

During 1920 the Bolsheviks, Red Army, had almost completely defeated, the Czarist supporters, White Army.

The Red Army no longer needed the bandits to wreak havoc and confusion so the bandits were forced to move out of the Mennonite villages and back to their own towns. Never before or after had the surviving Mennonites been so glad to see soldiers with the red five-pointed star emblem on their caps.

The Red Army also moved into their homes, but they gave no more cause for fear. There were no more beatings, torture, or plunder. There had been another sweep of typhus and the Red Army helped with burying the dead, cleaning their homes and land for better living conditions, and brought in medicine.

In the fall of 1920 they were even sent seed to plant for the spring. People were very guardedly becoming hopeful. It seemed that things would finally improve.

Sarah's father had a good reputation in Molotschna. His way of farming and dealing with his worker's was known and respected by many. Because of this they were able to find work on a farm that was of fair size. They had been given the foreman's cottage to live in and the task of working the fields.

The land was in terrible shape. Years of no planting and destruction by all of the warring. Because of lack of horsepower they were unable to do a good job of ploughing the fields.

All winter long food had been rationed. Mentally this was a very difficult thing to do. Not allowing yourself to fill your stomach to satisfaction was painful. But everyone stayed dedicated and honest about not taking more than their share because they were all hopeful that when spring arrived they would see the fields come to life with new growth and sustenance.

March turned into April, April into May, and no rain came. Every morning Henry walked out to the fields hoping to see some sign of life, but he always came back with his head hung low in worry. The fields were barren.

Henry noticed Sarah sitting under the shade of a tree watching Nicholas play with rocks and sticks. Slowly he made his way in his "schlorren" towards her. This is the footwear most of the Mennonites now had to wear. The soles were made of wood and the front part of the foot had a leather covering. He still remembered how good it had felt to put on his good quality leather shoes. To keep these "schlorren" on your feet you had to completely change the way you walked. Not so easy to do at his age.

Henry wondered if little Nicholas would ever have the pleasure of putting on some new soft socks and brand new leather shoes. It was a right that he had always taken for granted. Now he took nothing for granted. Everything good in life could be but for a fleeting moment and he now took all the joy he could out of every little blessing. If in the day they all had the pleasure of each eating one piece of bread this was a wonderful thing. If at night you could lay your body down on a soft surface, this was a wonderful thing.

His daughter Sarah. Now, she was truly wonderful. Six years ago he would never have seen the strength that was in her spirit. Her ability to accept and truly love everyone had saved their life many times over the years. Her genuine caring and respect showed through and anger and hate had melted away in the soldiers and bandits.

Knowing that Sarah's loss of Nikolai was just as deep as his loss of Margaret and at the same time watching her move forward with so much vigour had helped Henry cope with his grief.

Sarah had made him realize and believe that Margaret was still there. That he would in time be reunited with her spirit, and even if it was fifty years from now, he had to keep looking for the good in life, so as to keep his own spirit healthy and free.

Sitting there watching Nicholas play Henry could see that Sarah was taking in the goodness of that moment to treasure. Henry sat down on the ground beside Sarah. "You look beautiful sitting here enjoying your son."

Sarah looked at Henry in amazement. He had never given her aesthetic compliment. It took her a second to say, "Thank you father."

"I don't think that I ever sat to watch you children play the way you do with Nicholas," said Henry focusing his eyes on Nicholas. "I was just always concerned about getting everything done and at the end of the day I just wanted peace and quiet and to be left alone."

"If the world hadn't changed so much maybe I would be that way too," said Sarah.

"No Sarah," said Henry. "You have always been different. I tried to squelch that difference. I'm sorry."

Sarah reached over and took her father's hand. "I was a pretty strong willed girl, father, and you tried to teach me to behave in ways so that I would be protected. You worked hard to provide the basic needs of food, shelter, and clothing, and I definitely see that and appreciate that now. You cared for all of us the best way you knew. I feel completely forgiven by you for all of my wrong doings and I forgave you a long time ago for any area where I may have felt that you lacked."

"Thank-you Sarah," said Henry as he gently squeezed her hand, "Life is wonderful."

Nicholas had just noticed his grandfather sitting beside his mother. "Opa!" he shouted excitedly as he ran towards him for a hug. Even with no food in his belly he still managed to have energy to run when he saw Opa.

"So, whose birthday is it tomorrow?" asked Henry as he gently tickled Nicholas' stomach.

"Mine," answered Nicholas while giggling.

"Are you sure?" Henry teased, "I thought that maybe it was my birthday."

"No, it's my birthday," said Nicholas with much gumption.

"Well, if it's your birthday, then how old will you be?" asked Henry.

"You know how old I'll be Opa," Nicholas teased back. "I'm going to be five years old."

"Well, if there's going to be a birthday, I had better go and get some things ready," interjected Sarah as she stood up and dusted the dirt off of her skirt. Henry and Nicholas were already so busy playing that they just looked in her direction, kind of nodded and kept going.

Sarah loved the way her father played with Nicholas, all rough and tumble. In the evenings he would sit with Nicholas on his lap and tell him stories about the farm.

Herbert had managed to trade some of their milk for a bit of sugar so Sarah was going to bake a few cookies to celebrate Nicholas' birthday. Sugar was a rare commodity and treat during these times.

For months now they had lived on thin watery soups and small pieces of bread. Everyone wanted to keep Nicholas healthy so they always gave him a little extra share of their own. Sarah herself was already very thin. Her cheeks were very hollow and her clothes hung loosely on her body.

Sarah didn't know how her father still had the energy to play. Just baking these simple cookies seemed to be quite draining.

When Sarah finished baking the cookies she wrapped them in a towel and hid them away in a wooden box. She wanted to make sure that they wouldn't be found until tomorrow.

If people heard that they had sweets then too many would come to enjoy some. She wanted to make sure that Nicholas had a little taste so that in the future he would remember this as a special time.

Across the yard she could see her father with Nicholas in hand, making their way towards the house. It seemed that the afternoon would be quite warm and they'd agreed to lie down during this time to conserve energy. From the other direction Herbert and Jakob were also making their way towards the house.

That morning they had all eaten a few fried potatoes and although they were already all hungry again they would need to wait till evening before having any more food.

Nicholas walked into the kitchen area and gave Sarah a big hug. She sat down in the chair behind her so that he could put his stocky little arms around her neck. Sarah cherished the genuine love of these moments. Sarah took his hand and said, "Let's go have a little nap and then we'll have dinner."

"Yes mother," said Nicholas. No fighting, no fussing, he must be tired too Sarah thought. She felt quite drained.

Sarah fell asleep right away. She slept a dead sleep. A few hours later her father was gently pushing on her shoulders to wake her. "Sarah, it's time to get up for dinner," Henry called even though he was right beside her.

"Mmm?" Sarah questioned almost not able to open her eyes.

"Mother, we can eat now," said Nicholas jumping on the bed beside her. The force of the mattress going down and his body landing against her got her attention.

"Dinner? All right I'll get started right away," said Sarah as she forced her body into a sitting position.

"It's already ready mother," said Nicholas with his usual spunk.

"It is?" asked Sarah.

"Yes, I helped Opa make it," said Nicholas.

"Nicholas helped to stir the leftover potatoes into the soup," explained Henry. "You were having such a good nap we wanted to do something special for you."

"Thank you father. Now if you'll get off this sheet I'll come and try your soup Nicholas," said Sarah. Nicholas smiled and scooted off of her bed. He took her hand and guided her into the kitchen.

They sat down at the table and thanked God for putting one more meal on the table.

Even though their portions were very meagre it still felt good to have something warm in your stomach.

After dinner they all sat outside to enjoy the warm evening. Rolf, the dog which had come with the farm, came by to play with Nicholas. The family was no longer able to feed him off of their table but somehow he was still hanging on. They thought that he must be catching birds and mice to feed himself.

Sarah had such a good nap that when the rest of the family was ready for bed she decided to stay up. In other times she would have used this time to catch up on chores like sewing or folding laundry but there really wasn't much to do.

There was no thread available to patch clothes, and no one had any extra clothes to be folded. In the garden nothing grew so there was nothing to tend to. They had managed to hold onto a few books during all of their travels but there was not enough light to read by.

So she sat in a chair outside in the moonlight with Rolf at her feet and thought about all the events of the last six years and contemplated what the future of Russia would be.

A while back her father and both of her brothers Herbert and Jakob had been ordered to "participate" in the first communist election. The balloting was designed to fill all positions of district administration.

When they had arrived at the building where they were supposed to vote they had been surrounded by a sizable detachment of the Red Army troops. The opening remarks had left no doubt as to how the people were supposed to vote, "We know who you are. We know what some of you are planning. We know your sentiments. You see those Red Guards behind you? You make one false move and they will take care of you."

After several more remarks and further threats, accompanied by the vilest of curses he proclaimed, "We are now ready to proceed with the election of officers."

A list of names of candidates was read and the only question asked was "Who is against this candidate? Just raise your hand."

No one had dared.

They all knew what would happen. They had all heard the stories or known someone who was a suspected traitor of the Bolshevik party. You would be taken aside and held prisoner till the evening. At that point you could state your case and if the presiding officers found you guilty you would be shot.

While waiting to be shot you would be able to hear the officers argue about who would get to do the shooting of prisoners. This would be a much wanted duty because whoever did the shooting would be able to keep all the clothing and belongings of the prisoners. In these times they were a much coveted possession.

This had been her families and many others first experience of election under the new system of government.

The recording secretary had then written down that each candidate had been unanimously elected.

Sarah wondered what all of this would mean for their future. Would they always be ordered as to where to live, how to live? Would they always have to watch every word that came out of their mouth and every action that they did to make sure that it could not be misinterpreted as some type of plotting against the Russian government? In a few years she would want to send Nicholas to school. Would he have any freedom there at all?

At this point she had no answers. Her stomach started to growl and pinch. For now just staying alive would have to be foremost on her mind. Even though she was very hungry she somehow wasn't too worried about that. She felt that they would survive this dry year.

Sarah went to bed. If she could sleep maybe her mind could be taken off the thoughts of food.

*****

Sarah was the first one awake on Nicholas' birthday. Quietly she rolled out of bed. She put on her dress over her tattered slip that she slept in and made her way to the kitchen. She chopped up a potato into tiny pieces and mixed it with some flour and bit of water to form a soft dough that she could fry in some of their butter. She knew that they were very fortunate to own a few cows to provide them with this commodity.

Carefully she set the table and put the cookies that she had baked the day before in the centre. It had been so long that she had tasted sugar that she could smell its sweetness. Her mouth watered. Sarah was so excited to have Nicholas try some.

They had decided to have Nicholas' birthday celebration in the morning so that Henry would have the energy to walk into town for Sunday morning worship. This would be a very special treat for him. People just didn't have the energy for these long trips by foot.

The scent of the frying food must have woken everyone at the same time. Nicholas, too, must have been able to smell the sweetness of the sugar. His eyes opened wide and his face had an expression of glee as he entered the kitchen and headed straight for the table.

Sarah smiled with delight. It felt so good to see such excitement and surprise on Nicholas' face.

"What are those mother?" Nicholas asked pointing to the cookies.

"Those are a special treat for you for your birthday. They're called cookies. As soon as you go and wash up we will eat and you can try some," answered Sarah. "Come, I'll go with you to get some fresh water."

Their home was located near a well which supplied water for eighteen other homesteads. The well was twenty five meters deep and lined with rocks and mortar. A pulley system had been devised where a horse was used to walk around the well, back and forth scooping water with large buckets. As one bucket went down the other came up and was emptied into a large tank. Pipes were attached to this tank and fed to each of the nineteen farms.

The well had a brick wall on three of its sides built around it with a roof overhead to make the work possible in the winter months.

Sarah was thankful that there was still water for their basic needs of cooking and cleansing. She took Nicholas' hand and a bucket and headed to the barrel on their yard which contained the family's water rations. Sarah filled the bucket three quarters full and together they carried it back to the house.

When everyone was clean and refreshed they sat down for breakfast. Henry took the plate of cookies and handed it towards Nicholas. "Happy Birthday Nicholas," he said, "Why don't you take two cookies because it is your birthday."

"Thank-you Opa," said Nicholas as he eagerly took two. He had been very patient while waiting for Henry to finish the morning prayer before taking any food. Now he quickly took a bite of the cookie. He wasted no time eating the rest, looking at the cookie in his hand the entire time, concentrating on the delicious flavour in his mouth. Nicholas finished the first cookie and looked up to see that everyone was watching him. Opa was still holding the plate and no one else had taken any other food yet.

"That was the best thing I have ever tasted," Nicholas said as he looked at his mother.

Sarah smiled at him and everyone laughed. "That is wonderful Nicholas, but you had better eat the rest of your birthday meal a little slower so you don't get sick." They had been eating meagre amounts of food for so long that she didn't want his stomach rejecting this treat.

Nicholas' birthday was a day that would be long remembered. It was the most food that they would be able to enjoy at one time for a long time to come. That morning they had allowed themselves the feeling of being satiated. It had been much appreciated after all the months of rationing your portions.

Henry had surprised Nicholas with two wooden dolls that he had carved.

One of the dolls was supposed to be Sarah and the other one Nicholas. Sarah had felt truly touched by this gesture. She had no idea that her father had been working on these. He had even carved the image of clothes on the dolls knowing that there was no thread available for Sarah to sew some.

These toys were Nicholas' constant companions in the years to follow.

*****

Living so close to the well it had made sense with the community that the Doerksen family should be the ones to take care of it and work it. By the time someone else walked the two or often many more kilometres to the well their physical energy would be exhausted.

Those who had managed to hang onto some horses donated them to do the work. The people within the community, in exchange for the work, also took turns giving them small portions of cornmeal, a few eggs, or any other food source that they still had available to them.

Sarah headed towards the well. Although the distance was not great, trudging along in her wooden schlorren in this late August heat was a difficult task. Sarah was relieving Jakob and taking her turn at guiding the horse.

In the beginning she had taken Nicholas with her, thinking that he might enjoy doing something a little different in the day, but this had not been a good idea.

Just trying to grow, his body already used up so much energy and walking and playing in the heat on an empty stomach had made him feel sick. Nicholas stayed home with Henry. They kept each other company, becoming best friends. Henry spent much time telling Nicholas stories about farming, history, life, people, and biblical concepts.

Nicholas readily absorbed all of this teaching. He asked interesting questions to help him understand those things which did not make sense, keeping them both mentally alert. Often Henry had to repeat over and over Nicholas' favourite parts. He wanted to know the emotions that Henry had felt while waiting for Nicholas to be born. He loved to hear what the fields had looked like on a hot summer's day just before they were hayed and so on.

Henry had worked and worked all of his life. Never would he have thought that he would have all of this time to become a storyteller. Looking back on and telling of these highlights and events of his life did his soul good. He couldn't believe how truly blessed he had been and even still was right now. His need for food was minimal compared to the joy he felt each day.

As Sarah neared the well she could see that two beggars were already sitting against the outer wall on the shade side. A lot of people who had lost entire families and homes due to the ravages of the revolution and disease now wandered from village to village in search of food.

At night the beggars would go to sleep under the cover of the well house. It broke Sarah's heart to see these people so forlorn, helpless, and near death. Yet there seemed to be nothing she could do. She, too, was just barely surviving. At times it seemed that they were just waiting to die.

Sarah smiled at the beggars as she approached them and asked if they would like for her to bring them a drink of water before she went to work. They smiled back at her in appreciation and nodded acceptance. Even speaking took too much energy at this time.

Sarah brought the men some water and noticed a woman staggering down the road towards them. She was obviously almost starved to death. Sarah put down the pitcher of water to go to help her. Just then the woman collapsed. The heat and lack of food had weakened her.

Sarah went into the well house to get Jakob to help her bring the woman into the shade. She knew that at this point she too did not have the physical strength to move her alone.

Jakob tied up the horse that he had been working with and went out to help Sarah. Together they dragged her against the wall and into the shade. Sarah moistened the woman's lips with some water and poured a bit of water onto a part of her skirt to wet her forehead.

After a few minutes the woman became conscious and motioned to her skirt saying food. Sarah searched the woman's skirt and found a pocket with a leather pouch inside. In the pouch there seemed to be a mixture of grains. The other two beggars offered to cook the grain for the weak woman.

Sarah went into the well house and started her turn at hauling water for the community. She felt at ease that everyone outside had been taken care of. She was also glad that no others had arrived before she got to work because it was too hard for her just to leave them and not want to take care of them.

When it started cooling off inside the well house Sarah knew that the sun would just be starting to set and that she had better head for home.

Sarah walked around the well house to see how the people were doing that she had helped out that afternoon. A few more had arrived and were making themselves comfortable for the night. The two men who had prepared the food for the woman seemed to be sleeping peacefully.

The woman appeared to be spread out in an unusual position. Her arms were out away from her body and her legs seemed to be in an extremely stiff position. Her back and neck appeared to be arched and her head was in a slightly twisted position. Sarah approached her and noticed that her eyes were wide open but not moving at all. There was no life there.

After seeing so many dead from brutality and disease Sarah was not at all alarmed or panicked.

She did feel a deep sadness for yet another loss.

Sarah saw that some of the food was still on part of the woman's cheek. She must have regurgitated her last meal. Her body had no longer had the ability to accept this bit of nourishment. She had died from overeating. She must have died after the men beside her had fallen asleep because they appeared to be oblivious to the situation.

Alone Sarah could do nothing for the dead woman so she headed home to get her brothers to help. Sarah knocked on her front door to be let in. They now had to keep all windows and doors locked because so many people were frantic for food and would do anything to get some, even if that meant stealing or fighting for it. Everyone was just barely surviving themselves and there was just none to share.

Sarah knocked again. Henry came to the door and asked, "Who is it?"

"It's Sarah, father. I'm by myself, please let me in," Sarah answered.

"Just a minute," said Henry as he unlocked the door.

Once inside Sarah said, "One of the beggars at the well died tonight. We need to go and bury her."

"First you have to rest and have something to eat," Henry said in his authoritative voice. "Then if you feel alright you can go and help your brothers."

"Yes, father," answered Sarah obediently.

Nicholas looked up from playing with his dolls. "Can I come along too?" He was tired of being cooped up inside the house and he did not yet grasp the seriousness of the situation that they were all in.

"Actually Nicholas, I'm going to stay home with you and maybe we can play with Rolf for a bit," answered Sarah. She wanted to spare him as much of their reality as she could so that he wouldn't be frightened and worried about any of their welfare.

Sarah sat at the table with the rest of the family to eat some broth made from weeds and boiled leather just to give their bodies a bit of nourishment. They each had a small piece of bread that they dipped into the soup to make it seem more palatable.

After dinner Jakob and Herbert went to the barn to grab some shovels to dig a grave for the woman. Even though they were still young and had been very strong men this would now require great effort from their bodies.

Sarah, although exhausted from working at the well, followed them outside with Nicholas to find Rolf. Because they spent so much time indoors now he didn't come around too often. They called and called and still no Rolf. "Where is he mother?" asked Nicholas.

"I don't know Nicholas. Maybe he found a good rabbit and is enjoying himself too much to come and play right now," Sarah answered.

Nicholas was not about to be put off so easily, "Or maybe he's thirsty and can't walk to get a drink. Can we look for him a bit more?"

"All right. We'll go behind the barns one time but that's far enough." Sarah responded.

They walked and called but got no response from the dog. It was starting to get quite dark now and they really couldn't see too well. They each kept one hand in contact with the barn wall just to help guide them around. Nicholas was still hopeful and ahead of Sarah. He was walking so fast that he almost fell over Rolf. He managed to catch himself before hitting the ground.

Sarah could just make out his stumbling body and looked to see what Nicholas had tripped over. It was Rolf. He was as rigid as the woman at the well and Sarah knew that he too had died.

"Mother, it's Rolf!" Nicholas said excitedly. "I think he needs our help."

Sarah went to Nicholas and hugged her son while saying, "Nicholas, I'm very sorry, but Rolf is now in heaven with God. This is just his body that is left here. "

"No! Nooo!" Nicholas screamed. "He just needs some water, then he will be fine. We just need to get him some water." Nicholas broke free from Sarah's grasp and went to pet Rolf.

As he pet him and realized that there was no response from the dog Nicholas started to cry. It was the most sorrowful sound that Sarah had ever heard. Nicholas was intensely wounded by the loss of his furry friend.

Sarah had not grasped how deep the connection had been for Nicholas with this dog. As she thought about it she realized that Nicholas had not spent time developing any friendships with children his own age. There were no siblings to play with and share secrets with. Their constant travelling and fight for survival had not allowed them the chance to form bonds with any people.

From the way that he was crying she could see that he was already comprehending the loneliness that would now be his. There was no way to solace him. She could not give him false hope by saying things like, "Oh, it will be alright. We can always get another dog," or, "Soon you will go to school and then you will make lots of friends." Sarah had no idea when and if life would change. If she gave him false hope and these things would not come to pass than Nicholas would lose trust in her.

So she sat down beside Nicholas and put one arm on his shoulder, while she used her other arm to pet the dog and said her good-byes. Sarah said nice things to the dog so that Nicholas would see that she understood why he was so sad. "You were such a good dog Rolf. In the evenings you sat at my feet and listened to stories. And in the daytime you were a wonderful friend to Nicholas. You boys had so much fun playing together. I'm really going to miss you."

"Me too!" whaled Nicholas through his tears. "You were the best dog in the whole world!" With that he reached for Sarah and clung to her and cried.

When he started to relax a little Sarah said, "Let's go and tell Opa about Rolf. I'm sure that he is starting to worry about us being gone so long."

Sarah started to get up off the ground and Nicholas just nodded as she pulled him up with her.

Slowly now, arm in arm, they made their way towards the house.

Sarah knocked on the door again and Henry let them in. Without hesitation Nicholas flung his arms around Henry and blurted out, "Rolf is dead Opa! He's in heaven with Oma."

Sarah looked at her father in warning not to say anything that would upset Nicholas any further. He had probably never thought of animals as having a spiritual body and also going to heaven. He recognized that Sarah had tried to comfort Nicholas with this thought and decided to go along with it.

"I'm very sorry about Rolf. We will sure miss him around here. Tomorrow, first thing in the morning, we will dig him a grave and have a small funeral," announced Henry.

Sarah looked at him with gratitude and put her arms around him too, "Thank you father."

They sat at the kitchen table and quietly sipped water until Herbert and Jakob came back.

Nicholas told them about Rolf right away and by this time he was already much more composed. Surrounded by all these people that loved him so much he had already been able to accept the idea. He had even decided that he would find a nice stick to bury with Rolf as a reminder of all the fun that they had when playing together.

With all of the added work and trauma of the evening they had all worked up an extra appetite, but there was not enough to eat to allow themselves even a small snack. Although sleep would be difficult they all decided to head for bed.

Hours later Henry lay in bed, wide awake, tired, his stomach growling. As he lay there quietly he could hear the other's stomachs also making churning noises. He wanted desperately to find relief in sleep but could only think of the emptiness in his belly.

He felt completely helpless and destitute. He felt himself getting weaker and weaker. He felt that he was perishing. He was dying, slowly. Every night these thoughts drove him nearly to insanity.

Henry wanted so much to be able to take care of his family. He wanted nothing more than to be able to feed them. Every night he thought what can I do? The answer was always the same. Nothing.

A tear trickled down his cheek. His children were so courageous. No one complained. There was no point in it. It would not bring them any closer to food. His children continued to work hard just to keep bringing in whatever little bit of grains people would give them.

Well, he would keep giving extra little portions to Nicholas. He did not want his grandson to feel as though he was living near the brink of insanity caused by this hunger.

After hours of dealing with these emotions and thoughts, Henry finally joined his family in a restless kind of sleep.

Nicholas woke up early and went to rouse Sarah. "Mother, I want to go outside and start digging a grave for Rolf."

"All right Nicholas," said Sarah, slowly turning over to face him. "Just wait until I've woken up your uncles and we've all had a bit to eat."

"Uncle Jakob already went outside to milk the cow," said Nicholas.

The owners of this property had managed to hang onto a few head of cattle during these turbulent years and once a week the Doerksen's were granted the opportunity to milk them for themselves. This privilege alone already gave the Doerksen family much more sustenance than many around them.

Sarah could already taste the sweet, creamy texture of the milk. Just the thought of the warmth filling her tummy was enough to make her get out of bed.

"That's wonderful Nicholas," smiled Sarah. "I'll cook some of the grain and we can have it with some nice, warm, milk before we get to work." Sarah was about to tell Nicholas that he could go and wake Opa up but changed her mind as soon as she looked over at Henry.

Henry did not look well. As she looked at him, for the first time he looked old to her. Henry looked haggard and worn out. It seemed as though his vitality had been taken from him during the night. "We'll let Opa sleep until everything is ready so let's be very quiet."

Sarah handed Nicholas the bowls and spoons to set the table with while she stoked the fire in the oven, added more of the hardened cakes of dung for fuel, so the temperature could increase enough to boil some water.

A few minutes later Herbert came into the kitchen, his body waking him to the smell of food."Is breakfast almost ready?" he asked.

"Yes, we're just waiting for Jakob to come back with the milk," Sarah answered him.

"I'll go and help him carry it back to the house," said Herbert, "That way we can start eating sooner. I think we're probably all extra hungry from last night."

A little while later Herbert and Jakob were knocking on the door to be let in, each of them carrying a bucket of milk. Carefully, they set the buckets on the counter for Sarah to take care of. They could not afford to waste even a drop. What they had been blessed with today could potentially have to do them for a very, very long time. This treat was not taken for granted by any of them.

There was always the possibility that there would not be enough to feed the cattle and then at some point they would dry out. The cows which the owners had managed to hang onto were also not so young anymore and could at some point just die from old age, or be stolen.

Milk with their porridge was definitely a much appreciated treat. Henry could smell the sweet aroma of the warm milk from his room. Slowly he inhaled enjoying the smell and realizing that today his family would have a bit more to put into their stomachs and he instantly felt a bit more at peace.

This morning especially they made sure that all the windows and doors were locked before sitting down to enjoy their porridge. All, except Nicholas, felt a pang of guilt for doing this. He, of course, did not remember different times when people were readily welcomed into their home to share a meal.

Strangers who had just been passing through their town of Terekeransiedlung to visit or do business in other towns would stop in and ask for a bit of refreshment for their horses and always Margaret would have invited them in to share a meal with their family. This type of hospitality was customary and much enjoyed by the Mennonite community.

Now they made their home look as uninviting and unwelcome as possible. They even tried to prevent the scents of the cooking food from reaching any passersby on the street.

As soon as they tasted their porridge that morning any remaining qualms of guilt disappeared. It was so good. How they managed to eat slowly was unknown, but they all knew that they needed to give their stomachs time to adjust so it could actually process the food and nourish their bodies.

Sarah and her brothers remembered all too well what the woman beggar at the well had looked like after consuming too much food too quickly.

Nicholas was so used to emulating his grandfather that when he saw the time that Henry took to enjoy each mouthful, Nicholas did the same without being told. They all smiled at each other without saying anything, but all enjoying watching Nicholas be just like Opa.

An hour later they were all outside making preparations to bury Rolf. There was a section of land off to the west side of the barns that was coarse sand and rock and not used for much of anything. Herbert and Jakob started to dig the hole there while Sarah and Henry went to get the wheelbarrow to bring Rolf over to the burial site. Nicholas went in search of a good stick that he would place in the grave with Rolf and two more sticks that they could tie together to make into a cross and use as a marker for the site.

Half an hour later they were all converged at the grave to say their good-byes. Herbert and Jakob carefully placed Rolf into the hole which they had dug and then slowly covered him with the pile of dirt. They could see that to Nicholas the distinction was not yet totally clear that Rolf no longer felt pain, so it didn't matter what was done to his body. For Nicholas they handled Rolf with consideration.

When the ground was once more even and tamped down, Nicholas stuck the cross into it to mark the spot. As he looked up Sarah reached her arms out to him and he walked over to be embraced and consoled by his mother. Henry, through the years, had been able to keep a portion of his bible intact, and now read Romans, Chapter 5 versus 3 to 6. The message here was to be joyful and triumphant even during times of trouble, suffering, hardship, and affliction because it would produce patience and unswerving endurance.

This endurance would build maturity and character which could maintain the hope of eternal spiritual life. Henry went on to talk about how much God loved each and every one of them and that he believed that in all of this God's purpose was being done. They had already faced much sadness but they would need to continue to be strong in their faith and belief that one day they would all see each other again.

Both, Sarah and Nicholas, were now quietly crying together. Sarah was reminded of how she longed for the day to be near Nikolai's spirit once more and Nicholas was once again feeling the loneliness that would be his without Rolf.

Henry finished with a prayer for the family and guided everyone back to the house. Their spirits were subdued as each of them went to work on their daily chores. Herbert would begin his day at the well and Jakob would head out to the field to turn over the dried squares of cow and horse dung for their winter heating material.

Sarah would spend her time scooping the cream from the top of the milk to turn into butter.

Nicholas spent his day playing quietly in the house with his wooden dolls. It was quite unusual for Sarah to see him so solemn. Even with reduced portions of food for the past months, Nicholas still always maintained his spark, his radiance.

Sarah knew that there was nothing she could do right now to make him feel better. She did not want to give him false hope and she knew that it was best for him to feel his feelings rather than be so distracted in hopes that he would just forget about this day. Sarah did not want him to bury his feelings along with Rolf.

It was a day of reflection.

That night Sarah lay close to Nicholas as she had done when he was younger. She stroked his head and his shoulders just to give him some physical comfort and to help him see that loving was still safe. If felt good to have him relax and succumb to sleep under her touch. When she was sure that he was in a deep sleep, Sarah returned to her own bed. She, too, felt relaxed and had no trouble sleeping.

Commotion near their home woke them up very early. People outside were speaking very loudly. It almost sounded as though they were arguing.

Sarah quickly sat up in bed and looked across the room to her father's doorway. Henry was already up and putting on an overcoat. "What's going on out there, father?"

"I'm not sure," replied Henry, "but you'd better get dressed and be ready for anything!"

Were people coming for their milk? Quickly Sarah got dressed and tried to think of some place where she could hide it. As she was carrying it to her room there was banging on the front door.

"Who is it?" called Henry.

Rather than answering they heard, "Open up! We want your dog."

"We don't have a dog," yelled Henry not understanding what they wanted. "You must have the wrong house."

"We don't want anything except your dog! If you open up and show us where he is we'll leave you alone," shouted the person who had taken over leadership of all the commotion.

Still confused Henry slowly opened the door partially and started saying, "The dog which lived on this property died and yesterday we buried . . ."

"Exactly," interrupted the stranger. "We would like to have your buried dog. If you show us where he is buried we will leave your family alone and be on our way."

Nicholas by this time had also been woken by the commotion and now ran past Sarah and Henry through the partial opening of the front door straight towards the spot where Rolf had been buried, "No!! You can't have my dog! He is mine and God's! I won't let you take him!" He sprawled his body over the dirt where Rolf had been buried and dug his fingers into the ground as though clasping the dirt would help to hold him down hard enough so that no one could pull him off.

The small throng of people instantly followed him knowing that he would lead them straight to the dog.

They were a faceless group. No one that the Doerksen's recognized from their past. They looked like all the other beggars that passed by them on the street. Dirty and worn out, their skin just hanging on their bones, completely destitute. There were two children in the crowd, their bellies completely swollen from lack of food. Their faces so sad.

Sarah felt a mixture of deep, deep sadness well up inside of her for these people as well as anger and protectiveness for her son as she walked past the throng to her son lying in the dirt. What to do? They would not be able to keep these people away from Rolf. There were too many. To physically fight them over the carcass of a dog would be a precious waste of their own limited strength.

These people were desperate for food. Even if it meant a day old dead body of a dog, one way or another they intended to have it.

Sarah went on her knees beside Nicholas and gently placed her hand on his back and stroked him, hoping to calm him down."Sshh," she said softly leaning towards his ear. Sarah hoped that the crowd would give her enough time to gently remove Nicholas rather than force him off of the mound of dirt kicking and screaming. "Sshh. It's alright Nicholas. It will be alright."

At first it seemed as though her voice had not reached him at all through his wailing. Then his crying turned to a whimper and Sarah kept consoling him, looking up at the crowd to see that they were still keeping their distance. Her father and brothers now stood behind her not interrupting or arguing with the crowd. They, too, could see that the minute Nicholas was gone the crowd would go at this carcass like a pack of wild animals.

As Sarah kept whispering to Nicholas Henry walked closer to the crowd and politely asked if they could just wait with digging up the dog until they had Nicholas back in the house. A few of the throng nodded in agreement and Henry went back to Nicholas and Sarah and also kneeled down.

"Nicholas, I need you to come with Opa now. We will go into the house to talk about all this."Henry said in a stern voice. Henry surprised even himself at how difficult that was. Years ago he would have given his children a command and the thought of explaining any of the reasoning behind it would never even have crossed his mind. Now he felt that Nicholas had to be removed either willingly or by force but that he still wanted to spare his feelings as much as possible. Well, he had certainly been softened over the years. But, somehow he didn't feel as though it was a bad thing. Inside he felt quite at peace. It had taken much more energy to hold onto the constant sternness that he felt had been necessary to run the farm and his family.

Henry put his arms out to pick up Nicholas. Nicholas feeling the familiarity of the strong safe hands allowed himself to relax and be picked up by his grandpa. As he was pulled off the dirt he released the sand that was still in his hands and put his arms around his grandpa instead.

As Henry walked away towards the house with Nicholas, Sarah and her brothers situated themselves in front of the grave, just to remind the throng of people that they were to wait. As Henry rounded the corner of the barn and Nicholas was out of sight of the grave, Sarah and her brothers quickly stepped away from the grave.

Without delay the small grave was surrounded by people digging at the dirt with their bare hands. Their eyes had an eager and expectant look in them.

Sarah knew that she should go back into the house and yet she felt rooted in her spot. What she was witnessing was just so shocking. It seemed as though only seconds had passed and people were already pulling at parts of the dog. A woman at one end held the head tightly to her chest while two men at the other end were each pulling at one of the legs trying to secure their portion. Would they actually be able to just pull the dog apart? Wouldn't the fur hold him together?

Before any of these questions could be answered Sarah felt herself being turned around and guided away from the frenzy. Herbert and Jakob had kept their senses about them and realized that Sarah was in shock and shouldn't be exposed to anymore.

Nicholas came towards Sarah with outstretched arms as soon as she came inside. "Opa says that Rolf is still in heaven and that those people can't actually take him away."

Sarah snapped out of her reverie, "No, they can't. Rolf will always be in our hearts and in heaven. He is already safe from any pain." Sarah put her arms around her son. She felt so thankful that they still had enough to maintain their sanity and hoped that the day would not come where they too would have to eat someone else's pets.

She knew that it was just a fine line that kept her family from being in the same situation as these people that were wandering from homestead to homestead just hoping to get a few crumbs to fill that awful ache in their stomachs. Even now she could already feel her own gnawing pains start.

They had not yet had a chance to have breakfast and did not dare start anything till all the people had gone. If they smelled food cooking in the house who knew what they would do to get it.

"Maybe to show our goodwill Jakob and I should build a small fire for the crowd and bring them a pot of water to cook their food in," offered Herbert.

Sarah nodded in agreement. "Yes, then they will know that we don't hold any ill feelings towards them and perhaps they will treat us with respect and move on when they're done."

"That's an excellent idea Herbert," said Henry. "And when you're done come in and we'll split a raw potato before you head off to the well. Make sure that once they've calmed down a bit that you tell them that they can come to the well where you work for more water."

In no time Sarah could smell the smoke from the fire that Herbert and Jakob had built. A little while later they were back in the house each nibbling on a fifth of a raw potato.

While they ate quietly they could hear that the commotion outside had also died down. The crowd must have relaxed a bit knowing that they would each have a bit of food and feeling more humane.

Herbert went to work at the well and Sarah went with Nicholas on her bed to play with his dolls to keep him occupied. Jakob stayed in the kitchen to peek through some of the small slats in the wooden window closures so that they would know when it was safe to go outside again. Henry went to lay down for a rest. Carrying Nicholas back to the house had completely sapped his physical strength.

As Sarah played with Nicholas she was worried about Henry. He did not look well at all. No one looked well and healthy these days but he seemed to look even worse than the rest of them. Was he giving too much of his own food portions to Nicholas? She would need to watch him to make sure that he ate.

By mid afternoon the last of the throng was gone. Sarah convinced Nicholas to stay inside with Henry while she and Jakob went to see if the pot was left behind. There was still a thin stream of smoke coming from the dying embers. The pot was nowhere to be seen. Someone must have taken it along to see if they could trade it for something else or in hopes of preparing more food. It didn't matter. At least the Doerksen's were still all safe and they still had other pots and pans available to them.

Nothing was left of Rolf. Sarah could see a part of his skull still smouldering in the fire. Jakob went to get a shovel to put the fire out with dirt. Sarah made sure that he carefully removed the skull and that it was placed back into its original grave. They put all the dirt back in place over the grave and made it look as it had before.

Sarah would be able to tell Nicholas that he could still visit Rolf's grave.

*****

Weeks had passed and not much had changed except for the weather. The days and nights were now much cooler and occasionally they even had rain. Unfortunately this did nothing to raise their hopes for food for the coming winter. It was too late to plant anything. There was no time for anything to grow before the oncoming frost. And there was no seed available to plant anyway.

More and more people were dying. On many occasion Herbert and Jakob had been asked to come and help a widow dig a grave for her husband and remaining children. No one had any physical strength left. People would dig a grave for a loved one and when they brought their loved ones body to be placed into it they would find that someone else had already put their own loved one into it. If not enough manpower was found to dig another grave than more than one person would be buried in the same hole.

Henry now got out of bed just to join them for meals. Physically he was now nothing more than bone and skin. Mentally he was still sharp and was still able to make his presence as head of the family known.

October started with a very mild temperature so before the family sat down to have their thin soup and portion of bread Henry asked Sarah to open the windows to let in some of the nice sunshine.

Very few people now wandered past their homestead in search of food so it felt a bit safer to keep windows and doors open. The Doerksen's had surmised that either the population had dwindled drastically from all the deaths or that everyone was now too weak to keep moving. They were here in their own little world and not much effort was spent in going into town or visiting with others to find out what was happening. They could not physically afford to.

Everyone took their place at the table and slowly started eating their soup.

Nicholas, who was facing the window, suddenly had an excited look on his face. He pointed and exclaimed, "Mother! A boy at the window!"

Everyone quickly turned to face the window. Staring at them was the most dismal faced child Sarah had ever seen. He was completely swollen due to starvation and almost unrecognizable. "You're Karl Wolf!" Sarah cried out suddenly.

She recognized him from their own years of travel to safety. Karl was four years older than Nicholas and a few times they had played together. There had been a few more children in his family and without thinking Sarah asked, "Where is your family?"

"My brother Harold was with me but he couldn't make it any further. He collapsed a ways down the road," Karl answered barely able to speak because his mouth was so dry.

Henry took lead of the situation. "Sarah, bring Karl inside and boys go and get Harold." Without hesitation they left their lunch table to do as their father had requested.

It was apparent that Karl was near death. No time could be wasted in supplying him with nourishment.

Sarah opened the door and brought Karl in and placed him on the chair that had been vacated by Herbert. Henry pushed his bowl of soup over to the boy and told him to eat. Sarah gave her father a worried look. The look he gave her was

very stern and told her not to argue with him or say anything.
"Sarah, you can put Herbert and Jakob's soup back in the pot
and then when they come back divide it between them and
Harold. Then, please come back and finish your own lunch."

Jakob and Herbert hurried down the road in the direction
that Karl had pointed out to them in search of Harold.
They looked ahead but couldn't see anyone either laying or
walking on the road so they each walked on opposite sides
of the road to check the ditches as they walked.

About half of a mile from their home Jakob spotted him
lying in a curled up position. "Here he is," he said.

Herbert crossed the road to join his brother and looked
down at the boy. He looked up at Jakob. Jakob's face had
taken on a funny colour of white, green, and gray. Quickly
Herbert took a hold of his shoulders and turned him away
from the body of Harold and towards a spot of dry grass.
Within seconds he was retching. There was nothing in
his stomach so it was only dry heaving. "It's alright," said
Herbert while rubbing his brother's back. "Just try to relax
and breathe in between."

Jakob caught his breath. "When will it end? When will
people stop dying such an ugly death?"

"I don't know," said Herbert solemnly. "I can't remember
the last time someone just died peacefully in their sleep from
old age." Herbert took a few minutes to sit quietly beside
his brother and reflect. "You go on back to the house. I will
bring Harold."

Herbert took Jakob's arm and pulled a bit to help him up
and send him back. "Thanks," said Jakob and slowly walked
back towards their house.

Herbert took a deep breath and braced himself for the
prospect of carrying Harold back. Harold's eyes were wide
open and bugs were already crawling on them and trying to
dig their way underneath the eyelids. His body was covered
in filth and louse. He must have died as soon as he collapsed.

Herbert placed each of his hands underneath Harold's
armpits and picked him off the ground and slung him

over his shoulder. The boy was very small and quite light. Carrying him back to the house did not take too much effort.

He took Harold to the barn and removed his clothing. He would get Sarah to boil them to kill the louse and then Nicholas would have something else to wear. What Nicholas was currently wearing was getting small on him.

Herbert wrapped Harold in a few tattered sacks which were still there from years before for grain storage. He used some twine to secure the sacks to the body than brought the boy and a shovel out to the same spot where Rolf had been buried. He would dig the hole before going back in the house.

Jakob had informed Henry and told Karl that his brother had not made it. He told them that he had not felt well so Herbert had sent him back. Herbert would take care of Harold. Henry told him to have his soup and lay down for a bit. They made sure that Karl did not get too much too eat so that he would not die from overeating when his stomach was no longer able to retain and digest food.

After a little bit of soup and a small piece of bread Henry told Sarah to take his clothes off, wash him down, then put him to bed.

When Sarah went out to get more water from their storage barrel she noticed Herbert out near the barns digging with the shovel. She went over to Herbert, "How are you doing? You haven't eaten yet."

"I'm alright. I don't think that I could eat right now anyway," he said looking over at the wrapped body of Harold.

Sarah was thankful that Harold was already covered up. "Very bad?"

"Yes, it's very sad. Enough to make your stomach turn," answered Herbert.

Sarah nodded in understanding. She had seen enough pain over the past years to last a lifetime.

"I left his clothes in the barn for Nicholas. They're covered in body louse though so you'll have to boil them first. We don't want to give typhus another chance at our family," said Herbert.

Sarah brightened a little, "That's just what I was going to do with Karl's clothes. Thank-you. I can take care of all of them at the same time." She paused for a second, "When you're done come in for a little rest and I'll heat up your soup. Karl will probably be sleeping by then anyway and we can have the funeral this evening."

Sarah started walking towards the barn where the clothes were then turned back towards Herbert, "Should I help you carry him back to the barn. We could place him on one of the work benches in there to keep bugs and things off of him."

"Thanks," said Herbert. "That's a good idea but I'll manage. You have enough to do. I'll be in a little while for some of that wonderful soup."

Sarah smiled at him and headed towards the barn to get the clothes and get on with her chores.

That evening they woke Karl up and fed him a bit more of the thin soup before taking him outside to say goodbye to his brother. They placed Harold in his grave and Henry led them in song as Jakob covered the body with dirt.

Jakob thought that he had better force himself to hold back the nausea and continue being strong and contributing or mentally he would not be able to hold on. He was still always so amazed at Sarah. She was a woman. Weren't they supposed to be weaker? Well, his sister had certainly defied that notion. She just kept going day after day. Never with resentment or anger.

Here he was the older of the two and a man and yet Sarah possessed twice his strength and endurance.

Back in the house Karl still had a bit of energy. Everything he had eaten had stayed down and the family was hopeful for him. He was so happy to be taken care of again. He told them how his parents and other siblings had died of starvation a few weeks prior. They had heard that their relatives in Molotschna still had some food available to them and had hoped to make it that far for help. When his father had collapsed on the side of the road he'd pulled Karl close to him and told him to keep going with his brother Harold. "Don't stop!" his father had ordered. "Just keep going and get as much help for yourself along the way as you can. Don't wait for us! We will catch up when we can." His father had gripped his shoulders with both hands and shook him, "Stay strong, boy. You hear me? Stay strong and help pull your younger brother along."

Karl had nodded, "Yes father." His father had pushed him away, "Now go. Right now!" And off they went.

Days had passed and they had never seen their family behind them. Occasionally they'd met others along the way who had spared them small portions of food and water. They'd slept in ditches and snuck into people's barns on the colder nights.

Then a wagon had passed them by and the family on it had recognized them. The family had been very kind to them. After preparing them a bit of food they had told them that their father and mother and siblings were no longer alive. They had passed by them lying on the side of the road and they were still recognizable.

The family had given the boys a bit of extra food for the next day and left them. They had no more room in the wagon and would be heading in a different direction. So, now, here he was. And he was so thankful that the Doerksen's had helped him.

There wasn't a dry eye in the room. A nine year old child just should not have to fend for himself. Sarah couldn't even imagine being that young and trekking across the land without an adult for love and protection.

She held Nicholas extra close to her. He was only five. She could not imagine him surviving on his own. He too seemed to sense the loss that Karl had already faced and snuggled extra close to Sarah.

"But I couldn't save my brother," cried Karl."I promised my father that I would look after Harold and now he's gone too!"

Henry walked over to Karl and put his arms around him, "Karl, you did the best that you could. You're only nine years old and look, you made it all the way to Molotschna by yourself. Your father would have been very proud of you. And you came here looking for help for your brother. Even an adult could not have done anymore than you."

Karl clung to Henry and allowed all the emotions that had been built up inside of him to release. Finally he was safe to let go. For a child to stay strong for so long was a huge responsibility. Karl started to relax. "There, there," comforted Henry. "You can stay with us till your strong and then we will take you into town to stay with your Uncle. Now, it has been a long day and I think that it's time we all went to bed."

*****

Lazily, snowflakes were making their way to the ground. Sarah watched the boys trying to catch them on their tongues. It was such pleasure to hear them laugh. For those moments the emptiness in their stomachs was forgotten.

Henry came to stand behind Sarah and watched the boys play as he said, "I think that it's time that we brought Karl into town. Winter is now starting and I think that there will be even less food to go around." Sarah looked at Henry with concern. Henry continued, "The snow will not stick today. It's still too warm out but if we wait any longer it will be a difficult trek."

"I will take him," offered Sara. Henry was just about to protest but Sarah held up her hand. "I feel good and strong today father. Herbert will need Jakob's help at the well. Because of the cold nights there are more and more beggars seeking shelter there for the night. I have a difficult time getting them to move outside so that we can work properly."

"All right," said Henry. He wished that he could bring the boy to his relatives himself but knew that he would never make it. That would just mean that Karl would once again be left alone to find his way into town and seek help for Henry. It was a circumstance that could be avoided.

"The horse that Paul Wiebe brought over to do the well work is not in good health so I will take him with me to return to the Wiebe's," said Sarah. "That way we don't have to worry about feeding him and use our energy to return him another time."

"But that means extra walking Sarah," countered Henry.

"It's only about half a mile more," assured Sarah.

"Well, I want you to take half of my lunch portion of bread for yourself for your walk home," said Henry. This time Sarah was about to protest but he held up his hand before she could speak. "Nicholas needs his mother and I want to make sure you don't feel so weak that you lay down for a rest on the side of the road. It is too cold to sleep out there no matter how tired you are."

"Don't worry father," assured Sarah. "I won't stop for a rest. No matter what I'll keep going till I'm back home, "she said defiantly.

"That's good," said Henry. "You use that fire inside of you. I'm so glad that God made you so feisty. I was never sure what would become of you. You just always refused to conform, but it certainly has benefited all of us during these meagre times." Sarah smiled at Henry as he went to sit down.

When he was comfortable, she pushed the window open and called out to the boys, "Boys! Come inside for a bit!" They turned to look at her for a bit just to see if she really meant it. They were having such fun. What did she want? It wasn't time to eat yet.

Sarah had a serious look on her face. They were obedient and started towards the house. This would not be easy. Sarah braced herself. The boys had grown to be very good friends over the last six weeks. Now she had to tell them that they would not see each other for a while.

"Why did we have to stop playing?" burst Nicholas with annoyance as soon as he stepped inside.

Sarah ignored his tone and his question. "Come with me in my room. I need to speak to both of you for a bit."

"Did we do something bad?" asked Karl fearfully. In his home being taken into the bedroom in the middle of the day usually meant a spanking.

Sarah gently took his hand to ease his fears. She remembered all too well the horrible feeling in her stomach as her father had reached for his belt that was always slung over their bedroom door in readiness for discipline. "No Karl," Sarah soothed. "You are both wonderful." She guided each of them to sit beside her on her bed and encouraged them to get comfortable.

"First of all," started Sarah, "you boys have become very good friends haven't you?" Yes, they both nodded and smiled at each other. Sarah put an arm around each of their shoulders. "And we want you to know that you will always be great friends. Karl, remember when we said that once you were strong we would take you to live with your Uncle Wolf?" Sarah hesitated so that what she was saying to him would sink in.

Karl nodded as he realized what she was saying to him. "I have to go now?" he asked almost in a whisper because he felt as though he was going to cry.

"Yes," answered Sarah firmly. Nicholas was just starting to understand what was going on and had no trouble protesting vehemently, "No! I don't want Karl to leave! Why can't he stay here?" he demanded to know.

"With winter coming people are bringing us even less food for the well work and we don't think that we will have enough to feed Karl, "Sarah answered as directly as she could.

"I'll share my food with him," offered Nicholas. He could fix this problem.

"Do you remember how swollen Karl was when he first looked through the kitchen window?" asked Sarah. Yes, nodded Nicholas sadly. He, too, had not forgotten that image. "If you give half of your portions to Nicholas than both of you will soon look like that again. And I don't think that Karl's body is ready to go through that again."

Karl was already thinking of the future. "Will we see each other again?"

"Oh yes," answered Sarah quickly and excitedly. "In the spring we will be coming into town to do business and we will always bring Nicholas over to play." The boys looked at each other happily again.

"Is winter a long time, mother?" asked Nicholas.

"Well, it really isn't a very long time, but it will feel as though it is," answered Sarah emphasizing the word Feel. "Because mainly you will need to stay inside and there isn't that much to do. So you need to just keep telling yourself that spring will come, soon, and that you can wait that long."

"You promise that Nicholas will come to see me?" challenged Karl. "Yes, I promise," answered Sarah putting her hand to her heart. "Well, then I'll get ready to go," he said determinedly and got off the bed. Sarah was pleased at his bravado. It was a good example for Nicholas and this had gone much better than she had thought it would.

They had no winter coats so a few weeks ago Sarah had used some of the sacks from the barn to turn into warm coverings for their bodies. She had cut holes in the sewn up section for their heads and created opening on each side for their arms. She had found some old string and used that to tie off any frayed sections so that the bags would hold together.

Walking that long distance with the wooden schlorren was also not a very practical idea. She had also found pieces of leather in the barn that had not been stolen or taken by bandits and soldiers and managed to make a bit of a shoe to protect their feet. Walking completely barefoot would also not be good because their feet would be frozen very quickly.

They were ready to go. Sarah had hidden a bit of food in her dress and now all they had to do was get the horse.

The horse was extremely thin and Sarah hoped that it would make the walk back to its owners. Even when Paul Wiebe had brought them this horse some of its ribs were already showing. Now you could see its entire skeletal structure underneath its skin. To touch it felt as if its fur was just loosely draped over its body with no more muscle tissue connecting it to the frame.

Sarah slung a rope loosely around its neck so that she could guide the horse along the way. There was little fight left in this horse and no more restraint would be needed.

Nicholas stood on a chair near the kitchen window with Opa and waved to Sarah and Karl as they passed the house to leave. He would try to be brave and remember his mother's promise that it wouldn't be long and he would see Karl again.

Once Sarah and Karl were out of sight Henry lifted Nicholas off the chair and asked, "Now, would you like me to teach you how to make your own toys out of wood?"

"Oh, yes, Opa!" answered Nicholas excitedly. Henry had been saving some soft pieces of wood for a time just like this. It was too cold to do anything outside and yet Nicholas needed a task to keep him occupied and his mind sharp. Henry took Nicholas' hand and together they went to Henry's room to get all of the supplies.

*****

The sun was in the middle of the sky and Sarah thought that it must be close to noon. They had almost reached the small bridge which crossed a shallow creek just before town. As they progressed on their journey the snow clouds had drifted away leaving the sky clear.

Along the way they had met very few other people. Sarah looked around her now to see if there was anyone else in sight. She wanted to make sure that they were alone to eat a bit of their lunch before heading into town.

Everything looked clear. Maybe they should eat by the bridge so that the horse could have a drink of water from the creek.

Sarah looked over at Karl. He hadn't complained along the way at all but she could see that he was very tired. "We'll rest at the bridge just up ahead," she said as she pointed.

Karl looked ahead in the direction she pointed and nodded, "All right." He was too weak for much more conversation.

Karl sat down on the bank of the creek and waited for Sarah to lead the horse to the water. She left the horse at the creek and returned to Karl and took out some of the bread that she had brought along for them. She handed Karl his piece and sat down beside him to enjoy her share of the bread.

She had just swallowed her first bite when the horse collapsed in front of them. It took Sarah a few seconds to realize what had happened. Before she even got to her feet her mind replayed the image of the legs just buckling from under the horse and the horse falling over. Firmly she took a hold of Karl's arm to keep him where he was and said, "I think the horse just died. You can stay here and I'll go see."

She was just about to go over to the horse to check and see if it was still breathing when the people came. From every direction there were people running towards the horse. They were pushing, shoving, yelling at each other, swarming around the horse. Sarah just stopped in her tracks. Where had they all come from? She was sure that they had been alone. There must have been people watching them.

Everyone was holding in their hands either a knife, hatchet, shovel, or some kind of sharp tool.

Before Sarah could say or do anything the swarm of people was already hacking at the horse. Everyone wanted a piece. The smell of the fresh blood filled her nostrils and Sarah felt as though she would be sick. She could almost taste the blood in her mouth.

As quickly as the swarm of people had arrived they left. The horse was completely gone. All that was left was a pool of blood on the ground where it had died of starvation. There was not a single piece or section left that Sarah could return to the owner. Sarah felt completely baffled. She just stood there.

Karl stood up and walked over to Sarah. He took her hand and pulled her a little, "Let's go find my Uncle."

Sarah just looked at him blankly but followed. By the time they had crossed the small bridge and were nearing the town Karl had helped Sarah come back to the reality of the world in which they lived. "Sarah, there was nothing you could do. Those people were wild and would not have listened to you."

"Yes," Sarah nodded. "I know you're right. I just feel so awful that I have nothing to bring back to Mr. Wiebe."

"Do you want me to come with you?" Karl asked still holding her hand and squeezing a little.

"No," said Sarah as she smiled at him. "How did you get to be so brave?" she teased. "I think I have a lot of things to learn from you. I can't wait to see you in the spring so that you can teach me lots more."

Karl by now was grinning from ear to ear. He felt pretty big.

It didn't take very long for them to find the Wolf's house. At first they'd been reluctant to open the door. Just like everyone else they were very cautious. You could never be sure if people were telling you the truth or of they were coming to steal what little you had left.

Mr. Wolf had Karl come over to the window so that he could get a good look at the boys face. Sure enough, this was definitely his brother's son. There was no doubt about it. He had the same dimples in his cheeks and the deep cleft in his chin that distinguished this family.

"Well, what are you waiting for boy? Come on in the house and tell us all about yourself and your family. I have lots of questions for you. The last time I saw you I think you were just learning to walk."

"Well, I can assure you, that he has become very good at walking," said Sarah. Patting Karl on the back she added, "and very good at many other things. Karl is a wonderful boy and we've really enjoyed his company. I'm sure that he'll be able to help you with many things. He's very wise."

"Wise? Is that so?" asked Mr. Wolf with no antagonism in his voice. "We can certainly always use more wisdom."

"Well, I should go," said Sarah. "I still have one more stop to make before I head back home."

"Not before you have a bit of tea with us," said Mrs. Wolf. "You've taken care of our nephew for several months. The least we can do for you is offer you a bit of tea."

"That would be very nice," said Sarah.

Before leaving and saying good-bye to Karl Sarah enjoyed some watered down tea with just a hint of sugar. She was quite thankful for the bit of refreshment remembering that she had not even eaten the bread because of everything that had happened with the horse. She was thankful too that she had gotten to know Karl's family a bit. She now felt much better leaving him feeling that he was in good hands. Karl, too, seemed to sense that things would be alright for him here.

An hour later Sarah sat in the home of Paul Wiebe and told him the story of what had happened to his horse. She was telling him how awful she felt and how terribly sorry she was that she was not able to save the horse for him but he graciously stopped her. "Please, child, just relax." He was a man at least in his seventies and Sarah looked to him like a very young girl. He could tell that she was being completely honest. "This isn't the first time that this has happened around here. I know that you are telling the truth. It sounds as though one way or another my horse would have died. If it had died on your farm there is no way that the meat would have made it to us and there is no way that the meat would have made it to us had you been able to fend off all of those people."

Sarah nodded in relief at this gentleman. Bringing bad news was never an easy task. His reaction could have been very different.

"Now, I do not want to be an ungracious host, but I know that you still have to walk all the way home. I think that before it is evening we will still have more snow. I noticed dark clouds coming in from the east and I would hate to think of you trudging home in that wet stuff. So, would you like a drink of water before you leave?" he asked.

"That is just what I need, Mr. Wiebe," said Sarah. "Thank-you."

Once she was well out of town and underway heading home Sarah checked around her to see if she was alone. She was pretty certain that she was so she dug out her other piece of bread to nibble on as she slowly continued on her way. When she finished her bread she picked up her pace. The sky was starting to cloud over and she felt her body becoming colder. She still had a few hours of walking left before she would reach the safety of her home.

By the time she reached the entrance to her yard it was already completely dark out and the snow was once again falling but now it was sticking to the ground. Through the cracks around the windows and door Sarah could see the light flickering in her home. It was a very welcoming sight. She took a deep breath and felt herself relax and feel safe once more.

Before she even knocked she called out, "It's me, Sarah. I'm home!"

Nicholas was the first at the door letting her in. He wrapped his little arms around her hips and hugged her very tightly. He had actually been very tense about her being gone all day and worried that she might not make it back. "Mother, I'm so glad you're home!" he said excitedly.

"Me too!" answered Sarah with the same enthusiasm. "Let's go and sit near the stove. I need to warm up." Her face was all red from the cold and her hands felt completely numb.

Nicholas ran to the table to get his new toys. "Look what I made. This is Rolf." He had made a wooden dog. It was a very rough imitation but Sarah could see that it had four legs and a rounded head and a part that stuck out at a bit of an unusual angle to represent the tail.

"Did you make that yourself?"Sarah asked.

"Yes," he nodded proudly as he watched his mother examine it. "Well, Opa did help a little."

"This is very good work Nicholas. It looks just like Rolf. Soon you will be able to make us anything." Sarah pulled him over and gave him a big hug.

Then he held out his other toy, "And this is Karl. Opa made this one. See, it looks just like Karl. It even has the cleft in the middle of his chin. Now I can play with Karl and Rolf all winter long."

Sarah was truly impressed."That is brilliant, Nicholas. What a good idea you and Opa had."

"Yes," Nicholas said proudly, "and when I see Karl in the spring I'm going to give him a set of toys of our family so that he can play with them whenever we're not around."

"Well, I think that he will like that very much, "said Sarah.

Without trying to put a damper on all the excitement Henry asked, "And how did everything go?"

"Very well," answered Sarah. "Karl's Uncle and Aunt seem like very nice people. They were very kind to both of us and I think that they will take good care of Karl. They seemed quite happy to have him there."

"Very good," acknowledged Henry. He too, had become quite fond of the boy and wanted him to be in good hands.

"And the rest," said Sarah, "I'll tell you about tomorrow. I'm very tired and think that I should just go straight to bed."

Henry and her brothers did not push for anymore information sensing that the rest Sarah did not want to talk about in front of Nicholas.

"Well, before you go to bed you should at least have a little bit of warm soup," said Henry in a fatherly tone.

Sarah, although entirely exhausted by now, obeyed her father and allowed him to serve her a bit of the warm broth before going to bed. After her long day in the cold her bed felt so good. Sarah took time to appreciate the comfort of lying down in a soft bed and having blankets to cover up with and slowly feeling your body gently warm up.

Having gone to bed so early Sarah was also the first awake in the morning. Sarah tried to stay very quiet. Rather than add more fuel to the fire to keep warm she took her blanket to the kitchen with her and wrapped it around her to stay warm. She opened the window just a tiny bit to see what the day would be like. It must have snowed most of the night because the ground was covered in at least two feet of snow.

Sarah sat quietly near the stove facing the window and watched the snow continue to fall. Years ago on days like this in December everyone would have been very excited. Her mother, Margaret, especially loved how the snow brought this extra sense of peacefulness to the approaching Christmas season. The house would have been filled with busyness, preparing new dresses or updating older ones, and all kinds of baking to enjoy over the Christmas festivities.

The snow still left a sense of quiet, but rather than excitement, Sarah felt worry. Christmas day this year would be like every other day had been for months and months. She didn't even have a quarter cup of sugar to bake anything. She did not know how she could make this Christmas special for Nicholas. Sarah wondered if perhaps they should just let the day go by this year and not even mention it. Nicholas would probably not even know. He had been so little the last time they had had a big family Christmas celebration.

She would talk to her father about her worries when he woke up.

A little while later she heard Henry stirring in his room. It sounded as if he was calling her. Sarah went to his door to listen more closely. Sure enough it was his voice she heard. "Sarah!" Henry called softly.

Sarah gently pushed open the door. "I'm right here father. What is it?"

"Come inside so I can speak to you," said Henry.

Henry was still in bed and Sarah thought that it was a bit odd that he was calling her over to his bed to talk to her. "Are you alright, father?"

"I'm fine, Sarah. I just feel a bit weak and dizzy. I think that I will probably stay in bed for most of the day, but I want all of you just to have a normal day, and not act like I'm some sick man in bed," Henry answered. "I don't want everyone to tip toe around quietly like I'm sleeping. Alright?" he asked as he looked up at her.

Sarah looked a bit perplexed but agreed with him, "Alright father."

"And you can leave my door open too," said Henry. "Now tell me about the rest of your day yesterday before my grandson wakes up." Henry motioned with his hand for her to come into his room and sit on the edge of the bed.

This was a very unusual request, to sit on the edge of her father's bed and talk to him. Sarah did not question it. Her father had definitely changed over the last five years and this must just be another change of behaviour.

Sarah spent the next half hour telling her father every detail about the horse dying and trying to convey her emotions as she had watched the swarm of people just hacking it to pieces. Henry listened quietly and patiently.

"Sarah when the time comes we too may need to eat whatever we have available to us. If the two cows that we have stop giving milk and if you and your brothers think that they might not live any longer than between the three of you I want you to decide to butcher it. Of course, no one must know. You must do this very secretly. I do want you to go over to the landowners though and give them some of the meat. But when the time comes, I want you to promise me that you'll turn every last bit of those cows into something to eat," said Henry sternly.

Looking at him, Sarah nodded. Around him she still often felt just like a little girl. You did what he asked and you did not question. But as an adult Sarah now knew that this was for her own good.

Henry was trying to make sure that the last of his children would survive.

"Now, what else has been on your mind? You had a worried look on your face when you first came in here."

"I was thinking about Christmas father. I was wondering if we should just let it pass by this year and not say anything to Nicholas."

"Oh, Sarah. I do not think that would be a good thing at all. Even if we have no gifts to give or special food to eat we must still remember why we celebrate Christmas in the first place. You need to make that day special by telling Nicholas the story of baby Jesus and everything that he did for us to allow us to become closer to God. I'm sure that better years are ahead for us and that will make future Christmases even more special for Nicholas. We must still sing the special songs and have extra prayer times," encouraged Henry.

Christmas would be here in less than three weeks and Henry knew that he would not have the strength to take the lead in Christmas worship this year. He must make Sarah see that she was in charge of Nicholas learning the true meaning of Christmas. "Yes, father. You're right," acknowledged Sarah. "I will teach Nicholas about the true meaning of Christmas."

Over the weeks that followed Sarah took time everyday to read parts of the Christmas story from the pieces of the bible that Henry had left. Henry's strength did not return to him so they would all bring chairs into his room at night and Sarah would read to all of them. There was great warmth and love in that room and they would all cherish these memories forever.

Nicholas would even scoot into bed with Opa during these times and cuddle while they had their discussion and prayer times.

When Christmas day arrived Sarah no longer felt any anxiety. Nicholas had accepted that this is what Christmas was. He did not have any other expectations and was very happy with all the attention and love that he received.

Jakob had found a dead bird lying on the ground on his way to the barns on Christmas Eve. This was an unexpected gift and they all thanked God that they would be able to enjoy a bit of meat. Sarah was just ladling out portions of the bird soup that she had cooked when there was a knock on the door.

Everyone was inside their house and they had not expected anyone to come by. Who could it be? Sarah felt a bit worried. She was sure that the smell of the meat boiling could be smelled outside. Cautiously she went to the door. "Who is it?"

"It's Mrs. Neufeld," came the reply.

Now Sarah was even more surprised. It was the owner of the cottage in which they lived. The Neufeld's had never come down from their much bigger house to see them. What could she possibly want? A quick knot formed in her stomach. Hopefully they were not being asked to leave. Her family had not provided any of the crops for which they had all been so hopeful, but then neither had any other homesteads. No, her thinking was silly. Of course, they would be given another chance to work the fields and make this farm prosperous once more. Quickly Sarah opened the door.

Her worry still showed on her face as she said, "Please come in. It's so cold out there."

"Yes it is," said Mrs. Neufeld as she stepped inside followed by Mr. Neufeld. Mr. Neufeld was carrying a fair sized box with some obvious weight to it because he headed straight for the kitchen table to put it down.

"We just came by to wish you all a Merry Christmas," announced Mrs. Neufeld. "And we've brought your family a small gift."

By this time Herbert and Jakob and Nicholas had come out of Henry's room to see what was happening. Herbert quickly took hold of the situation. "Thank you very much. That is very kind of you. Would you like to join us for a bit of soup?"

"Oh, no, no," said Mr. Neufeld putting up his hand in protest. "Our children are waiting for us to come and have our Christmas dinner with them. We just thought you might enjoy a bit of dessert."

"A bit of dessert is an absolutely wonderful Christmas gift, "said Herbert enthusiastically. He could already smell the apples in the box.

"Could I say hello to your father?" asked Mr. Neufeld.

"Certainly," answered Herbert as he led Mr. Neufeld to Henry's bedroom.

Mrs. Neufeld took this opportunity to walk over to Sarah and spoke quietly so only Sarah could hear, "In the box there is also some blank paper and some writing tools as a gift for Nicholas. I thought that he was probably old enough for you to teach him the alphabet."

Sarah could barely contain her excitement and keep her voice down. "Oh, that is so thoughtful of you. Nicholas will absolutely love that. He loves to learn new things and it is a wonderful way to spend the winter months. Thank you so much."

Mrs. Neufeld gave Sarah a little hug, "Think nothing of it child. He is a bright and happy boy. You have done a good job of raising him. I think that he will be a strong man and good leader one day."

After the Neufelds left Sarah along with her brothers and Nicholas went straight for the box. They had felt it kind of rude to open while the Neufelds were still there but now they let all of their excitement show. Smiles were on their faces and laughter in their voices as they each reached in to take an apple.

Nicholas sat right down on a chair to enjoy his treat. As he took his first bite he closed his eyes so that he could shut out all that was around him and just savour the flavour and sweet juice of the apple.

Sarah stepped close to Jakob and pointed at Nicholas while whispering in Jakob's ear, "Look at how he's enjoying that apple. I think I will do the same thing."

"You go ahead and do that. I will bring father his Christmas apple, "said Jakob.

Sarah sat down carefully beside Nicholas so that she wouldn't disturb his pleasure. She, too, took a bite and closed her eyes to enjoy the sensations. Their bird soup would just have to wait till later. Today they would have dessert before dinner.

Their stomachs had shrunken so much over the past months that after eating a whole apple they all felt quite full and satisfied. It would probably be the last time that they would feel that way again for a long time. There were still five more apples in the box but they all agreed that rather than each of them eat another whole apple the next day they would all share one apple a day to make the nutrition and pleasure last longer.

Sarah spent the rest of Christmas day working with Nicholas on the alphabet. He was absolutely thrilled that this writing package was for him. He certainly understood that he had to work seriously and conservatively with what he had been given. He did not take this gift for granted.

Later when Sarah went with Nicholas to show Opa all the good work that Nicholas had done Henry seemed to be asleep. Beside his pillow lay half of his apple. Nicholas spotted it right away. "Opa didn't eat his apple."

"No," said Henry, "I saved it for you Nicholas. It is my Christmas present for you."

"No!" exclaimed Sarah just as Nicholas started reaching for it. "You need the food father. It will help you get stronger."

"Please Sarah, "pleaded Henry."Truthfully, by the time I had eaten half I did not feel at all well. If I have anymore I don't think that it would stay down."

Sarah looked her father in the eye and felt that he was being honest with her. She looked at Nicholas and nodded, "Al right, go and enjoy the apple."

Forgetting all about showing Opa his writing, Nicholas scooted out of the room to enjoy his second treat for that day. Henry and Sarah both smiled contentedly. It was wonderful to see the exuberance of a child.

Christmas had brought with it some unexpected and delightful gifts. They had been completely happy with what they had but these extra blessings had been much appreciated.

*****

The snow kept falling and piling higher and higher. They just hoped that this would mean that this coming summer there would be enough precipitation to grow plants to maturity. It was a new year, 1922, and with that fresh hope of good things to come.

It was difficult to keep thinking this, when everyday their portions grew smaller and smaller and they didn't know if anything would be found to eat the next day. They had managed to make the apples last till the middle of January but now at the end of January they just did not know how they would keep going.

Sarah now wished that they had a dog or cat that they could eat. The hunger was now so overwhelming that they couldn't even think of anything else. She decided that she would go to the Neufelds and beg. She just couldn't think of anything else. There were no more crumbs left. Her father was now so weak. When he spoke it was completely incoherent.

She had to do something.

Sarah put on the sacks that she had turned into a coat and tied on the makeshift boots. She told her brothers that she would see the Neufelds about something to eat. Everyone was so weak now that they didn't bother try to argue with her or tell her that it was not a worthwhile idea.

Walking the three quarter mile to the Neufelds home took every bit of strength Sarah had left. She was so thin now that she looked as though she was just skin on bone. It was just pure determination that got her to the Neufelds front door. After knocking several times and yelling, "It's Sarah! Please let me in!" did the door open.

Mrs. Neufeld opened the door with Mr. Neufeld standing right behind her, "Oh, child!" exclaimed Mrs. Neufeld."Look at you! You look half frozen. Quick, come over to sit by the stove in the kitchen. We must warm you up."

Sarah's feet stung as sensation returned. Mrs. Neufeld handed her some watered down tea that Sarah gratefully accepted. "Now, tell us Sarah, why have you come here on this awful day."

Sarah felt a knot form in her stomach. She felt just horrible needing to ask for food and not even having anything to give in return. Nothing these days had any real value anyway unless it was somehow associated with sustenance. A strand of pearls could not feed you. It could not even be exchanged for food. Only one food item could be exchanged for another, like some butter for flour, or eggs for milk. Then you had made a good deal.

"I came here hoping that perhaps I could get a bit of food from you. We have absolutely nothing left. We did make those apples last for three weeks, but I don't know what to do. My father is so weak and limp, I don't know if he'll keep on living."Sarah swallowed the lump and tears started to roll down her cheeks. "I'm worried about Nicholas. Even he is just lying around now with little strength to talk or play."

"There, there, now," soothed Mrs. Neufeld."You just relax. I'm sure that we can give your family enough to last for a while longer. You just sit here while Mr. Neufeld and I go and discuss our situation."

Sarah sat by the stove, drank her tea, and wiped away the tears. Her emotions were just so uncontrollable these days. She could hear the Neufelds quietly whispering in their bedroom. She looked around the room and for the first time since entering noticed the three Neufeld children sitting at the kitchen table and watching her. She had been completely oblivious to them when she had first entered. Sarah started to laugh, almost hysterically. She must look quite a sight to them in her sackcloth coat, sitting here, and blubbering.

She wiped the tears from her eyes again just as the Neufelds came back into the room. This time they were the tears from her laughter.

Seeing the emotional state that Sarah was in Mrs. Neufeld thought that it would be best if they fed her a bit before sending her home again. With her irrational behaviour Sarah might not make it otherwise. It looked as though the physical exertion of treading through the snow had pushed Sarah close to the edge of delirium.

Mrs. Neufeld guided Sarah over to the kitchen table and brought her some of the watery porridge that she had just cooked for her own children. "Now, you eat all of that before you head back home. Your family needs a strong woman to take care of them."

"Thank-you," whispered Sarah as she looked at the food in front of her. She was so hungry. It took all the self control she could muster to eat it slowly and properly with the spoon. What she really wanted to do was take the bowl, lift it to her mouth and drink the porridge as though it was water as quickly as she could. Not only would that be rude, it would also not be good for her stomach. So, Sarah restrained herself and with proper etiquette, ate in unison with the Neufeld family.

After her meal the Neufelds invited her to sit once more near the stove and get good and warm before heading home. A half an hour later Mrs. Neufeld was gently shaking her awake. Sarah had dozed off from the warmth and good food. "Oh, I'm so sorry," said Sarah, "I must have been very tired. I do feel so much better now. Thank you."

"That's quite alright," said Mrs. Neufeld. "You needed the rest to bring your energy up." She could see that Sarah was once again stable. "Here are a few things to help you for a little while." Mrs.Neufeld handed her a bundle of food tied up in a sack.

As she stood up to accept the bundle Mr. Neufeld said, "We've heard that food supplies are coming from Canada and the United States. The Mennonites there are working together to help us. Hopefully we've given you enough to last till the help arrives."

"Oh, that is wonderful news. I can't wait to tell my family. I don't know how we can ever repay you for this," said Sarah as she held up the bundle.

"Just try to keep everyone healthy until the help arrives, "said Mr. Neufeld, "That is all we want for repayment."

"I promised my father that we would butcher the two cows that we have left when things seemed to be too bad, but we have had a difficult time deciding if this is the right time," confided Sarah.

"Tell your brothers to be patient and hold on for a little while longer. It shouldn't be too long before food arrives from America. Once we hear where to go we can go together," offered Mr. Neufeld.

"Oh, they will be very happy to hear that," smiled Sarah. "I will tell them everything you said. I had better go now."

"Yes," agreed Mrs. Neufeld. "We will see you very soon."

Heading back home Sarah felt almost a lightness to her step. Somehow the snow did not seem even near as difficult to traverse as on the way to the Neufelds. She definitely felt refreshed. It seemed to take no time at all before she arrived back at her own home.

Back inside her own small home everything seemed very quiet. The house felt very cold. Sarah felt a shiver run down her spine. It was as though she was surrounded by death. Quickly! She had to work quickly to restore the warmth and spirits of her family.

She went to the box to where the squares of dried cow dung were kept and took a few extra than usual so that she could heat up their stove to a higher degree than what they had been during these conservative times.

Once this was done she cleaned her hands and opened the package that the Neufelds had given her. To her eyes it looked like a feast. There were at least ten potatoes, a small bundle of dried corn, another bundle of grain, and there even appeared to be some dried meat. How they had managed to hang onto all of this through this past year was beyond her but she was very thankful. They must have planned very well.

Sarah put a pot with water on the stove and while it warmed up she chopped up one of the potatoes into very small pieces. She would make a thin soup for her family. It was probably all that they could hold down after this long period of time with almost nothing in their stomachs.

As the stove became hotter and hotter and the soup boiled, Sarah could hear movements in the other rooms. Her family was rousing. The warmth and the smell of food was invigorating their senses.

Several hours had passed since she'd come home and the soup was almost ready. Sarah went to wake up Nicholas. She sat down on the bed beside him and gently stroked his arm. "It's time to wake up Nicholas. I have some nice warm food ready for you."

Slowly he turned over and faced her looking at her with a dazed expression. Because of the cold and the lack of food, waking up and the ability to comprehend, was a very slow process. "Would you like to come and have something to eat?" asked Sarah. His cheeks looked so hollow. The baby fat which should still be there at this age was all gone. None of the adorable roundness which was still associated with a normal five and a half year old was left.

As Nicholas realized that his mother was offering him food there was a spark in his eyes and once again he looked like a child with hope and delight. It was the look of a child on his birthday when just the toy or gift that he'd been hoping for is opened.

Sarah felt herself glowing with pleasure as she saw that look in his eyes. Nothing could be more satisfying for a mother than to know that she had everything available to her that she needed to take care of her child. The desire to care for, nurture, and protect was just so strong.

Sarah removed the covers from Nicholas and put her arms out to lift him out of bed. He reached his arms out and wrapped them around her shoulder as she pulled him up and he pushed off the bed with his legs. When he was in a standing position Sarah pulled his hips towards her body and lifted so that he could also wrap his legs around her waist. "Let's go and tell your uncles that it's time to eat," she said in a conspiratorial tone.

Nicholas smiled mischievously and nodded catching on to the playful tone in his mother's voice.

Nicholas felt so light now that Sarah had no trouble carrying him to her brother's room to tell them to get moving into the kitchen.

"Tickle his toes, "whispered Sarah as she bent down with Nicholas so that he could reach his uncle's feet.

Nicholas giggled and lifted the covers off of Uncle Herbert's feet, "It's time to get out of bed Uncle Herbert. There's food." Nicholas tickled his feet and Herbert made a grumbling noise.

"Come and eat boys!" announced Sarah.

Jakob bolted upright in bed. "Did you say food?"

"Yes," answered Nicholas impatiently. "Hurry, I'm hungry."

"Are you sure?" asked Jakob teasing Nicholas. He could definitely smell the boiling potatoes.

"Yes!" shouted Nicholas. "Mother says that we can eat."

Although Herbert and Jakob would have loved to jump out of bed with youthfulness they just did not have the strength so they slowly got out of bed and made their way to the kitchen. Once they were seated at the table Sarah brought each of them a bowl of soup. "Be careful so you don't burn your tongues. It's still very hot. While you eat I will go and feed father."

Nicholas looked up and with a worried look asked, "What about you, mother? Aren't you going to eat?"

Sarah went to put her arms around him and assured him, "When I was at the Neufeld's I already had some food there. So, right now I'm alright. I will have some soup later."

Happy that everything would be alright Nicholas picked up his spoon to start enjoying the soup that was in front of him. Sarah looked at her brothers to assure them that she really was feeling good and that they could feel good about enjoying their meal.

Henry lay motionless in bed, listening to the stirrings of the house. It was the sound of the beginnings of life. He sensed a shift from the hopelessness of their situation. His children had a reason to get out of bed. "Thank-you Lord!" he whispered. His children would survive.

His body ached lying in bed, but his mind did not even have the strength to will it to move. His weakness was encompassing. Even the basic, primal act of relieving oneself was an activity that took every ounce of strength that he could muster.

Sarah knocked on her father's door before entering with a tray of food. She sensed that he was awake but did not bother waiting for a response before entering. She knew that speaking took a great deal of effort from him right now.

"Father, I've brought you a bit of fresh warm soup," said Sarah as she put the tray down on the chair. "I'll just prop you up a bit so that it's more comfortable for you." She took one of the blankets off of him and rolled it into a ball to put behind his back. The house was much warmer now and he should be fine.

Henry tried to smile at her in appreciation but the corresponding muscles did not respond correctly. Sarah saw the small glimmer in his eyes that accompanies a smile and smiled back.

Once he was comfortable she picked up the tray and dragged the chair over beside his bed. As she held the first spoonful towards him she started chatting to him. She knew that this must be just awful for him not to even have the strength to feed himself. She wanted him to feel that his dignity was intact and that he was still the head of the household here and that he had all of their respect.

"The Neufelds were very generous father. They gave us corn, grain, potatoes, and some dried meat," said Sarah.

Henry stopped mid bite and looked at her. Before he had a chance to speak Sarah continued, "It's alright father. They have heard that help is on the way from Canada and the United States. I know that you would not want us to take their last food from them. I just went there thinking that if I could even just get a little bit of food from them then we would perhaps gain enough strength to butcher one of the cows." Sarah looked into her father's eyes with tears of the severity of their situation. "Father, that's all that we have left that we could eat. Even if we could dig through the snow, there is nothing left on the ground."

The food was starting to work in his body and Henry nodded. "Tell me more about the help that's coming."

"Well, they did not have too much information, but said that we could go with them to get food when the time came. They will let us know. They said that we should wait with doing anything with the cows and just to get everyone healthy, "answered Sarah.

The bowl was not yet empty but Henry held up his hand in a motion telling her no more. Sarah looked at him, "Are you sure you've had enough Father?"

"Yes, it doesn't feel as if it's agreeing with me too much. I had better just let this bit settle in. My body just doesn't feel as though it's working quite right," said Henry. "You can just leave me in this position for a while. Maybe it will help the food stay down."

"Would you like for me to come and read to you a bit later?" asked Sarah.

"That would be very nice," said Henry. "If Nicholas is feeling better you could ask him if he wants to play in here with his toys."

Sarah nodded. She was delighted to see him desire a bit of lively company. She desperately hoped this meant that he was on the road to recovery.

The impact of the nourishment was definitely most noticeable in Nicholas. In no time he seemed to just come to life with energy. He was thrilled at the idea of playing with his wooden toys in his Opa's room. He was so excited. It felt like old times. If such a thing was possible for someone so young. But he had already witnessed a lifetime of trauma.

Chapter

11

It was a beautiful, sunny day in February. Everyone's spirit had lifted from the daily portions of food and there was a slight sliver of hope that life would continue this coming spring.

Henry was once again in his bed. Jakob and Herbert had occasionally helped him get to the kitchen to sit there with the rest of his family for small amounts of time. But he just wasn't getting stronger and this took a great deal of exertion. Right now he was quite content to lie in his bed and enjoy the rays of sunshine that were shooting through the cracks.

Soon Sarah would be coming to feed him. He had to talk to her. His body had not resumed functioning the way it was supposed to. He felt that his time left with his children would soon end. What he ate was just going through him. At least today he felt alert. He had to talk to her, to all of his children.

Sarah arrived with the thin, watery, soup. She smiled as she saw her father enjoying the beam of sunlight on his face. Before she had a chance to pull the chair near his bed to feed him Henry stopped her, "Put the soup tray on the floor and come here to sit by me."

Sarah put the tray down and pulled the chair over, "Alright." She had a perplexed look on her face.

Henry reached out to take one of her hands and gently touched them with both of his own. Her hands felt rough and worn, and yet so strong. "Sarah, you have turned into an amazing woman. There are just so many things that I want to say to you before my time here is up."

"Father, don't . . ."interrupted Sarah. Henry took one of his hands off of hers and put a finger to her lips to stop her.

"It's alright Sarah," he consoled her. "I will not be here much longer and there are many things that I want to say to you. Knowing that you will be here with your brothers and

Nicholas, I have complete confidence, faith, and peace. I am so proud of the woman that you have become."

A tear rolled down Sarah's cheek. These were not words and emotions her father would have expressed years before.

"Sarah, years ago I said that you would never be allowed to get married. I want to take that back and change it. That was a big mistake on my part and I am so sorry for the love that I took from you." Sarah was shaking her head, no. She herself had never thought of marrying or even loving someone else.

"Yes, Sarah. Look at you. You are a beautiful and young woman. You still have many years to live. You have so much love in you. You need and have every right to share that. Any man should be very proud to have you as a wife. There is nothing dirty or shameful about you and I want you to work on changing the way you think about yourself. "Henry took a deep, slow breath and looked down in shame himself.

"The way you were treated by people years ago, that was shameful. It must have torn at your very soul. Instead of showing an innocent young girl love and support, we treated you with disdain and arrogance. As if any of us were better than you. We have all made mistakes in our lives. You were a young woman with so much life and vitality that we all felt threatened by you." Sarah looked at her father in surprise. Why would they have felt threatened?

Henry nodded as he said, "Oh yes. People felt threatened. We had no idea how to harness and control all of your energy. You would just speak what was on your mind. Everyone thought that you would pollute their young children with all of your radical ideas. We did not want a mass of undisciplined children running around. And then when you became pregnant it just confirmed all of our beliefs." Henry took a deep breath.

"People could say, Oh, yes. See? That could have been my son or daughter if I would have let them spend more time with Sarah. I knew she was trouble." Henry shook his head in remorse.

"We were so narrow minded. We missed all of the wonderful goodness that you brought with you. The resilient joy in your spirit. The way you view everything as wondrous and miraculous. The strength and energy that you possess. It is just way beyond that of the average person." Henry looked Sarah directly in the eyes and squeezed her hands. "Don't hide anything of all of your qualities anymore. Be the person that God made you." Sarah was astounded and speechless.

"Sarah don't be afraid to fall in love again. You have my blessing with whomever you choose. I know that you will choose wisely. Find someone who can love both you and Nicholas with all of his heart. There are now many women with children and no husbands. There are many husbands who have been left with children and no wife. You are no longer an outcast or different. Hold your head high with dignity."

Sarah was overwhelmed by all that her father had said. Henry motioned for Sarah to stand up, "Maybe just let me rest a bit before you feed me. I'm kind of tired now."

"Alright father," said Sarah, "Thank-you."

"I love Sarah, "replied Henry before closing his eyes as she left the room.

Tears were rolling down her cheeks as she walked into the kitchen. Nicholas noticed right away and came over to her and put his arms around her waist, "Mother, what is it? Did Opa get sicker?"

"No, Nicholas. Opa just said some very nice things to me and they made me so happy that I'm actually crying."

"That's funny mother."

"Yes it is Nicholas. Sometimes when people feel very happy they cry." Sarah was actually filled with such a mixture of emotions that she had to make sense of them herself. Her father had said so many things to her. Was he really dying? The thought hurt more than she could bear. He had become so dear to her. She was still too young to be without a father. She felt a moment of panic. Like she was still a child and what would she do without a father. She was not ready to let him go.

Marriage. Life had been so focused on just survival that thought had not been a part of her at all. Even now thoughts of herself with a man felt completely foreign and ridiculous. She would somehow try to open her heart to that possibility, but for now that idea seemed a lifetime away. She would keep focusing on strengthening her father. Her energy had to remain on those she loved in this house. Other thoughts were just fanciful and distracting at this time.

Later that day Sarah went in to feed Henry his small portion of soup. It would not stay down for him. It was an agonizing sight to watch someone already so weak lose all control of his body with the spasmodic vomiting. Tears were rolling down his cheeks and breathing was difficult for him.

When it was finally all over and Sarah had cleaned him up and laid him back down to rest, she went into her room and closed the door behind her.

Her brothers stayed with Nicholas in the kitchen.

Sarah slumped down on the floor and held her knees to her chest and cried as silently as she could. It was the most awful sensation to have watched her father suffer like that. A part of her wished that he would just pass away peacefully rather than to endure any more pain. And she felt just horrible for even wishing that. "Lord," she prayed looking towards the heaven, "I just don't want him to suffer anymore. I don't want anyone to have to feel any more pain. Please, God, let him get strong again."

After a long time her tears subsided and she went to lie on her bed. Right now she did not want to move again. Loving could feel so wonderful and yet hurt just as deeply. And yet what was life without it? An empty and dull state of being. Love heightened all of your senses, making you tingle, giving you reason to live.

Maybe she should just thank God for all the love that she had already been able to share during her time in the world. She had enjoyed much pleasure at both giving and receiving love to and from family, friends, and especially Nikolai and their precious son Nicholas.

With these thoughts Sarah allowed her body and soul to feel peace and drift into a restful sleep.

As the days progressed and March arrived nothing changed for Henry. When he awoke and felt mentally stable he called his sons in one by one and also gave his love and last words of advice and wisdom to them.

With Nicholas he cuddled and told him "Don't worry one bit about your old Opa. I've got Jesus waiting for me and he's going to reunite me with my beautiful wife, Margaret."

"Are you really going to die Opa?" asked Nicholas so innocently.

"Yes, Nicholas," he answered matter of factly. He felt completely ready to leave this world. He felt that his children were all more than capable of looking after themselves and that they would be alright. He yearned for the peace and comfort that heaven promised him.

"Heaven is a wonderful place Nicholas," said Henry.

"Can I come and see you there?" asked Nicholas.

"Well, not for a long, long time Nicholas. First you have to be an old man like me. But then, I will be ready and waiting for you."

"What about my father?" asked Nicholas.

"I will have a long talk with Jesus and I'll make sure that he is right there beside me waiting for you. But first there will be a lot of things that you need to do here on earth," answered Henry.

"There are?" asked Nicholas in surprise.

"Oh, yes," returned Henry. "You need to grow up and then find a job. And you will probably have your own children one day and they will need you to teach them many things for a long time to come. And Nicholas, always have fun and enjoy everything that you're doing. Even work. Be like your mother. Learn to see the beauty in everything and life will always be beautiful."

Nicholas snuggled closer to Opa and thought about these things. Pretty big things for a five and a half year old to think about. But than his life had already been part of many big things. And maturity and growing up quickly were just part of what one reaped during these type of turbulent times.

When Nicholas started getting sleepy, Sarah took him from the room and put him to bed.

The next morning Henry's spirit was no longer with them. Sarah felt the emptiness as soon as she entered his room. She looked at the body lying there but knew that there was no more life inside. "Good-bye, Father," she whispered as tears formed in her eyes.

Sarah walked to her father's bed and sat on the edge. His hand lay on his chest and gently she touched the thin and delicate skin. There was still a bit of warmth. A little bit earlier and he would still have been alive. "Boys!" Sarah called with urgency, trying not to be too loud but get all of their attention. Her voice was raspy, "Boys!"

Herbert, Jakob, and Nicholas quickly came into Henry's room. Abruptly they all stopped, looking at Sarah they knew that Henry had passed away. Standing behind Nicholas, Herbert put his hands firmly on Nicholas' shoulders, to offer comfort. Nicholas just stayed there for a second than raced over to his beloved Opa. He flung himself on Henry's chest and cried, "Not yet Opa! Don't go! Please God?!"

Herbert and Jakob walked to Sarah and Nicholas and kneeled by the bed embracing each other and embracing Nicholas and Sarah. Together they all cried and shared in the sorrow of letting their father go. When everyone's tears subsided they carried Nicholas to the kitchen and sat down by the table. "What should we do?" asked Jakob.

"You and I will go out and prepare a proper grave for father," answered Herbert. "Then we will go and tell the Neufeld's that father has passed away. Perhaps they will allow us to use parts of the fence to build him a casket. Sarah, you can stay with Nicholas and comfort him. Later when we come back we can prepare father. And tomorrow we will give father a proper burial."

"Yes, that would be the best way to go about things," agreed Sarah.

Jakob and Herbert went out to work on the grave. They picked a spot under a tree where the snow did not seem to be as deep. The work was very difficult. The ground was frozen solid. This was not something that could be put off till the spring though, so they kept at it. By mid afternoon they decided that the hole would be sufficient. Herbert went to talk to the Neufeld's alone and sent Jakob back to the house to help Sarah.

An hour later Herbert was back home and asking Jakob to come and help him build the casket. The Neufeld's had readily agreed to allowing them to use material from the fence. "I want to help too," said Nicholas with determination. They all looked at him with surprise.

"Are you sure?" asked Herbert.

"Yes, Opa would be happy to know that I am helping and learning something new. I want to do something for him," he answered without hesitation.

"Alright, I'll put warm clothes on you and you can go and help your Uncles, "said Sarah.

Sarah watched the three males remaining in her life trod off to the barn. The house felt so silent. It wasn't just the boys leaving. It was not having her father there. For months now her father had been a very silent part of the home but you could still always feel his presence. Even when he was asleep, his vitality was still there. Now it was gone. The world had changed once more. How would they all adjust? At this moment Sarah felt as though she had no strength left to adjust.

For just a little while she would allow herself to give in to the weakness. She was tired. She was so sad. Their world right now felt very dark. There was so little light. She could hear her father's voice telling her over and over how wonderful he thought she was. How she could always find the goodness. "I don't feel that way right now father," she cried and whispered. "I miss you so much."

She sat by the stove and let the memories of life with her father envelop her. She laughed and she cried. He had been quite a man. Hard working and dedicated to his family.

Tough and yet fair. He had changed so much over the years. As a teenager she would never have thought that they would someday become so close. Her father's heart had melted with the hard times and gold had flowed from it. It had been a beautiful and amazing process to watch.

She felt so thankful and blessed that she had been able to witness his transformation of character. She wished that Annie could have seen their father like this. Maybe he could have helped Annie turn to gold too.

Sarah prayed for her family that was no longer with her and for those remaining.

A part of her was really missing Frieda right now. Frieda should still be here. Life had been so full of challenges over the past years that not much time had been left for the thought of having people around just for company, but right now she really wished that she could have the companionship of her sister Frieda.

To have another woman to talk to right now would just feel so good. And by now Frieda would definitely have been a woman.

Sarah prayed that her sister had found peace. She hoped that the spirits of all her family member, who were no longer part of this life on earth, were all giving each other comfort and love.

Soon her brothers and Nicholas were back with the casket. Sarah had been so deep in reflection that the time had passed in the blink of an eye.

Earlier Jakob had helped Sarah clean their father's body. They would have loved to put a nice, clean suit on him, but the clothes on their bodies was all that they had. Their father deserved so much, but he had always lived a humble life and his body would be put to rest in humble attire.

They lined the casket with Henry's blanket, than put him inside it. Together they all carried the casket back to the barn to remain there overnight.

Nicholas was with them every step of the way. He wanted to make sure that he did all that he could for his Opa, just as his Opa had always done all that he could for him. Although he was only just over five years old he was well aware that Opa had spent more time with him and given him much more than he had any of his own children. Opa had taught him so much. He would always try to be a man like Opa.

The night had passed slowly for Sarah. She was not looking forward to saying her final good-byes to her father. By afternoon they were all as cleaned up as they could get and went out to get the casket and put it in the grave that Herbert and Jakob had prepared.

The Neufeld's with all of their children came down to join them for the funeral. They read scripture, they prayed, they sang songs of worship, and they cried.

Sarah couldn't help but think of how different her father's funeral would have been years previous to the war and all of the political upheaval in their country. The entire village would have showed up at their church. There would have been many people present to speak about all that he had meant to them and their community. He had been a leader and man of great respect within their community. Many people would have come to their house to continue mourning his passing. They would have brought food for the family.

Those times were so long gone that it was difficult to even visualize such events.

Each of them realized that had it still been in those times though, that none of them would have been as close to their father, as they had been privileged to become over the past years of difficulty. Although life had been very hard, this had definitely been a blessing for those family members still remaining.

They would each always take with them the love that their father had time to show them in these past years. They would all always look back on him with love, respect, warmth, and no regrets. Here was their gift of these past difficult years.

Chapter

12

March 13, 1922. It was a day that would never be forgotten. For Sarah's family and many other families it would be remembered as a memorial of being saved from death by starvation.

If only her father could have been here to celebrate with them. Had this day come just a few months sooner Henry would still have been with them. They could have coaxed his body back to being able to accept food.

Sarah so needed the man that her father had become over the past three years. She would have loved a chance to work beside her father with his new character and the old physical strength that he'd possessed.

But it was too late for Henry.

She would now focus on Nicholas. He was still young and although he'd seen and endured much hardship, this would now be the beginning of giving him a chance to enjoy life the way that Sarah and the rest of her family had at one time.

Sarah would teach him never to take anything for granted and always appreciate everything they had. These humble and treacherous times would not be forgotten.

There had been great excitement throughout the village as news spread that the American food had arrived at the railway station. Herbert along with many others had gone to the railway station to watch the railway cars being opened.

As they were opened and people could see that they were completely filled with food, their joy was overwhelming. People smiled, hugged, and cried at this generous gift.

It was very difficult for Herbert to walk home empty handed. It was very tempting to stay near these railcars till everything had been organized. But it was still winter and very cold.

Everything would be done in an orderly fashion. He had to have faith that his family would get their share.

Now, three days later, they were standing in line at the American soup kitchen waiting for their first real meal in years. There were hundreds of people all waiting patiently in the cold.

Sarah huddled with her brothers and Nicholas. At times Herbert or Jakob would pick Nicholas up just to make it a little easier for him. It was difficult but they were all happy and thankful.

The food that they'd received from their generous landowners had been just enough to tide them over till this day.

Finally it was their turn. They stepped inside the old school house. Inside tables had been set up for people to enjoy their meal. You had to eat slowly so that your body could adjust, but at the same time you knew that there were many others waiting behind you, out in the cold looking forward to their turn.

They each received a good chunk of white bread. Sarah estimated that it must have been about 1/3 of a pound and a dish of soup. Soup that actually had flavour and a mixture of vegetables. Warming their bodies from the inside out. Such a pleasure!!

Sarah and her family ate only half of their bread and saved the rest for the next few days.

This was more food than they'd been able to enjoy for a very long time, but the hard times were not yet completely over.

They'd heard that they would still need to wait for more food to arrive before people could actually take food into their own homes. For now they would have to rely on daily trips to the soup kitchen.

Hope had returned once more. They would be patient and keep thanking God everyday for all that they had.

Word was sent throughout the village that food drafts had arrived and people could pick up their portions in Ekaterinoslav.

The journey there would take days. Only the strongest men would be able to survive the strenuous endeavour. Sarah so wished that she could go, but they would never consider taking a woman amongst a group of men.

Both of her brothers were chosen. Herbert seemed quite excited to be heading off on an adventure, but Jakob was a bit apprehensive. Every day for a week now they'd had nourishment and they could feel their bodies improving and functioning at a normal level, but a bit too much exertion and he would quickly feel weak.

Others from the village provided horses and wagons. The men were given enough food from the soup kitchen to sustain them for about three days and sent on their way.

Sarah and Nicholas waited at the fence on the roadside of their house for the procession to pass and say good bye to her brothers.

"There they come!" exclaimed Sarah, pointing towards the group of people approaching them.

As soon as Nicholas saw them he jumped off the fence rail that he'd been standing on and ran towards his uncles. His body seemed to be bouncing back to health much quicker than the rest of them. It was so wonderful to see his youthful energy return.

Sarah smiled. Weeks ago they would not have trusted anyone on the streets and now Nicholas could freely run towards his uncles. Such a simple but wonderful pleasure.

Freedom and safety. How to live in a world where this could be for everyone?

As the group passed their house Herbert and Jakob each stopped for minute to hug Nicholas good bye and waved to Sarah. Sarah smiled and waved back to everyone, calling, "Be careful, have a safe journey!"

Nicholas ran back to her and hugged her. "In a week mama, we will have our own food in our kitchen, I can't wait!"

"Neither can I Nicholas," said Sarah. She took his hand, "Let's go and take care of the cows."

Throughout the day the group of men took turns walking and sitting on the wagons. They did not want to over burden the horses. The strength of the horses would be needed on their way back with all the food.

Towards nightfall Herbert could see that Jakob was already having a much greater struggle than he was so he gave up his turn in the wagon for Jakob.

Jakob felt a bit embarrassed. He did not want to be the one to slow the group down. "It's alright, Herbert, I'm fine," he stressed, creasing his brow together and giving his brother a stern glare.

Herbert made the same expression back to Jakob and said jokingly, "That's all right, I'll just take a longer turn on the wagon on the way back with the food." He tried to relieve his brother of some of his embarrassment.

About an hour later they arrived at a relative's home of one of the other men. Here they took time to make themselves comfortable in the barn. While they did this and took care of the horses, the family that lived there prepared them some interesting rolls.

They had beaten the branches of a Russian thistle weed. When doing this little black seeds fell out. The family put this seed through a feed mill to grind it down. Then they mixed it with some of the flour the group of men had brought and baked it. The rolls were dark in colour and quite tasty.

After all the walking it was very comforting to eat something warm and tasty.

Morning would come soon so the group went straight to bed after eating. They did not want to waste any daylight hours.

After a few more days of walking the group arrived at Ekaterinoslav. There were already many other groups at the American Relief Administration waiting for their turn to receive their food drafts.

Herbert and Jakob did not complain while waiting and neither did anyone in their group. This meant survival for themselves and their families. Everyone helped to load up the wagons. It was hard work. Each draft weighed about 100 lbs. The wagons were overloaded. No one would be sitting in the wagons on the way back home.

It was mid-day so they decided to head home.

By early evening it started to rain. At first it did not seem so bad. One of the men knew of a location about an hour away where they could lead the horses and wagons off the road and find some shelter under some trees.

It did not take them long to realize that the one hour would stretch into at least two hours. None of the men were wearing shoes. All they had on their feet were the makeshift wooden sandals. Their feet slipped around inside the sandals, making it difficult to walk quickly.

As the rain continued to fall, the temperature also dropped. The mud and water on their feet was freezing. They were so cold now, it felt like a stabbing, burning pain.

"We can't continue on like this," said Jakob through chattering teeth. "Look at the road, it's getting all soft and the mud is getting too thick. With all the weight on these wagons we are going to lose one."

Some of the men mumbled in agreement, "Yes, we should just pull over right here and wait for morning," said one of them. "I can't even feel my feet anymore," called another.

Others just wanted to continue on towards shelter. "We won't get any rest here. It's starting to get windy and the tarps won't stay on the wagons. Herbert, what do you think?"

It was a difficult decision. Staying where they were could be just as treacherous as moving onwards. The rain could last for days and all their food could get ruined.

His feet hurt just as much as everyone else' and he wanted nothing more than to take the pressure off.

Everyone had turned to look at him while he was thinking all of this through. They waited on his answer. "If the rain continues, even well into tomorrow, then the roads will be even worse. We may be able to keep the water off the food for a few more hours, but not for the next few days. I know that none of you can even feel your feet anymore, but this is for our families. I think that we need to pray and then gather all the strength that we have left to make it to that shelter."

Those that had wanted to stop now agreed with Herbert. As difficult as this was for them right now, they had wives and children and brothers and sisters that were counting on them. They had to continue onwards.

Jakob looked at Herbert to show his support to his brother. Herbert, as always, was thinking of the future and making his decision based on that. Jakob on the other hand was living in the here and now, but he appreciated his brother's reasoning. It had kept him out of trouble more than once.

"Herbert is right, we have to continue onwards for our families," said Jakob.

The men who'd been leading the horses pulled at the reigns to get them moving and the others pushed the wagons from behind to get them out of the mud that they'd begun to sink into.

When it was so dark that they could not even see directly in front of them one of the men spotted the group of trees that they'd been heading for. "There! There they are!" he shouted.

No one could see anything, but the group headed in the direction he'd pointed. The ground here was rough and the wagons bounced around as they made their way towards the trees.

They pulled the wagons as close to the tree trunks as possible, wanting to get as much protection from the rain as they could. They secured sections of the tarps to the trees to keep them from blowing away during the night.

They had decided just to leave the horses harnessed and hitched to the wagons. Herbert and a few of the other men got some of the straw out for the horses.

It was so windy now that they had to hand feed the horses, to keep the straw from blowing away. This would not be an easy night.

After the horses had been taken care of and everything seemed as secure as they could make it the men huddled together and ate some of the food they had tucked away.

As they ate they noticed the sky light up in the distance. All they could do was hope that the lightening did not come their way. It did not matter where they were, at this moment they were in danger of the elements. There was no escape.

Each of them found a place on the wagons to spend the night. They tucked themselves amongst the bundles of food and underneath the tarps to stay as warm as possible for the night.

Herbert fell asleep quickly but not for long. Sleeping in moist clothes as the night got colder and colder kept waking him. By morning their blankets and tarps were frozen stiff.

The only thing they could do to try and get warm was to get moving. Fortunately the rain had stopped and the wind had died down. They moved as quickly as their bodies would allow after a freezing and uncomfortable night.

Getting the wagons back on the road was quite arduous. Pushing and pulling and lifting the wheels out of ruts or over rocks, all the while protecting the food drafts.

By the time they had all the wagons back on the road, it was a relief to just make their way forward in their wooden sandals. They were all hard working men by nature but at this point their bodies still needed to recover from the years of hunger and they could not afford to labour so strenuously.

By mid day the sun came out and slowly the clothes on their bodies dried and everyone became more comfortable.

That night they made it to the home of one of their friends, who allowed them to use his barn and the use of his stove.

The rest of the journey home was without incidence.

As the men turned onto the main road leading to Molotshna they were all so thankful to be coming home safely.

So much could have befallen them, but they had been spared. At any time they could have been assaulted by thieves and everything would have been taken from them. They could have been murdered without hesitation.

Everyday Sarah and Nicholas had kept an eye out for the group of men returning from Ekaterinoslav. Today Nicholas was playing with his wooden toys near the entrance of their property, all the while checking for the men.

"Mamma, Mamma! I see them!" he shouted to Sarah who was just finishing hanging the bit of laundry they had on the clothesline.

"All right! All right, I'm coming," Sarah replied while drying her hands on her skirt. Briskly she made her way to Nicholas, but he could not wait, he was already running towards his uncles.

When they both joined the group of men, Nicholas asked, "Can we go along into town with them? I want to see everything they brought!"

"Sure ," answered Sarah. She was just as curious as he was. "It's so good to see all of you! People were starting to worry that maybe something had happened." She did not need to explain further. They all knew what she meant.

"We had some bad weather and walking quickly in these sandals is just not possible," answered Herbert.

"I knew that you were just fine," said Nicholas making everyone smile. The sweetness of a child lightened their hearts.

Sarah could see that the journey had taken quite the toll on these men. It had not been an easy task.

It seemed that the entire town was there to meet the men. Some of the women had tears running down their cheeks. Tears of joy and gratefulness! The children were jubilant.

Others came forward to take care of the unloading and dividing. The horses looked in pretty bad shape and were quickly released from their loads and cared for. These horses were an extremely important resource and not taken for granted.

The American people had sent them flour, bacon, tea, and evaporated milk.

There was so much tea. Years later they still often wondered and laughed at the amount of tea they'd received. They could not figure out why so much tea.

Both Sarah and Nicholas helped to carry as much of their food draft home as they could.

Even Nicholas sensed the exhaustion that had over taken his uncles once they'd safely delivered the food to town.

Once they got home Sarah prepared warm water for her brothers to bathe with. She ordered them to sit and relax while she soaked their feet in warm water and allowed them to sip the hot tea and fed them.

The next morning they all slept till almost mid day. Full bellies and a warm home. Their bodies were recovering.

By mid April life had become almost pleasant. People smiled and the skin no longer seemed to hang lifelessly off their bones. Children played and slowly their cheeks became soft and round.

Sarah and her brothers were respected in this community. No one shunned her or her son, but then no one asked about her husband either. There were many other families where fathers had survived with their children or mothers had outlived their husbands. In many cases both mother and father had died and now brothers and sisters looked after each other.

Everyone assumed that she'd lost her husband to famine or disease, or worse-through torture by the bandits or soldiers.

For the first time in years Sarah was enjoying the comfort of community. Nicholas was forming friendships. She would keep any of the facts about their previous life in Terekeransiedlung as vague as possible.

She had not spoken to her brothers about this, but it seemed that she did not have to. They never mentioned Nikolai or anything that had happened during the years before the war.

It was easy to see that Herbert and Jakob were also enjoying community life. They had all started going to church on Sundays and Sarah noticed a lot of women paying attention to her brothers. Herbert was now 29 and Jakob 24. Neither of them had ever been married and everyone in town knew that they were solid and hardworking family men.

Life had been so difficult the past six years that Sarah had not given any thought to her brothers marrying and making a life for themselves. She wanted nothing more than to see them find love but she was also not sure of how she would cope if she were to live alone with Nicholas.

Herbert and Jakob most certainly enjoyed the attention but at the same time they seemed almost oblivious to the intentions of these women.

The four of them had become such a close knit unit. Life had become a comfortable routine.

Chapter
13

Receiving those food drafts in 1922 had seemed like the return of freedom and life as they'd known it. Most definitely many lives had been saved, but freedom was not what any of them had experienced since.

Sarah watched her young son in amazement. She'd been busy putting away some of their clean clothes when she looked out their bedroom window and noticed him weeding in the garden alongside her brothers. The sun had reflected off of his blond hair the same way Sarah had noticed the sparkle off of Nikolai's hair fourteen years ago.

Nicholas was thirteen years old and already taller than Sarah. He was lean and muscular and everyday Sarah was reminded of how much he looked like his father.

Sarah leaned against the window with her elbows and crossed her arms. She thought about the conversation that she'd had last night with her brothers. The Neufeld's were leaving their farm and travelling to Moscow to leave Russia.

The decision to leave Russia was absolutely heart wrenching. They loved their country and they had loved their life here.

But it was no longer the same country. Everything had changed. The first few years under communist rule had not seemed so bad.

With the end of the fear of constant violence, people had been happy to get back at the task of repairing the land.

1922 really had been a very good year for their community. With the return of rain the Mennonites had put their heart and soul back into the land. They'd enjoyed an abundance of melons, watermelon, potatoes, vegetables, millet, barley, and corn.

Children were amazed to watch the crops grow. Nicholas had absolutely flourished. All day he kept his uncles busy asking them the most interesting questions about farming. He was not afraid of the hard work involved. Being outdoors brought him the same kind of peace that it brought Sarah.

Slowly order was restored within communities. Businesses were re-established and people went back to work at what they'd previously been doing.

Sarah and her brothers worked the farm together with the Neufelds. Everyone had to pitch in and do their part. Gone were the days where there was an abundance of labourers available for hire. They dug out cellars in the yard to store milk, cream, and eggs.

They exchanged their produce and dairy products for items they needed on the farm.

Teachers went back to teaching and children went back to school.

In September of 1923 Nicholas started his first year of school. Two weeks before his first day of school Sarah had taken him into town to buy him his first pair of shoes.

Nicholas had been so excited. It had felt so strange to him to have his feet enclosed. It had been so much fun for him to tie and untie the laces. Every day for those two weeks Sarah had allowed him to wear his new shoes for a few hours. She'd wanted him to get used to them so that his feet would not be sore. He would be to walking many miles to and from school every day.

Nicholas thrived in school. He excelled in his studies and put equal enthusiasm into getting to know the other students.

Halfway through the school year his friend Karl had joined the class. Nicholas was overjoyed. Karl was like a brother to him. Their bond was as strong as ever and it had been a pleasure for Sarah to watch their friendship grow.

Then in 1924 a Government official had come to visit the classrooms. The inspector asked the students if their teacher taught religion. Did they start and end their school days in prayer?

The children had been so uneasy. By now they'd come to love their teacher. Should they tell the truth? What would happen if they did? Praying, teaching the Bible, was all part of the Mennonite school curriculum. Glory was given to God for all things. They lived their life for God.

Their teacher spared the children from having to betray him. He admitted to the inspector that they had been praying during school times. Honesty was something that they valued and he did not want to let these children down by telling a lie in front of them.

Right in front of the children he was told that he was no longer allowed to do this. He was given two choices. Either sign a form to verify his compliance to this order or his teaching certificate would be taken away.

He had a family to take care of. Teaching was his life. He really did not have a choice. He signed the form.

What happened next made him sick to his stomach. He could not comprehend how he would do this. He was given new instructions. He was to actively instruct students that there was No God!! The whole Christian belief was a fantasy and the Bible a fairytale.

The inspector smirked as the teacher slumped into his chair in shock. It had given him pleasure to crush this teacher's vision. Then he eased the blow just a bit by telling the teacher, "If you cannot teach against God than you are to teach with no reference to God."

They could no longer worship in public. The ramifications were too great.

In 1924 Lenin, Russia's first communist leader died. Joseph Stalin took over. News spread quickly of how ruthless and ambitious he was. Stalin had all former colleagues of Lenin put on trial and then executed. Any other opponents he had sent to prison camps in Siberia.

As a symbol of the seriousness with which the new government would deal with anyone practicing religion the communist soldiers destroyed churches. Many church leaders who refused to follow the communist way of thinking and become atheists were arrested and killed.

Members within the community became Secret Police for the communists. They spied on their neighbours and informed the government of any activities that were suspicious of anti-communist views.

Victims were either shot or sent to prison camps.

It became increasingly difficult to know whom to trust. Someone could appear to be your friend one day and then betray you the next day.

You could never truly express what was deep in your heart for fear of being taken away from your loved ones. Everyone had learned to be quiet and fake being satisfied with life as it was. When people smiled it was with their lips but not with their eyes. The eyes glazed over to mask all the thoughts and emotions that were deep within.

It had become a commonplace event for men to disappear suddenly and never be heard from again. Every time one of her brothers ventured into town Sarah had been worried that she may never see them again.

And even worse, Sarah was so afraid of losing Nicholas. In many cases, parents who trained their children in the faith of God, had their children taken away from them. The communist authorities would remove these children and place them in communist homes.

Everything belonged to the nation. The government controlled and owned everything. This included your wife, your husband, your children, or your animals. If you wanted to butcher an animal to feed your family you had to obtain a permit. You no longer had a say in anything.

Everyone was re-educated.

The communist government closed down all newspapers. Any political activity was prohibited. The government took over all the banks, factories, country estates, and stores. It was declared that all property belonged to the worker.

Although this declaration sounded quite good, especially to those that had not owned anything before, in reality people were no longer interested in working hard when it was not to their own personal benefit.

People were forced to become agricultural labourers. Those who worked in factories to develop Russia's economy worked in severe conditions.

Over the years many more people died unnecessarily from over work and starvation. It was just so much easier for the government to force starved people into submission. If the people had been well fed and well clothed they may have banded together to overthrow this heartless leader.

The communist government taxed its citizens beyond reason. The taxes were three times higher than the harvest. Sarah and her brothers had barely paid off the required fees and then more was required. Anything and everything of any value had to be sold to pay the taxes.

They were even required to pay a tax for the privilege of having a cow.

If they did not have money to pay these taxes they risked being put in prison. For many it meant selling their last cow or horse.

All wealth and possessions were lost to the communist government.

To ensure full cooperation from its citizens the communist government had gone throughout the towns and appointed several men of each town as hostages. They picked those men that were considered the best or most honoured and respected men.

These men were free to go about their lives in a usual manner, but if anything went wrong within the community these men would be put in prison or executed.

Of course, Herbert had been chosen. He was liked and respected by many and the government officials felt that as long as he stayed in line with the communist rules than so would the rest of the community.

Back in 1922 when Sarah had actually for a moment entertained the idea of her brothers marrying and leaving her on her own, she actually had nothing to worry about.

Herbert, being such a thoughtful man, had no intentions of starting a family, and then take the chance of being ripped away from them. It was enough that Sarah and Jakob worried every day that he might be whisked away from them. The last thing he needed was a wife that would be left lonely and helpless.

People spoke in private about leaving Russia. Their future here was completely beyond their control. They could not raise their children as they pleased. Every day they felt constricted in their actions. They'd been placed in a mental prison.

It came with no surprise that in 1926 a large group had immigrated to Canada. The news of how this had all come about spread throughout the Mennonite villages. People did not have any money for travel. They'd heard that a big company in Canada called the Canadian Pacific Railway had provided money for passage. It was arranged in the form of long term loans to would be immigrants.

Immigrants had to sign legal documents to agree to loan re-payment as soon as possible once in Canada. In order for these immigrants to leave Russia they had to purchase Russian passports.

This was the last group to receive regular Russian passports and exit visas.

The Russian government had begun to realize that they were losing their best farmers.

And now, three years later, in 1929, Sarah and her brothers had seriously discussed finding a way to leave Russia themselves.

For her there was only one choice. Nicholas was thirteen years old. Soon he would be old enough to be drafted into the Soviet Army. She did not want to lose her son and she did not want her son to lose all of their values and beliefs.

Although Sarah did not view herself as a traditional Mennonite, deep inside she believed strongly in an Almighty God. She just wanted to be somewhere, where they could have the freedom to live as they wished. She wanted so desperately to live without constant fear. They had nothing here and starting somewhere new with nothing would not be unfamiliar.

Sarah continued watching her brothers and Nicholas work in the lush garden. The answer came from deep within her and she knew without a doubt that they had to leave Russia.

Chapter
14

Among the thousands of Mennonites that descended on Moscow during the summer months of 1929 were Sarah and her family.

Agreement to leave had come easily between Sarah and her brothers and once the decision was made so were their preparations.

They quickly sold anything that they had which was still of some value. Sarah took time to meticulously sew money into the hems of their clothing to conceal it. She toasted buns and prepared as much food as she could so that they would not starve upon their arrival in the city. Herbert and Jakob worked on securing train permits to travel to Moscow.

Travelling by train was free but one had to have good reason to use the system. The Russian government did not want its' citizens just spending endless days on the trains for no purpose.

At first Nicholas had not been happy with the decision. He now had many friends here and since he'd never really known any other life he felt secure.

A few days later though, he heard that his friend Karl along with his aunt and uncle were also preparing to leave. For the boys leaving was now an exciting adventure.

Although the trip to Moscow had just taken a few days on train, arriving there, had felt like arriving on another planet to Sarah.

Sarah had never seen so many people or buildings. Sarah found both the ancient and modern buildings equally impressive. How anyone could put structures like this together was beyond her comprehension. Sarah was in awe of the skill and talent and time it must take to build such massive structures.

Moscow was a beautiful city. It was surrounded by many well kept parks and evergreen forests. The Moskva River flowed right alongside the city adding balance of nature and life to the stone and brick buildings.

Sarah was so thankful to have her brothers with her to guide her through this place. She felt utterly lost in the streets of Moscow. Years before when Herbert had left to work with the injured soldiers during the war he had been through Moscow.

He thoroughly enjoyed the look of wonder in the eyes of Sarah, Nicholas, and Jakob as he walked them through the Red Square. The Red Square was located in the centre, at the heart, of Moscow. It was a large open area of cobbled ground surrounded by ancient buildings known worldwide.

St. Basil's Cathedral was absolutely splendid in the mid day sun. Sarah thought the onion shaped domes atop each tower looked like upside down radishes. The very centre of these domes each had a much thinner tip which tapered to a point resembling the radish root to Sarah. The cathedral was multi coloured and looked to Sarah like a child's fantasy palace. Each onion shaped dome had different designs on it with multiple colours. One had swirls of yellow and green and another seemed to have dots of red and green, and yet the other had what looked like a wave pattern of white, green, and red. To Sarah and Nicholas it had almost a playful appeal.

The Kremlin was anything but playful. It was a very serious looking building with formidable walls. The onion shaped domes atop its towers were coated in gold and glistened brightly even when the skies were overcast. Originally it had been built as a medieval fortress and refuge. Within its walls were palaces, armouries, churches and living quarters. It was now the government headquarters.

On many of the buildings there were tall and striking columns leading to equally impressive arches with ornate designs.

Before the communist government there had been one more cathedral lining The Red Square, The Kazan

Cathedral. The communists tore down the Kazan Cathedral and Iverskaya Chapel. They'd felt that it was not appropriate for the new regime. The grounds were now used for military parades and demonstrations.

Years ago the Red Square had been used to celebrate church festivals, public gatherings, hearing government announcements, and watching executions. On the days where there were none of these big events going on, the Red Square was used as an open market.

Centuries ago the word for red in Russian also meant "beautiful". Sarah felt that the square was appropriately named.

Herbert explained to Sarah that she should imagine the roads of Moscow like a spider's web with the Red Square being the centre of the web. From the centre roads went out in all directions as rays from the sun. Then there were circles of roads around the square. Each ring larger than the previous, in effect forming the picture of a spider's web.

Leaving the square there were many roads much wider than any Sarah had ever seen before. There was still work being done on some of the roads. Stalin had ordered that many of the older buildings were to be tore down to create these wider roads and to build new apartment buildings to house each and every one of Moscow's citizens. It was Soviet policy to provide housing for each of its citizens and families.

Sarah and her family had been most fortunate to get one of the smaller log cabins near the Perlovka train station. In other times these simple dwellings had been summer homes for vacationing czars and their families. For the first time in years life seemed much simpler. There was time in the day for things besides constant work and struggle just to stay alive.

For the young people life in Moscow was very enticing. They were having fun. On the hot days they found places to swim and play. They obtained month long train passes into the city and spent days exploring.

The city had entertainment for Nicholas and Karl unlike any they had ever enjoyed before. They spent hours meeting new young people in the Red Square. They formed large groups and went to the zoo and watched the circus.

These were young boys and girls who had spent their whole life toiling on farms or any chore that was given to them to help their family survive. They had an independence and freedom here unlike any they had tasted before.

One day Nicholas came home with the intention of convincing his mother to stay. "Mamma, why can't we stay here?!" he said in his high pitched teenage voice. "I really don't see what's so bad about the communist government. Every day we get food vouchers and we have a place to live. No soldiers harass us when we go into the city."

"Nicholas, I know that you are having a lot of fun here, but it will end," Sarah replied with emphasis. She had felt that soon he would be begging her to stay. "Every day more and more Mennonites are coming to the city. There is no way the government will let all of us stay. And this house, it's fine for now, but when winter comes, we will freeze." There was no stove in the log cabin for heating. "You know that temperatures can drop to minus forty. And then there is the matter of school. You would be put into a communist school." Sarah lowered her voice as she continued, "Them trying to convince all of you that there is no God. You know what they do to people who believe otherwise. And I don't want you drafted into the army, besides your friends are leaving Moscow too."

Nicholas was not convinced but knew better than to keep arguing with his mother. He loved and respected her and deep down he knew that she was looking out for his best interests.

"Alright, I want you back home early today," continued Sarah. "Tomorrow your Uncles have lined up some work for you, so you need to be well rested."

Herbert and Jakob had been working on the city's railway system. Sand had to be moved from one location to another.

They had to load up a wheel barrow with sand then push them uphill to empty box cars. Each box car could hold from eight to ten tonnes. The brothers were paid per tonne.

Nicholas was good and strong now and they'd decided that he could help with the shovelling. Although the family had bare necessities, they could all use some new clothes for the journey out of Moscow. They did not know when they would once again have the chance to earn money.

About four kilometres from the Perlovka Station, deep within the forest, there was an ammunition depot. The brothers had been offered a chance to work there but had decided they would rather do this. At the ammunition depot weapons from the war had been collected. They were now being dismantled and re-made into new weapons and tools.

Many of the Mennonites worked on this assembly line. Others found work on some of the farms surrounding Moscow.

Sarah had met a women named Helena Neufeld who had years of experience as a midwife. Helena had heard that Sarah had only one child and since he was already a bit older, had wondered if Sarah would be interested in helping her with her work. With so many Mennonites coming to Moscow there was no way that she, herself, could deliver all the babies.

At first Sarah had been a bit hesitant. After witnessing her first birth Sarah was in awe of the miracle of life. Helena was a kind hearted and patient woman and loved teaching Sarah everything she knew. Helena's love for the women she helped was apparent. The women relaxed when Helena entered the room and trusted her completely. Sarah felt quite honoured to be working beside this woman.

Helena could see that Sarah also felt both the joy and the pain of the women they helped. She felt that she'd made a good choice in Sarah. Together they made a compassionate team.

It was a beautiful Sunday afternoon. Sarah had taken a train into the city center with Nicholas and Karl. She did not feel at home here, but she did want to take another stroll through the Red Square just to impress the sight to her memory.

Sarah knew for certain that once she left here she would never again return. Even though this was not where she wanted to spend the rest of her life, she did appreciate all that had gone into creating this city. Soon this would be an imaginary place in her memory.

Sarah slowly walked around the square keeping a good distance between herself and the buildings. She wanted to be far enough away so that she could see entire buildings at once and imprint the image.

As she stood gazing at St. Basil's Cathedral and just allowing her mind to relax and take it all in she took a few steps back in awe. She felt herself bump into someone who had obviously been walking a lot quicker than she. The push startled Sarah and she lost her balance almost falling forward. "Agh!" she exclaimed recovering her step and turning around to apologize.

Whoever she had bumped into quickly grabbed a hold of her arm to help pull her back up before she hit the rock ground.

As she turned to face the person who had helped her she was about to apologize in German, but stopped herself when she saw the gentleman's face.

He was much taller than Sarah, with thick dark hair and the lightest blue eyes Sarah had ever seen. The color of his eyes seemed to be intensified by the dark brows forming a perfect arch above them.

She quickly decided he must be Russian and said in Russian, " Excuse me sir." At the same time he said in perfect German, "Enschulde mich, bitte."

Sarah blushed as she realized that he was also German. He continued on in German, "It's alright. People have often mistaken me for being Russian. I just don't have the usual lighter coloured hair. We think that somewhere along the way there must be some Greek blood in us." Then he gave Sarah the most dazzling smile she had ever seen.

His teeth were so white and perfect and his lips full and luscious. For an instant Sarah's eyes widened and her mouth opened speechless before she caught herself. Then she stuttered, "I didn't think that you, that you were Russi . . ."

"Oh, yes you did," he interrupted and teased her while enjoying watching this woman all flustered. There was something about her. He sensed that she was most likely a woman that was quite used to being in control and in charge. And absolutely beautiful. She was stunning, even in her shabby old dress and hair pinned to her head.

Sarah straightened her body defensively, pulling her shoulders back. "Well, in any case, I'm sorry I bumped into you. I took a step back without looking first."

"I'm sorry too," he responded sincerely. "I was walking forward and not watching where I was going. My eyes were fixed on the golden globes on top of the Kremlin. It's so fascinating how these buildings were made."

Sarah relaxed as they both turned for another look at The Kremlin. "Yes, that's why I came here today. I don't want to live here, but I do want to remember this place."

"Well," he paused, "After today I will never forget this place," he said while looking deep into Sarah's eyes.

Once again Sarah was taken off guard as he held her gaze. "Please, let me introduce myself," he said as he held out his hand to Sarah, "I'm Eldon Enns."

As Sarah reached for his hand she said, "I'm Sarah Doerksen." As soon as their hands touched an energy flowed between them. Sarah felt the sensation flow from her fingertips and throughout her body. She felt her knees weakening but could not let go of him both with her hand and her gaze.

In an instant it was both electrifying and terrifying. If it had not been for the sound of her son's voice calling her she may never have let go. "Mother, we have to go! The train will be leaving soon!"

Sarah quickly let go and turned to walk towards Nicholas. "It was a pleasure meeting you, Sarah," said Eldon softly as she walked away. Sarah gave him a confused smile and went to catch up with Nicholas.

Nicholas watched the man who was watching his mother walk towards him. He'd never seen anyone looking at his mother like this. Spending time in Moscow with his friends Nicholas and the other boys had often spent time trying to get to know the pretty girls.

Nicholas wasn't sure what to make of this. A part of him wanted to tease his mother and the other part was defensive. If he'd seen one of his buddies eyeing a girl like that he would surely have teased them, but this was his mother. He decided on the latter. "Who was that?" he asked defensively.

"Oh, Uh," Sarah hesitated, "I accidentally bumped into him when I was strolling." She smiled, "I almost fell on my face, but he caught me before I hit the hard ground."

"So you don't know him?" Nicholas asked, still not sure of what to make of what he'd seen.

"No, I've never met him before. But he introduced himself and he seemed nice. His name is Eldon Enns," Sarah answered him.

Nicholas' curiosity seemed to be appeased and he turned his attention to his friends as they boarded the train home.

Sarah turned her attention on the man she'd just met. She could not get his handsome face off her mind. The feelings that he'd stirred in her by just the touch of his hand. It had been years since she had felt anything like this. She felt a need within her awakening. A deep wanting to love and be loved.

As they stepped off the train at Perlovka Station and headed home Sarah brought herself back to reality. This was silly. She would probably never see Eldon again. And even if she did, their future was so unsure. This was not the time to start a relationship with someone. No one knew if or when they would leave Moscow.

In the weeks that followed Sarah busied herself helping Helena whenever she was needed and finding any other odd jobs she could to earn extra money for their family. Her mind and body were once again focused on tasks at hand and not frivolous thoughts of romance.

It was a warm summer evening towards the end of August and Sarah was sitting outside the log cabin with her brothers and Nicholas when Helena came by in a carriage. "Sarah, can you come with me? There's a woman in labour a few miles from here and we have to hurry."

Sarah quickly got up, "Of course, I'll just get my jacket."

When they were in the carriage heading toward the pregnant woman's home Sarah asked, "So, who are we going to see? I did not think that anyone was due to deliver for a few weeks."

"Well, her name is Justina and I don't think you've even met her yet. I just met her myself a few weeks ago when I was at the market. I told her that when her time came I could help her. But she was not due for several more months. I told her I could stop by and just check her to see how everything was going but she was worried about being able to pay me."

"You've often helped woman without receiving anything in return," Sarah said.

"Yes," answered Helena, "And I told her not to worry about that. I said that people give what they can, when they can, and that I was not keeping any kind of list. I just wanted to see healthy women and children and make the delivery as easy for them as possible."

With that the carriage arrived at their destination and Sarah and Helena headed towards the shabby cabin. Before they even reached the door it opened and out stepped a man. By now it was dark outside but there was just enough light to illuminate the features of the man's face.

It was Eldon. Sarah quickly recalled her conversation with Helena and realized that she had never told her Justina's last name.

With a quick, courteous nod he ushered them into the cabin. Sarah could tell that he recognized her but at the same time there was worry all over his face and there was no time for small talk. "Justina is right over here," he said as he pointed to the corner of the cabin.

Sarah assessed the home and quickly deduced that this must be his wife. It was a small, one room shack, with only one mattress on the floor. For an instant she felt like a fool, and then she felt anger. How could he have looked at her like that when he had a pregnant wife at home? What kind of man was he?

Sarah kept these thoughts to herself, but closed her heart to him and said matter of factly to Eldon, "We are going to need boiling water." She had not spotted any type of stove when looking around the cabin.

"We share a stove with the neighbours. I'll go get the water." Eldon left quickly. He'd been beside himself the past hour. Justina seemed to be in such pain and he had no idea what to do for her. Now he could finally do something useful.

Helena took the water from him and told him to just keep preparing more and wait outside. They would call him if they needed him. Usually Helena allowed Sarah to do the initial check to see how far along a woman was and what problems might present themselves, but this was an emergency and they could not afford to take the time.

Both of them washed their hands, washed Justina's bottom, and then Helena proceeded to check her out. Sarah did not allow her anger towards Eldon to interfere with her compassion for the woman they were working with. She completely focused herself on making Justina as comfortable as possible.

Justina was a tiny woman, very thin, but strikingly beautiful, with thick dark wavy hair. For someone who was seven months pregnant she barely even had a belly.

"She's already lost all of her water," said Helena. "She seems to be fully dilated. Your baby will be here soon."

When one of the contractions had finished Helena took Sarah over to the water bowl. "The child is breach. Because the baby is so small I think we'll be able to manage."

"All right," said Sarah. So far she had not witnessed a baby's death during birth, but she knew that it was quite common. Often both the mother and child did not make it. Especially during these times when people were still so weak and frail from everything they'd been through. Now she felt nervous.

They went back to Justina. "Aahhh, I want to push," Justina cried.

"That's good! You go ahead and push. But you listen to me very carefully!!" said Helena sternly, "When I tell you to stop pushing, you have to stop!"

Justina barely nodded agreement as she grunted and started pushing. Sarah pushed pillows against her back and helped to support Justina into a slight upward sitting position.

Every time she pushed Helena massaged her vaginal opening to help stretch the skin and keep her from tearing. "All right!" called Helena, "No more pushing now!" The baby's body was out but the cervix was already closing around the baby's neck.

Sarah held Justina's hand tightly, "No pushing! Just try to relax for a minute!"

Justina squeezed her face and clenched her teeth as the next contraction hit. It was so painful. Helena was sliding her fingers between the vaginal opening and the baby's neck. "Sarah I need your help. You need to also get your fingers inside to support the baby's head." It was very awkward but they managed to pry the opening just far enough to allow room for the baby's head. "Sarah, when she pushes, don't pull, just let her push our hands out along with the baby." Sarah nodded. "Justina, when the next contractions come, you push as hard as you can, and you just hold it there till the next one!"

"I can't, I can't anymore," Justina barely whispered. "I'm so tired."

"Justina, you have to!" demanded Sarah. Sarah softened her voice, "You have a beautiful baby girl here and she wants to see her mother!"

That seemed to be the inspiration Justina needed. With the next contractions she pushed with every ounce of her being.

What seemed like hours but was only minutes, the baby was out. Justina fell back onto her bed and relaxed her breathing.

Helena worked quickly to clean the baby's mouth and nose. They had to get this baby breathing on its own. Sarah had never seen such a small child before. The skin on this girl was almost translucent, so thin and fragile. Sarah said a quick prayer, "Please Lord, give this child breath." And with that the little girl made some quiet sounds.

Justina looked over at Sarah, "Would you go and tell Eldon that I have a baby girl?"

"Of course," answered Sarah.

Sarah washed her hands and took a deep breath preparing herself to talk to Eldon. She did not want him to see the effect that he'd had on her.

As soon as he heard the door creak open Eldon turned to face Sarah. He'd been pacing back and forth, hands deep in his pocket, whispering prayers. He could hear the pain that Justina was going through and it made his stomach ache in empathy. Sarah could see the apprehension in his eyes. He was prepared for the worst.

Sarah tried to smile as she said, "You have a beautiful baby daughter. She has thick black hair and . . ."

"Is my sister alright?" Eldon interrupted.

Sarah hesitated, did he say sister?

"Please, how is Justina doing?" he asked again.

"Uh, Justina is fine. She's just very weak and tired," replied Sarah.

Eldon relaxed, took his hands out of his pockets and took a step closer to Sarah. Sarah quickly folded her arms in a gesture to keep distance between them. Eldon realizing how all of this must have looked to Sarah said, "I know what this must have seemed like when you walked into our home. I'm sorry I didn't explain I was just so worrie . . ."

Sarah held up her hand to stop him. "Oh please, you have nothing to explain. It just did not seem like you were married when I met you at the Red Square. I'd better go back inside to help Helena clean up. I'll get you in a bit and you can see your sister and niece." Sarah turned to walk back into the cabin.

Eldon reached out to stop her from going back inside just yet. As soon as he touched her Sarah felt the flush throughout her body and it stopped her from moving forward. "Please," he spoke softly, "Just give me a minute." Sarah turned to listen. "Truthfully, I did not think that you were married either, but when your son called you, I thought, what was I doing? But then I asked around about you and people said that you were on your own. So since then I've been thinking about you and trying to figure out a good reason to come and see you. Things are just so different now than they were years ago," Eldon sighed as he looked at the shabby cabin he now lived in.

"But now that you're here, please, could I come by to see you? I would just like a chance to have a good conversation with you."

Sarah nodded "Yes" excitement growing within her. On the train ride home from the Red Square she had not even thought of the fact that he must have thought that she was married. She smiled at him, "I'd best get back inside now." Eldon gave her one of his dazzling smiles and unwillingly released his hold on her arm.

Sarah went back inside and told Justina, "Your brother is very happy that you're alright." She felt a kinship with this woman. She wondered where this baby's father was. Sarah knew all too well how it felt to give birth and not be able to share the joy of such a blessing with the one you loved.

As though reading her thoughts Justina said, "I wish her father could be here to see her."

"Where is he then?" asked Helena bluntly.

"He died about five months ago," answered Justina in anguish. "We were robbed. Everything was taken from us, and then he got sick, and he just never recovered. I guess it was all just too much for him." She started to cry. "He never even knew that I was pregnant, maybe if he'd known, he would have been able to pull through."

Sarah went to sit down beside Justina and wrapped her arms around her. "I know things have been very hard, and it's especially hard to lose the ones we love."

In the meantime Helena had stepped outside to tell Eldon that he could come in to see his sister and the baby. He saw Sarah comforting his sister and was deeply moved. Her compassion was so genuine.

Helena finished wrapping the baby and held her out for Eldon to take. Eldon was not quite sure how to hold this tiny child. He was almost afraid that she would slip right out of his arms. He did not want to hold her too tightly but he also did not want to drop her.

As he brought her close to his body he too was overcome with emotion. "She's beautiful, Justina, "he smiled. "A little angel."

Sarah let go of Justina and moved away from her to give Eldon room by her side.

Helena and Sarah busied themselves cleaning up and getting ready to go home. It was well after midnight and they still had a long walk ahead.

Helena spent a bit of time giving Justina advice on breast feeding her child and told her not to hesitate to call on either herself or Sarah if she had any problems.

"I'll walk you ladies home," said Eldon.

"Oh no," responded Helena, "We'll be fine."

"No, I insist! It's very late and I would not feel good if anything happened to either of you. Please, it's the least I can do," he said convincingly.

"Yes, I'll be fine," said Justina. "Please let my brother walk you home. And thank you!"

Walking home Sarah was not the least bit tired. The three of them kept the conversation light and spoke quietly. They did not want to disturb the sleeping families. Helena's home was the first one on the way so they walked her to her door step. Helena gave Sarah a warm hug and bid them "Good night." It felt wonderful getting a hug from this kind hearted woman. She felt like a mother to Sarah.

As they made their way to Sarah's house they intuitively slowed down the pace. They both did not want their time together to end.

"Helena's an amazing woman!" said Sarah.

"Well, I think you're easily her equal, Sarah, and then some!" responded Eldon. "I've heard some pretty great things about you, and what you did for my sister . . ."

Sarah blushed and was unsure of what to say. It had been a long time since she'd received any type of compliment. And Eldon was so serious. "Well, thank you, Eldon. So what have you heard?" She asked with a bit of spunk. She was giving him an opportunity to tease her and keep things light but Eldon did not take the bait.

"Well, for one thing, I've heard that your son has a great character. He's confidant, helpful, and apparently very intelligent," Eldon replied.

Sarah smiled thinking of Nicholas. She was proud, "Yes, he is certainly all of those things, and then some." She added borrowing Eldon's compliment to her.

"Surely, to be all of those things, one has to have a pretty great mother," said Eldon.

They were nearing Sarah's home. Eldon reached for Sarah's hand and gently pulled her under the cover of a tree. It felt so natural that Sarah did not resist for even an instant. "Sarah, can I come by to see you on Sunday? We could go for a stroll by the river and get to know each other."

A million thoughts raced through her mind, What would she tell her brothers? How would she explain this to Nicholas? But "No" never crossed her mind. She wanted to be with this man.

"Yes, Sunday would be fine," replied Sarah holding his gaze, completely mesmerized. With his free hand Eldon reached to release Sarah's hair which was already half undone from the evening of work. It seductively fell over her shoulders and softly framed her face. Sarah's lips opened slightly, waiting, anticipating what he would do next. Gently he touched her face and ran his fingers through her hair, meanwhile moving his body closer to hers. Then, ever so slowly he brought his head down towards hers and softly pressed his lips against hers.

Sarah melted. It was the invitation she needed to pull him even closer towards herself and there she held him as their kiss became deep, meaningful, and passionate.

Neither of them was prepared for the passion that flowed between them. It took all the strength they had to pull away from each other. "Sarah, I . . .,"said Eldon. Sarah put her forefinger to his lips. "Sshh . . . It's alright, I know. I'll be waiting for you Sunday afternoon." And with that she stepped away from him and he stood still and watched her walk the rest of the way home.

Sarah went to bed but could not sleep. All night she thought of what she should say to her brothers and Nicholas and how she would say it. She did not want to have another secretive relationship. Her teenage innocence was long gone. She was thirty years old and had already lived through more than a lifetime of events. She felt completely ready for love and would not let society dictate with whom or when the time was proper.

There was no doubt in her mind that her family would be shocked. Life had been so focused on mere survival the past years that there had been little if any talk of meeting a significant other. Nicholas had all of them to himself his whole life and the thought of his mother perhaps marrying would be quite an adjustment.

When everyone was settled for breakfast Sarah cautiously approached the subject. "So, the baby that I helped deliver last night, was that of the sister of Eldon Enns. Do you remember, Nicholas? He's the man who stopped my fall when we were at the Red Square."

"Yes, I remember," said Nicholas, thinking back on the look on Eldon's face as he'd been watching his mother. "So, he was there last night Mother?" "Yes, he was," answered Sarah looking Nicholas straight in the eyes. Nicholas saw the glimmer in her eyes and the slight smile on her lips. "You like him!!" Nicholas exclaimed.

Herbert and Jakob both stopped eating and looked up to watch Sarah.

"Yes, yes I do," said Sarah quietly. "There is something about Eldon that I find very appealing and the feeling is mutual. After your father, Nicholas, for years now, I did not think that I would ever meet someone that I would want to spend time with, but I would really like all of your support as I get to know Eldon."

Jakob was the first to break the silence, "So, when do we get to meet this Eldon?" He, too, had been thinking that it was time he started looking for a wife. Life was passing by and he would love to start his own family.

Nicholas and Herbert were still processing Sarah's announcement. "He'll be coming by on Sunday. We're going to be going for a walk by the river." She looked at Nicholas.

Nicholas was a confidant and secure young man. He'd received much attention and love from his mother and uncles and deep down he knew that his mother deserved to find love and happiness. "Soon I'll be grown up and making a life for myself mother. I'll be respectful when he comes by to see you."

"Thank-you Nicholas, that means a lot to me," said Sarah, reaching over to touch his hand. Sarah looked over at Herbert who was still quiet in thought. She knew her brother, and she knew that he was running all kinds of thoughts through his mind.

"Sarah, I just don't want you to get hurt. We don't know when we will leave here. We don't know how many of us they will allow to go at a time. We don't even know in which country we will find refuge. I would just hate to see you get deeply involved with someone and then be torn apart," he finally answered her. Herbert remembered how much Sarah had suffered when Nikolai had been forced to leave.

Overall Sarah was pleased with the outcome. As usual she was surprised by the maturity of her son. Sunday did not come soon enough. Sarah worked without end to finish a new dress that she had been sewing for herself. Weeks ago she'd bought material for herself from the money she'd earned helping Helena. Sunday morning she washed her hair in a basin and washed the rest of herself as well as she could with what they had.

When Eldon arrived by carriage Sunday afternoon she was already to go. She looked crisp, clean, and fresh. Like a new woman, transformed from the harshness of their reality.

Eldon helped her on the carriage. When they were underway he said, "I didn't want to say anything in front of your family, but you look absolutely beautiful."

"I feel beautiful sitting next to you," answered Sarah. Actually she felt like a queen. Eldon reached over and took her hand in his. "So, I know very little about you," said Sarah. "You already know so much more about me, tell me about yourself."

"Well, what would you like to know?"

"Everything! But how about what part of Russia did you come from?"

"My parents settled in Omsk, in the Siberian Steppes in the early nineteen hundreds. And life there was wonderful until the communists took over." Sarah nodded agreement. "The winters there were severely cold but the cold came gradually, with every month getting colder and colder, to the peak in January and than a gradual warming. By March we already had many warm days, and I remember running around and playing outside after school as a child. Are you sure this is what you want to talk about?" he asked looking at Sarah.

"It's exactly what I want to hear. You came from the north and I from the south of Russia. Tell me more," she stated. Listening to him reminisce was very comforting and relaxing.

"By mid April winter is over and farmers start preparing the land for spring sowing. And in the blink of an eye greenery starts to appear everywhere. I used to love to just lay in the meadows and watch all the life around me. The larks would hover motionless in the air, all the while just singing their hearts out. We always had an abundance of vegetables, fruits, raspberries, black berries, and currants." Sarah nodded agreement again, remembering their orchards and gardens.

"Our homes were surrounded by miles of undeveloped steppe land, where you could find many tracts of wild strawberries. Delicious!" he said bringing his lips together as though he could taste them.

"Now, our village was very beautiful. The main street had a sidewalk on each side and next to the sidewalk there was a neat and trim fence. Behind these fences people planted poplar and ash trees and a lot of shrubbery. I still remember walking down the street feeling so comforted by the charming and warm feeling."He squeezed her hand and smiled, "It was very romantic."

"Every home was set to one side of the property leaving room for a side drive which lead to a spacious farm yard. And of course, in the back everyone had barns, machine sheds, and all those other out buildings, that I'm sure you are quite familiar with."

"Yes, our farm was similar," said Sarah.

"And then behind all the buildings we had large gardens. We grew enough to feed our entire family, but here is the best part," he said with a mischievous smirk on his face. "Behind these gardens everyone planted a thick belt of trees with a road beside it which circled the entire village. We all called this "Lover's Lane"."

Eldon took a breath and looked into the distance and the happy look that was on his face dissolved and turned into a sad and mournful look, "But then everything changed with the Russian Revolution and the Communist government. Before long the shelves were empty. They came in and killed our factory owners and managers, destroyed machinery."

Eldon stopped talking. They'd reached the spot where they had planned to step out of the carriage and start their walk. Gracefully he held his hand out for Sarah to help her down from the carriage.

As they started walking he cautiously asked her, "So, when I asked people about you, I was told that you did not seem to have a husband, but no one really knew much more than that. Would you mind sharing more?"

Eldon was quite aware of how brutally many loved ones had been lost over the past years. He did not want to upset her.

Sarah looked at him so she could gage his reaction as she said without guilt or shame, "I was never married." She had wondered if he would judge her the same as people had judged her thirteen years ago when Nicholas was born. A wanton, wild woman not to be trusted or liked.

If he held any negative thoughts towards her his face did not show them. Instead he took her hand and they proceeded to stroll along the river bank. "So, tell me about Nicholas' father," he encouraged her.

Sarah opened her heart to Eldon. She told him about how she'd met Nikolai on their farm. How they'd spent blissful afternoons falling in love. And she shared how torn apart she'd been when her father had sent him away. She shared how receiving the gift of Nicholas had been her saving grace. He had brought all of them so much joy and in the end had brought their family closer than they'd ever been.

Tears slid down her cheeks as she reminisced about the loss of her father, and mother and sisters and brothers. So much pain along with so much joy of the love they'd all shared.

They sat down on a grassy section and Eldon put his arm around her shoulder and held her close. Silently they watched the river flow and allowed each other to live in the past and present simultaneously.

After a time Sarah turned to Eldon and asked, "Have you been married?" She thought him to be about seven or eight years older than herself and there seemed to be something about him that seemed as though he was well aware of deep and intimate relationships.

"Yes, it seems like an absolute lifetime ago that I was married. We were married for a number of years before my wife became pregnant. I think it was the stress of everything that was happening around us. She was very apprehensive about bringing a child into this world of upheaval and then she was worried about me."

Sarah interrupted, "Worried about you?"

"Yes, I was a school teacher in Omsk and quite involved in community business. When men started disappearing for no reason, just removed from their homes, she was so worried about me. But then, she did finally conceive, but when it came time for delivery, well there were complications." Eldon said through gritted teeth and a creased brow, "She suffered for days in labour. We tried everything but she just could not get the baby out. She started to bleed and there was nothing we could do to stop it. Sarah, it was absolute torture to watch her in so much pain, struggle, and finally bleed to death." Even now the memory still made him nauseous.

Sarah now did for him what he had done for her. She slipped one arm around his waist from behind and the other around front and clasped her hands together and just held him close.

In one afternoon they'd shared a lifetime.

Eldon turned to face her and a soft smile touched his lips, "And now I've met you and I feel joy and hope for the future. You are so strong and confidant Sarah. You are a woman filled with compassion and zest for life unlike anyone I've ever met before. I would really like to keep spending time with you and when it's time to leave Moscow, I want us to stay together."

Sarah was overwhelmed with emotion. They lived in a day and time when you had to be direct. They had all learned that life was much too short to waste on being illusive about one's intentions.

Sarah loved how he was able to express himself and not show any fear of rejection from her. He was showing her his heart and she would take it and cherish it always.

Chapter
15

Amidst the life that they had so quickly created for themselves in Moscow there was secretive work being done by many to get proper paperwork to flee.

Voting openly for leaders was much too dangerous. Discreetly, word was passed around during the day and at night many men gathered deep in the forest to discuss what they should do.

Eldon and Herbert were elected to help with the process. It did not take the two men long to realize that they shared many common traits and a friendship developed. Herbert's anxiety over his sister's welfare dissolved. He could see that Eldon's intentions were indeed honourable and that Eldon would care for and love Sarah as she deserved.

One gentleman, in particular, would be remembered by many for years to come for all the hard work and effort he put in for the Mennonite people in Russia. Henry Martins spoke to anyone in Moscow who would listen and tried to find those people that would have influence with the government. He found people in charge that he could trust and set up meetings with Ministers to put the plight of the Mennonite people before them.

It was rumoured that when talking to one of the sympathetic politicians he was told to tell the Ministers that soon winter will be coming. Tell them that if they don't allow you to leave, you along with your wife and children and all the other Mennonites will go to The Red Square and there you will protest and stay till you die.

As harsh as this threat sounded, it could become a likelihood, even if that's not what was wanted. Moscow was quickly becoming overpopulated as trains continued to unload boxcars full of Mennonites. It became tougher and tougher to find housing and the cost of rent was increased as the demand rose.

Everyone did what they could to fit as many people into their homes as possible. Sarah was quite surprised when Herbert suggested that Eldon and his sister move in with them to free up their current cabin for a larger family. Herbert said that he would rather live with someone that they were becoming close friends with than new people.

There was very little privacy for Eldon and Sarah but both realized that this was also a blessing. They had such a strong attraction for each other that being alone would have been too great of a temptation to unleash their passion.

Instead they spent hours talking about the future that they planned to build together.

All around the situation turned out to be a wonderful blessing. Justina, being all alone with her first child, really benefited from the help that Sarah provided. And her precious daughter became a delight to everyone in their home.

Herbert, who was always so cautious, opened his heart to love for the first time. It seemed that everyone around him knew what was happening even before he did. His eyes lit up every time he saw Justina and Sarah could tell that he would get nervous. He was very helpful and protective of Justina and the baby, who'd been named Frieda.

Little baby Frieda, reminded all of them of their young sister Frieda, who had left this world much too soon, but their memory's were of the joy she had brought them.

Sarah felt joy and peace with the thought that her brother could finally relax and think about himself. He'd been selfless for so long. It was time for all of them to live life and make the most of each moment.

Together they all joked about how they would all have a double wedding once their new homeland was established.

Then one night Henry Martins received the advice he needed to finally get the Russian government to give some serious thought to allow these Mennonites to leave. Late at night the men gathered in the forest and letters were prepared to each Russian Minister. Attached were lists of signatures of the people that wanted to leave.

That very same night Henry Martins risked his life once more by going to different mail boxes throughout Russia and dropping off these letters and lists. He wanted to arouse as little suspicion as possible.

On October 29, 1929 a wave of excitement swept over the Mennonite people in Moscow. Permission had been granted for a group to leave that night at midnight. Frantically people tried to find out if their name was on the list of families that were allowed to leave.

That afternoon Herbert, Jakob, and Eldon just left their job site without even a look back. Nicholas had come by to tell them that they were on the list and had only a few hours to get everything ready to leave.

Many people were in shock at the short notice. They were not ready. They still had wet laundry. The weather had not been very favourable for drying clothes. They just could not see themselves getting everything settled by midnight.

Now that permission had been granted many felt that they would still have many other opportunities to leave. It was even rumoured that another train would come the next day.

This, of course, never happened. It would be three weeks before another group was granted permission to leave and many unpleasant things happened in the meantime. Many people were forced to go back to the communities where they'd come from. Once they got there they would find that their homes were already occupied by others.

Many families were forced to go to Siberia in mid winter where the living conditions were impossible and many died. If the extreme cold did not take your life than a nervous breakdown could take away all hope of survival. Suffering is all that these people would know until they were granted the peace of death.

For Sarah and her family there was no confusion about what they should do. This is what they had been waiting for, dreaming of. Sarah was so thankful that Eldon and Justina were also on the list. They had discussed what they would do if they were separated, but their prayers had been answered, and they did not have to worry about trying to find each other once they left Russia.

Where they would end up was just so unpredictable. At this point they had no control over where they would settle.

Jakob was sent to find someone with a wagon that they could hire to transport all of their luggage to Perlovka Station. The rest of the family worked to fit all of their belongings into their suitcases.

A few hours before midnight Jakob arrived with a friend he'd made while working on the railways. The wagon they'd brought did not look very stable but the streets were very busy and they would not find anything else this night.

The men loaded up the wagon and on foot they made their way to the train station. It was very cold and it had already been raining for hours. The roads were all muddy but it did not matter. Dirty and wet feet was the last thing on any of their minds.

Herbert reached his arms out to Justina and said, "Here, I'll carry Frieda." Justina handed her precious bundle over to Herbert appreciatively. She was so grateful that this man treated her daughter as if she were his own. Sometimes she felt as if her husband must have had a hand in picking this caring and able man for her.

Softly she said, "Thank-you Herbert," all the while showing her appreciation in her eyes. Having been born premature, Frieda was only now the size of an average new born, but being so heavily bundled, the weight would soon have become too much for Justina.

"There are a lot of people here, mama," commented Nicholas. Besides the people that were leaving there were also a lot of others saying good-bye to their loved ones. Many people were crying. They did not know if they would ever see their sister again, or their brother, or a much loved aunt, and so on. So there was even more crying for those whose names had not made it on the list.

Sarah was so thankful that all her loved ones were with her. She did not know how she would have behaved if one of her brothers would have had to stay behind. Her heart had been broken before and now it went out to all the people who were hurting so deeply.

Nicholas spotted some of the young people he'd gotten to know during their months in Moscow. "Mamma, can I go and talk to my friends?"

Eldon had become quite fond of Nicholas during his stay in their home and answered for Sarah, "The train could leave any minute. There's so many people here we don't want to get separated. Just say a quick "Hello" and come right back."

"Alright," Nicholas nodded and headed off. He was used to taking direction from his uncles and knew that Eldon was just trying to keep him safe for the sake of his mother. Eldon was an intelligent and well learned man and Nicholas had also quite enjoyed getting to know him. It was like having his own private teacher and he felt quite privileged to have been living with him the past month.

Sure enough, minutes later they were allowed to board the train. At 10:30 pm the conductor closed all the train doors and said that's it. No more people would be leaving. It was a pity. There was obviously still much room left on the train. Only about three hundred people were taken on the train. Over half of the people that were on the list had been left behind. But the communists did not care.

Half an hour after the doors had been shut Nicholas asked, "So, when are we going to start moving."

"I'm not sure," answered Herbert, looking around. People were getting a bit anxious. All the rushing, hurrying to get to the train on time and now just sitting here.

"We should all just try to get some sleep," said Sarah. "It's already so late and we have a long trip ahead of us." They all got as comfortable as they could, leaning against each other.

Finally at 2 am the train started moving. The jolt woke Sarah. Others woke up also, but the train was moving so slowly that people did not get too excited. Soon they dozed off again. At noon the next day the train stopped. The doors were opened and they were given the freedom to step off the train.

Jakob laughed, "We did not even make it out of Moscow!" The train had only travelled from one end of the city to the other. It had stopped a hundred meters short of the Leningrad Station. This is where people usually boarded to travel to and from Leningrad.

"Well, we might as well go and buy some lunch. Our money will not do us any good once we cross the Russian border," advised Eldon. With so little warning about their departure they really had not been given any time to use up what little savings they had. Sarah and her family had tried to spend their money wisely over the past months. They now each had real shoes and decent coats and basic cookware.

While they were having their lunch they overheard some of the other people talking about heading into the city for some last minute shopping so they would not have to give the communists the last of their money.

"That's much too big of a risk," said Sarah, "We have no idea when the train will start moving again, and I really don't think that they will wait for anyone who is not on board."

As it turned out they would have had lots of time. They ended up spending the entire day just waiting at the station. Finally, a long time after dark, the train started moving again.

The communist government had sent two military guard's for each boxcar. One was stationed at the front and one at the rear to keep peace during the process of transporting the transients. The atmosphere was fairly relaxed though. They were given the freedom to move about in the train as they wished.

The next morning they could see that they were well on their way to Leningrad. Along the way they stopped at many small stations where they had the opportunity to leave the boxcar and shop at some of the vendors. Some of the stops were very quick so they had to hurry. Bartering over price was a common practice, but most people did not bother during these stops. There was no point in hanging onto their money and they wanted to make the most of the time they had.

On the evening of Oct. 31, 1929 they arrived in Leningrad. Here they were met by NKWD Agents, the Soviet Secret Service police. They were told to gather all of their belongings and come with them. They hauled everything out to the street where the agents proceeded to hold up the electric street cars. They made the people in the cars get out and told the Mennonites to go in. Once again an agent stood guard at the front and rear of the car.

Sarah and Nicholas had never been on a motorized vehicle before and this could have been quite exciting for them but since no one was told what was going on, they were more apprehensive than excited. They were taken to a big warehouse, located on the ship yard by the Baltic Sea, for the night.

"This is very nice," said Sarah in surprise as she entered the warehouse. Before her stood rows of nicely set tables covered in white tablecloths. Everyone was quite surprised to be treated so well. They were served a hearty meal. To be sitting at a table and served by others was a very foreign feeling to many.

When dinner was finished they were all taken to Quarantine. "What are they going to do to us?" asked Nicholas alarmed. They did not have to wait for an answer.

"Before we put you on a ship to Germany, we have to disinfect you and all of your belongings. Take everything off and then take a disinfecting shower!" yelled one of the guards.

This was a very humiliating process for the Mennonites who were a very humble and reserved people. Men, women and children were not separated. Everyone had to get naked or near naked. It was a shameful procedure.

Sarah had never been naked before her son or her son before her. Her family always changed and cleaned their bodies in private. Nicholas looked at his mother in horror!

He was a teenage boy! It was one thing to get naked in front of his uncles, but quite another to be naked in front of his mother and the other teenage boys and girls in the room! "Mother!" he cried.

Sarah could see his thoughts racing through his mind. "Nicholas, it's all right!" stated Sarah calmly. "Just keep your eyes down and cover yourself with your hands."

Herbert and Jakob were already starting to undress and Nicholas knew that he did not have much of a choice. He took a deep breath than started taking off his clothes.

Sarah paired up with Justina and the baby and the ladies took off their clothes, taking turns holding baby Frieda. Having been around many women giving birth the past few months Sarah felt quite comfortable amongst the unclad ladies.

Eldon had courteously turned away as Sarah and his sister undressed. He was fully aware of the fact that the woman that he had been falling in love with over the past three months was just feet away from him and completely and beautifully nude. But this was neither the time nor the place to admire and take in her God-given beauty.

Sarah refused to cower shamefully in the situation they were in. She was determined to hold her head high and proud. She'd never really given much thought to her fully grown womanly body. It had been so many years since her romance with Nikolai. He had made her feel quite lovely and aware of her curves. Through loving him she had also come to desire the masculine form.

Just for a moment she blushed as she caught herself wanting to linger on gazing at Eldon. It was an awkward situation for all of them, brothers and sisters and love interests. Reality set in quickly though as they realized that they would be left naked and cold for many hours.

Soon children started to whimper and cry. They were getting so cold and uncomfortable. It felt strange to them to have their naked parents trying to hold them close to keep them warm and give comfort.

Nicholas stayed close to his uncles trying to be brave. They all took turns holding baby Frieda to keep her as warm as possible. They did not want her to get sick.

Finally they were given their clothes and belongings back and brought back into the warehouse. They thought that they would now be allowed to sleep but this was only the beginning of the brutal and harsh treatment. All of their suitcases and belongings were brought outside in the yard and everything was searched.

The guards were well aware of where people might try to hide their money and they searched their shoes and hems of their clothing. The guards kept all the money that they found. The guards told them that since no one was paying for their trip to Germany they had to help out and hand everything over to them.

Many people were searched very seriously by having to succumb to strip searches. Since both Eldon and Herbert had been well known within their communities they were among those strip searched. Not a crease or crevice was left unchecked!

In the middle of the night they were all called out to the yard to come and get their belongings. There was constant activity in the warehouse and no one was really given any chance to sleep.

In the morning the whole procedure started again. "If we find any of you with money you will not be allowed to sail to Germany!" And the searches started all over again.

No breakfast was served. They'd had the kind treatment the night before. It would be their last meal in Russia.

By the time they were allowed to board the ship named "Felix Djerjinsky" their minds were almost in a stupor. People were tired and hungry and cold, but this was their opportunity for a new life.

During their ordeal in the warehouse everyone's health had also been checked. Sarah was so thankful that they were all healthy. A few of the families had sick children and were not allowed to board the ship. She felt awful for these families. What would happen to them now? Where would they be sent? And with nothing.

Midday on Nov. 1, 1929 the anchor was lifted and the ship set sail towards Germany. Without speaking Nicholas raised his eyebrows in question and smiled at his mother basically asking, "Now can I go and find my friends?"

Sarah could see that he was ecstatic! His long time friend Karl along with his Aunt and Uncle had made it onto the ship. Now they would no longer be separated unless it was by choice. She did not have to worry about losing her son. "Go, find your friends!" she said as she smiled back.

Sarah turned back towards the railing of the ship and held on, watching Leningrad become smaller and smaller. Eldon moved closer to her and placed his arm about her waist and held her close.

They both watched the horizon disappear, deep in thought. "This will be the last time we will ever see Russia," said Sarah looking up at Eldon. It should have been a joyous occasion, but it was mixed with sadness. They were leaving behind family and friends. Loved ones that they would most likely never see again. It had been their home for many years. Even though they would never forget why they were leaving, they would also always remember all joy that life in Russia had brought them.

Eldon took a deep breath and said, "I know." He turned Sarah away from the disappearing land line and turned her towards him, "From here on I just want us to look at the future together. I know that we still have many unkowns ahead of us but I feel that the time is right, right now." Surrounded by her brothers and all the people watching the horizon Eldon continued softly, "Sarah, I love you with all my heart. I would be so honoured to have you by my side forever. Will you marry me?"

Sarah was so caught off guard. They had talked about a future together and she knew that when he spoke to her about together he meant as in marriage but she thought that he'd meant when they had settled on a home country, once they had a home.

The words were like a sweet melody to her ears. Eldon was a man that possessed all the qualities that she admired and wanted in a man. He was confidant, strong, intelligent, kind, loving and the list went on. She felt like a queen beside him. "Oh, Eldon, yes, of course, I will marry you!" she said barely being able to contain her excitement. Sarah pulled his head down towards hers and just before kissing him said, "I love you!"

"Mother!" said Nicholas aghast. What was his mother doing kissing Eldon like that in public, in front of all these people? This was just not done in their society.

Sarah stopped kissing Eldon and looked over at her son who was so obviously embarrassed in front of his friends. She reached out her hand towards Nicholas and pulled him a little closer. Squeezing his hand she said, "Eldon just asked me to marry him."

"Really?" asked Nicholas showing his excitement. Suddenly he did not care about what his friends had just seen. "When?"

"Oh, well, we have not really talked about that," said Sarah looking at Eldon.

"Actually, I was thinking right here on this ship, tomorrow, before we get to Germany," said Eldon. He did not want to give anyone the authority to separate him from Sarah. As husband and wife they would be considered a family and taken seriously.

Sarah touched her hair and ran her hands down her clothes. Eldon could see what she was thinking. She would not be a bride that was all decked in finery, but what Sarah did not seem to realize was that she did not need it. "Sarah, you look absolutely stunning as you are. Having each other is all that matters!"

"You're right," said Sarah forgetting about her vanity. She did not need a fancy dress and fanfare. All she wanted was to make a lifelong commitment to the man she loved.

Herbert and Jakob who'd been quietly standing by noticed all the people heading inside. "Come on, let's go inside and eat. It's time to celebrate!" said Jakob.

One of the Mennonites took command of the situation and led the people in prayer and song before their meal. They took a big risk. The ship was still Russian property and on board there were soldiers to stop any rebellion in case Germany refused to accept these immigrants.

After lunch some of the older girls helped with clean-up as people got settled in their quarters. Eldon went to find one of the Mennonites who had been a minister to perform the ceremony for them.

Sarah should have been much too excited to even sleep that night, but after the long and cold night in the warehouse she was just so exhausted. That added to the gentle rocking of the ship, she had a very peaceful sleep.

The next morning they all tidied up the best they could and gathered on the deck of the Djerjinsky just before lunch. Word had traveled quickly amongst the passengers and many joined them on deck to witness the modest wedding ceremony.

For Eldon and Sarah it was a perfect day. They joined hands while they listened to the minister's message. The sky was blue and a gentle breeze touched their faces as they said their vows. They were at complete peace with each other and with God. This was most definitely a day "That the Lord hath made."

They were told by the ship's captain that when they arrived in Germany, they should make it official with proper documentation.

That night out on deck in the dark Eldon told Sarah "Although I want nothing more than to consummate our union this is just not the place."

"I know," said Sarah. "I want so much to be alone with you, but there is just no privacy here. But I feel completely at one with you."

They went to their sleeping quarters and joined their families who were already settling down for the night.

Their time to make love without reservation would come. If there was any one thing they had both learned during these years of hardship it was patience.

Chapter
16

Sunday afternoon the entire family was out on deck as the Felix Djerjinsky reached the Wilhelm Canal. Sarah stood close to Eldon with her body leaning on his. Eldon had his arm proudly around her waist. Herbert was holding baby Frieda and stood just as proudly beside Justina although much more reserved.

The sun shone brightly and it was a beautiful fall day. The anticipation of touching their feet to German soil was evident in all of the passenger's faces watching from the railings. They were here! They were free of Communist Rule!

Slowly the ship travelled through the canal till it reached the dock in Kiel. As they passed underneath a bridge Nicholas pointed and shouted, "Look, they are waving red towels at us!"

Quickly he pulled out his white handkerchief and started waving back. The other passengers also took out their handkerchiefs and waved back at the German citizens.

Sarah smiled and hugged Eldon. It felt so good to be welcomed with open arms.

After the ship docked, people quickly went below deck to gather their belongings. Everyone thought that they would now need to quickly leave the ship. "Where's the crew?" asked Jakob.

No one had an answer. All the workers on the ship had hidden themselves. Even the captain had made himself unavailable. The Mennonites on the ship received curious stares from the security guards on the dock.

What this group of Mennonites was completely unaware of was the political situation between the German and Soviet government.

In August of 1929 the Soviet Govt. had issued the last of valid passports. Since then they had refused to let any more people leave their country. But the numbers of people wanting to leave had continued to grow. All the Mennonites arriving in Moscow that same summer and fall had put great pressure on the Soviet Govt. With winter quickly approaching they'd been forced to do something, out of humanitarian reasons.

As much as the communist govt. wanted to keep all that was happening in their country quiet, people in the rest of the world were becoming more and more aware of the situation. They did not want to be seen as a heartless country.

At the same time Germany was facing serious problems of its own. Their unemployment rate was climbing higher and higher. As much as they wanted to help these immigrants, how were they to continue to support them. How could they promise to care for thousands of new immigrants, promise to help them start a new life? It was just such a big responsibility at this time. So the German Govt had halted Russian deportation the summer of 1929.

The Russian government had not made the German government aware of this ship full of Mennonites. They'd brought no documents for the passengers, they had not even prepared a passenger list.

It was obvious that the Soviet Govt. was hoping that Germany would not accept this shipful of Mennonites. They were hoping that Germany would send them all straight back to Russia. This way they could use this group of people as an example to all the other Mennonites still waiting in Moscow. This way Germany would be to blame and the other Mennonites would go back to their villages.

Once again Henry Martins along with Johann Funk took leadership of the situation. They decided to try and get the attention of one of the security guards. The security guard came on board and headed to the Captain's cabin with Henry Martins.

The passengers started getting anxious. They were so close to tasting their freedom from Russia and yet . . . what now?

Later they heard that the guard had asked Henry Martins if he spoke German. Henry had said "Yes" and worked as an interpreter between the guard and the captain. Everyone was quite shocked to hear that they had travelled to Germany without any documentation. This had been the last thing on their mind since making frantic preparations to leave Moscow.

The security guards had no idea that the Mennonites were coming. They did not know what to do with them. The guard contacted a Kiel immigration official. This official then reported the group to Berlin. Still no one was aware of these people arriving.

Finally Professor Benjamin Unruh was contacted. Professor Unruh had already spent years fighting for the plight of the Mennonite people. He was a man that would never be forgotten by any of the Russian Mennonites. Since 1921 he'd been tied to the MCC (Mennonite Central Committee) in North America.

Professor Benjamin Unruh dedicated his entire life to helping these people. He worked tirelessly to rescue these homeless refugees. To these refugees he became someone that they trusted implicitly. He became their advisor, mentor, counsellor, father figure and friend. In the future these Mennonites would come to him for help on all difficult problems. Although he never visited these future colonies his advice would always be taken.

Professor Unruh was in close contact with German President Hindenburg, both as an informant and advisor. Because of his influence, a short while later, all the Mennonites were allowed to leave the ship. That same afternoon the Djerjensky sailed back to Russia, empty.

They were taken to a warehouse nearby. Before long wagons full of hay arrived. They all worked together to unload the hay to make beds for the night. By evening they'd received blankets, clothes, sweets, cigarettes, tobacco, bread, milk, soup, and luxury items that they were unfamiliar with.

"How will we ever be able to thank them?" asked Sarah.

"I don't know," replied Eldon, "but we will never be able to thank them enough!"

Nicholas was beaming. The German citizens along with President Hindenburg had been extremely generous to these people and lifted their spirits in ways they would never know.

They had hope! Hope! They could relax and breathe! It did not matter that they were spending another night in a warehouse.

After a few days they were moved to another warehouse. Here they waited till enough wagons could be located to carry all of their belongings to a temporary residence in Hamburg.

Two weeks later they were moved to Hamburg. Because it was near Christmas they were given more gifts before leaving Kiel.

They'd been told that their home in Hamburg would be temporary. So far no one could yet answer the one question that they all so desperately needed to have answered. Where would their final home be?

Although Germany was very clean and orderly and the citizens very generous, Sarah did not feel at home here. This was not the place where she would build a home and family with Eldon. She did not feel connected to anything here.

After three weeks in Hamburg the group was moved to a more permanent residence in Molln which was located in Lauenburg. This would be their home until a land could be found that could take these refugees permanently.

Nicholas along with his friends adapted quickly to all the changes. For the adults getting used to everything took a little longer. Since travelling to Moscow and then on to Germany they were having so many new experiences. A world that they had never known any part of before was opening up to them. Travelling in motorized vehicles, sailing on a ship, and now living in a four story building.

The German Govt. had vacated a four story Officer Training School for the refugees. Here the classrooms were converted into large bedrooms for the families to share. For the teenagers finding their way through the maze of corridors was a quick accomplishment.

In the months that followed this building became the central registration location for all people fleeing the Soviet. People were always coming and going. At times there were anywhere from one thousand to fourteen hundred people calling this school home. It was an enormous change for the families.

At times Sarah just ached for the open land. To be alone. To smell the fresh orchard smells.

She really did not have too much time though to dwell on these thoughts. Helena, her dear friend, had not made it to Germany with this group. Sarah was kept quite busy working with expectant mothers.

People did what they could to keep busy while waiting for their turn to leave. In the front of the school there was a separate building. Anyone who wanted to either enter the school or leave had to ring a bell and give a valid reason for being there. The building was completely secured for the Mennonites protection. Herbert and Jakob took turns working as security guards in the building.

Eldon with his years of teaching experience ended up working with the new people arriving. He helped them with their paperwork.

Some of the refugees did find work in the city. People were allowed to leave the school in work groups. One person was made responsible for the group. Everyone tried to do this from time to time. It was a chance to leave the shelter and do something different for a few hours.

They found work as house-keepers, janitors, and kitchen helpers.

For Sarah and Eldon leaving the school for excursions into the city became a wonderful pleasure. It was a time for them to be alone. They would walk and admire the beautifully kept old buildings. They became like two young teenagers discovering love for the first time. Holding hands and trying to find private places between buildings where they could kiss with open abandon. They found bushes and trees where they could hind behind and discover each other's bodies.

It soon became apparent that they needed to find a private place where they could fulfill each other's needs completely.

The time had come. They no longer had to worry about their next meal. They did not worry about being taken away from one another by an untrusting government.

They had the opportunity to focus on each other.

It was a freezing cold day in February when Eldon convinced Sarah to come into the city with him. The streets were quiet. Sarah told him that they were insane to be out in this weather. Their noses would freeze together. When she wanted to pull him close for a kiss he said, "No, my darling, not yet."

Sarah was a bit perplexed. She did not know why he'd brought her out here on a day like this, unless it was to steal some passionate kisses. He took her hand and pulled her along. He too was starting to freeze.

He brought her into a building that she'd never been in before and once inside reached into his pocket and pulled out a key and smiled mischievously. Sarah still did not understand what was going on. He gave a sigh and rolled his eyes in exasperation, teasing her. Eldon took her hand and led her to the door that the key belonged to.

Sarah stepped inside to find herself in a beautiful bedroom. She had never been on a bed this size or of such comfort. There were heavy drapes covering the windows which were of matching material to the bedspread. Sarah started to tremble as she realized what Eldon had done for them. "Oh, Eldon, it's beautiful!" she whispered.

Eldon had been saving up his earnings so that they could consummate their marriage in luxury and privacy.

"One day Sarah, you will be able to spend every night in a room like this," replied Eldon.

"As long as all my nights and days are with you, you know that I don't need any of this. But it means so much to me that you want to give me this," said Sarah.

"And so much more," said Eldon.

Eldon took off his coat and hat and sat down at the end of the bed. "Come here, Sarah." Sarah walked over to him, never taking her eyes off of him. She stood right in front of him. Slowly he unbuttoned her coat and slid it off her shoulder and let it drop to the floor. He pulled her close to him and reached around her back to undo the buttons of her dress. Sarah was still standing and ran her fingers through his thick black hair touching his strong neck and shoulders.

Slowly Eldon pulled her dress and underwear off her shoulders and down the rest of her body till all her clothes were on the floor. He allowed his hands to slide down the sides of her body feeling and lingering on all of her beautiful curves. When he had his hands on her hips he pushed her away from him so that he could admire her exquisite figure.

Sarah stood before him naked and completely unashamed. She saw the hunger in his eyes and felt the warmth inside of her belly. He pulled her to him once more and starting touching and tasting her with no reserve.

In no time at all Sarah felt completely weak with the desire he had built in her. Eldon sensed her weakness and stood up and picked her up and placed her on the bed. Quickly he took off his own clothes and lay down beside Sarah to continue enjoying this gorgeous woman that God had given him as his wife.

They kissed deeply and passionately moving their bodies in unison, exploring each other. He was lean and muscular and Sarah felt safe and protected by this man. When she felt that she could wait no longer she slid her hands down his back and onto his buttocks. She opened herself up to him and pulled him deep inside of herself. They were a perfect fit for each other.

Together they reached a pitch of pleasure unlike either of them had ever known before!

Mind, body and soul in a complete universe of its own.

Throughout the rest of the day and night they slept and made love, slept and made love. In the middle of the night they cried together and thanked God for what they had found in each other.

The next day when they returned to the school house Sarah felt like a new woman. She was most definitely glowing. She was sure that everyone could see on her the night of passion that she had just experienced. But no one said anything and the days went on the same as before.

Occasionally when everyone in their room was sound asleep Sarah and Eldon made love very quietly and with as little movement as possible so as not to wake anyone. But they both waited till they could once again be alone and allow all the sounds that accompanied their love making to escape their lips.

Leaving the school became more and more dangerous as the months went by. There were Russian communists living in Germany and they wanted the German Govt. to send the Mennonites back to Russia. They said that everything the Mennonites were saying about their previous life in Russia was lies.

The climate was changing and you could feel that turbulent times were coming. The Russians were protesting loudly and completely unsympathetic to the Mennonites.

It was also during this time that Hitler started taking advantage of the political situation to fight his way to the top.

Professor Benjamin Unruh knew that these Mennonites were in danger if they were to stay in Germany. He continued working very hard with other Mennonite leaders to find a land that could offer them a permanent and safe home.

A council was put together to discuss and make plans as to where all of these people could go. They dealt with Canada and Brazil and later Paraguay.

Canada had very strict health criteria that many families could not pass. If one member of the family was sick then the whole family was denied acceptance.

The Mennonites were more than willing to work very hard in any country that would provide them land. They would work the land and make it prosperous. They would pay their taxes, but they were a peace loving people and did not want to fight. Brazil would not promise them "No Military Service."

No one had heard much about Paraguay before. The name of the country was quite foreign to most of them. But people started talking. Then one evening as people were just sitting and relaxing before bed, Sarah and her family overheard a conversation that gave her the answer to the question that no one had been able to answer before.

"So what is it like in Paraguay?"

"Well, it's warm year round and you can grow a large variety of fruits and vegetables."

"Really? What kind of fruit grows there?"

"I heard that they grow oranges, mandarins, bananas . . ."

"Is that true?"

"Yes, and many more like lemons, limes, watermelon, pineapple . . ."

"And the potatoes and corn that we're all used to," interrupted another person.

By this point in the conversation Sarah's mouth had started to water. She had only had the pleasure of tasting a few of these fruits that had been mentioned but they all sounded so delicious and exotic. For the Russian people a lot of these fruit were considered a delicacy.

Sarah started to envision a life with Eldon tending their orchard, relaxing under a canopy of fruit laden trees.

When she looked at him she could see that he was also envisioning the two of them side by side, sharing a life in paradise.

Eldon reached for Sarah's hand and squeezed gently as their excitement grew with what they were hearing.

As Sarah looked at her brothers and her son she could see that they too felt a pull towards Paraguay.

There were many people to thank for this promising possibility. Canadian Mennonites had already worked out privileges with the Paraguayan government in 1921. They would not be required to do any military duty. They were given the freedom of teaching whatever they wished in school. Religiously they could worship and build churches without government interference. They were also given the right to set up their own government system.

In 1926 the first Mennonite colony from Canada had already been established in Chaco Paraguay. These people would be crucial in helping the new settlers adjust and start a new life.

Professor Benjamin Unruh, who'd been tied to the North American MCC (Mennonite Central Committee) since 1921, had now created a help organization called "Brothers in Need (Despair)". Because of his dedication a variety of churches joined in along with the Red Cross to help these homeless Russian Mennonites.

Sarah could hardly believe the generosity of all these people. Since they would all be starting with nothing in South America much was given to them beforehand to start their new life. Containers were filled with dishes, clothing, bedding, wagons, and seeds from the German Govt and Red Cross and then shipped ahead of the immigrants. Every two weeks a load was transported by ship. Every family was promised oxen, cattle, and chickens upon their arrival in Paraguay.

In the weeks that followed after over hearing the conversation about Paraguay Sarah and her family had many conversations of their own. They were all in complete agreement that this is where they wanted to go and establish a homeland.

It became quite apparent that Herbert and Justina had become very fond of one another since meeting in Moscow. In February of 1930 they were officially married in Germany. Jakob, at this time, seemed quite content with being a much sought after eligible bachelor. Sarah felt that he should try to focus attention on just one woman so that he too would have a partner before they reached South America, but he was not at all worried about it.

In March of 1930 Sarah and her family received the news that they would be part of the first group to sail for South America.

For the first time in years Sarah felt certain of her future. She was completely ready for what lay ahead of her. She thought back on the days that she had spent with Nikolai and how they had planned on working the land together. She fully appreciated all that her parents had been through establishing the prosperous farm in Terekeransiedlung. And leaving their respective families behind in Germany when they'd decided to start anew in Russia.

She was also leaving her parents behind in Russia to start anew in South America. She realized that, of course, she did not have a choice in this. The Lord had taken them years ago, but there would now be a great distance between them and all she had known.

Through their toughest times she had come to know her parents, love and respect them, in a way that she would never have thought possible in her youth.

She wanted to take with her all the hard work ethics that she had learned and the character traits that they held of high value.

Watching Nicholas grow into a young man she knew that there was one thing though that she needed to work on changing. The Mennonite people kept their children so shamefully innocent that many were never told, even just before marriage, about sexuality and she did not want her son to go through what she had been through. Conceiving a child out of wedlock and not even realizing the actions that had made this possible.

Nicholas was truly her greatest gift and she wanted to be open and honest with him so that he could make choices with true knowledge. Sarah knew that her thinking and ideas would not be acceptable to others of her time. She would have to be very careful in how she went about imparting information to her son.

Nicholas saw his mother sitting on her bed deep in thought, "Are we all ready for tomorrow, mother?"

"Yes," answered Sarah. "I believe we are."

Nicholas came over to sit down on the bed beside his mother. "I'm so excited mamma! I know that everyone keeps saying that it will be hard work for many years, clearing land, establishing orchards, but I'm looking forward to all of it!"

"Me too, Nicholas!" said Sarah matching his enthusiasm.

"I still remember weeding the garden with Uncle Herbert and Uncle Jakob. Sweating and working hard! It felt good mamma! And now it will be for us, for our family!" Nicholas sighed, "I just wish Opa was here! He would have been so happy to be a part of this!"

"I know," said Sarah , "I was just sitting here thinking of him and Oma." Nicholas had been so young when his Oma had passed away that he really did not remember her at all, but his Grandfather, Henry Doerksen, had made quite an impression on Nicholas. "I know that they would be so happy for us, Nicholas! And your Oma and Opa would be so proud of you! You've been so helpful with everything in the past months and all the moving that we've had to do. Never knowing if your friends will follow or be left behind!"

"It will feel so good to put down roots and establish life-long friends in South America," finished Sarah.

"Mamma, I'm so happy that you met Eldon," said Nicholas holding Sarah's gaze in all honesty. "I know that you would have wanted me to know my father Nikolai and I wish that I could have known him too, but I know that Eldon truly cares for both of us."

Sarah's eyes started to get blurry with the tears that were welling up inside of her. Her son was only thirteen years old, but this conversation showed wisdom beyond his years. The hardship that they had all been through had definitely taught them great appreciation for the things that truly mattered.

"We have been so blessed Nicholas!"

Sarah leaned towards her son to give him a hug before joining the others in a farewell celebration.

On March 16, 1930 Sarah stood beside her husband Eldon, hand in hand, leaning on the railing of a ship named "Bayer." Close to them stood her brothers Herbert and Jakob, Justina holding baby Frieda, and beside Sarah stood her son, Nicholas.

Eldon watched his beautiful wife, tears streaming down her face as the ship pulled away from the dock. Sarah looked up at Eldon and said, "We're going home! We're going home!"

THE END

THE SEQUEL: Theresa Chevalier, author of 'Shameful Innocence,' has been busy at work, creating the sequel. Keep an eye out on the author's web page (www. theresachevalier.com) for the release. Escape into the wild, untamed jungle, with Sarah, Eldon, Nicholas, and the rest of her family as they continue their adventure. With all that they have to face in this new land they come to realize that the greatest danger to them may be the evil that followed them!

Special Thanks to all who helped turn my vision of the cover page into a reality!

Lindsay McCausland-Model/Actress

Verena Reardon-Authentic Costume Creation (talented artist 'beautiful warm paintings')

Margaret at Hair Alternatives-help in giving our model an authentic 1916 'Look' Check out all that their company does at hair-alternatives.ca

Dezirae McCausland-Hair Stylist and Make Up Artist

Photographer-Revival Art Studio-Jason & Darcy Brown www.revivalartstudio.com

Web Design-Darin Shepit-Nocturnal Studios

The Team at Strategic Book Publishing

Bibliography:

Durksen, Heinrich. 'Das du nicht vergessest der Geschichten'
Filadelphia: Druckerei ASCIM 1990

Kolonie Fernheim. '50 Jahre Kolonie Fernheim' South
America: Imprenta Modelo 1980

Toews, John B. 'Ein Vaterland Verloren' Winnipeg: Christian
Press 1971

Schroeder, Gerhard P. 'Miracles of Grace & Judgement'
Tenessee: Kingsport Press 1974

Unruh, Peter W. 'Biographie unseres Vater' Abbotsford, 1979

Wedel, Helen. 'A Museum of Memories' Autobiography

Penner, Jakob & Lena. 'Remember How The Lord Your God
Led You All The Way' Autobiography

Young, Laura. 'Russia-Then & Now' L. Young PC Sept. 1993

'Cultures of the World

Printed in the United States
146717LV00002B/3/P